THE LAST LOOK

LAUREN ECKHARDT

turning soul press

Book One of the Second Spark Series

Cover Design: www.creativeparamita.com

Part One
Before

Chapter One
Her

My eyes adjusted to the dim bar lighting, the casual lowlight that illuminated the smoke creeping through the room, sneaking and spying on its patrons as only the truly dingy bars do. I adjusted my shirt strap. Jessi had coerced me into buying a tight, off-the-shoulder blouse with a twist in the back, showing way more skin than I normally would on any given day. As she pointed out, red was a good color for my dark blonde hair and neutral skin tone, but typically it's a color reserved for date nights. Wearing it in this bar? It made me feel like I was a siren walking through the darkness, begging for all eyes to be on me. Not the right choice.

I assumed it would be crowded on a Friday night, but there were several open tables. The bar area itself was full, everyone hunched together as though keeping each other warm in a blizzard. I searched for Josh, eyeing the heads that stood above all the rest.

Eventually, I spotted the back of his head near one of the pool tables. With my eyes focused on his thick, brown hair, I weaved through the chairs and tables toward the back of the bar, where the light changed to a green hue as it filtered in from the plastic overhead lights marked with "Southern Tap." The locals jokingly called the bar, "Tap That Ass," which perfectly exemplified its classiness.

Sidestepping past a couple amid a heated discussion as they sat staring at a game of pool in session, unintelligible mouths rapidly moving, I made it to where Josh stood.

"Hey," I poked him in the ribs right as he was bent over the table, carefully lining up for a shot. He jerked in surprise and turned around. "Oh, oops." Not Josh.

Instead of the blue eyes I was gradually getting to know better, deep brown ones smiled back at me. Although the nose and chin were exactly the same, he stood about a half inch taller than Josh and had cheekbones that were meatier yet equally sculpted. Still, he carried the same killer smile that was enough to make my knees weak every time I saw it. God blessed the Claystone men with perfect teeth and the most kissable lips.

A kiss on my cheek interrupted my analysis as the real Josh appeared.

"Hey hon, thanks for coming out." He stuck a toothpick in his mouth as he put his arm around my shoulders. "Haleigh, meet my brother. Ryan, this is Haleigh."

Ryan stuck out his hand and I shook it, the warmth sending a shock through my system as I recovered from the chilly air.

"Nice to finally meet you. I've heard your name dropped a lot over the past few months."

Glancing at Josh with a raised eyebrow, I baited, "Hopefully the only name." Josh shrugged and mouthed *maybe*, and I rolled my eyes, turning back to Ryan.

"I'm glad you came down this weekend. Thanks for letting me intrude on your guys' night."

Josh sauntered to the pool table to line up for his next shot as he called out, "We needed a designated driver."

Ryan eyed his brother. "I don't know how you put up with him. That alone tells me you're a saint." He winked at me before reaching in his back pocket for his wallet. "Can I get you a drink?"

"Yeah, that would be great, thanks. A beer, please. Whatever you guys are drinking."

"Okay, cool. Josh, you good?"

Josh responded with a flick of his finger to suggest another round was needed.

I sighed emphatically. "I think that was a 'yes, another, please and thank you'."

Ryan laughed as he walked to the bar to grab our drinks.

I leaned against the table and watched Josh queue up and hit ball after ball. He was good at anything he put his mind to, and I was consistently in awe of what Josh could do with his hands. He could cook, fix cars, do just about anything that needed done around the house, and play any sport like an all-star. Jack of all trades. It was incredibly alluring.

Josh put down his stick and walked back to me, pulling me into his arms and kissing me again.

"I'm glad you're here. The two most important people in the world to me now in the same room."

I wrapped my hands around his waist, pulling him in close, and inhaling the scent of his cologne. "How was your day?"

He rubbed his nose against mine and said, "Just another day of going through the motions while all I could think about was seeing you."

"I think you may like me a little," I teased him.

"You don't even know the half of it," he whispered in my ear, before kissing me on the cheek and returning to the table.

"Special delivery," Ryan appeared again, balancing three filled-to-the-rim glasses of liquid amber. I took one out of his hands with a "Thanks for this." He delivered one to Josh who was already laughing and joking with the guys at the table next to us, his charisma on full display. Ryan returned to stand next to me.

"I've heard a little bit about you from Josh, but I may inundate you with questions about your life," I warned. "Josh calls it a constant interrogation, but I just love getting to know people."

Ryan chuckled. "He prepped me, but you don't need to

worry. One of my superpowers is rapid-fire questions, so you may meet your match here. Lindsay gets annoyed, too."

"And Lindsay is your wife, right?"

"Yep. We've been married for four years this November. She's a fitness instructor who bounces around gyms all over town leading classes. We had our first baby, Adam, six months ago and he's wonderful."

"Josh showed me pictures. He's absolutely adorable. It makes me want one of my own." When Josh showed me pictures of Adam on our first date, I knew right away I was in trouble with this one. He was so proud, as though Adam was *his* son, bragging about how Adam had started crawling and how smart he was. I could see in Josh's eyes the deep desire for a family, a desire that resembled my own. I could see us having one together.

Ryan flashed me that killer Claystone smile that I was sure would get passed down to Adam as well. "The cutest baby in the world. I'll admit, I'm still in that new dad euphoria. Leaving him is hard. Josh was hoping I'd crash at his place tonight, but I'm eager to get back home. Adam is a pretty good sleeper, but when he wakes up in the middle of the night, I'm the one running to him. I can't get enough of those baby snuggles."

"Baby snuggles," I sighed, wishing Ryan brought Adam with him, although the "Tap That Ass" bar would not have been appropriate. "Yeah, I thought you would be in town all weekend. That's sweet of you, though. I can already tell you're a great dad."

Ryan chalked his cue stick and winced when Josh sank the solid seven ball. "Well, Lindsay has a class at five o'clock most mornings, so it makes sense for me to get up with him."

"That just means you're a good husband as well," I pointed out.

Ryan's cheeks reddened as he chuckled. "Yes, maybe. I hope she thinks that, too."

He asked about my job, and the only word that came to mind was, "Tedious. It's hard for me to truly care about numbers even though I know they affect the bottom line. I don't know," I dragged my thumb along a crack in the table as I admitted the truth that I don't tell a lot of people, "I guess I always thought I would be doing something more life-altering, such as being a therapist—like you. Although, I will say, it's hard enough to get my own life in line, so I'd be rotten at giving advice to others."

Snorting, Ryan responded, "The words that tumble out of my mouth aren't always gold."

"But you're making a difference in people's lives. I wish my job had that impact. Sometimes it'd be nice to know I'm spending all of these hours each week doing something to change the world. Otherwise, it's easy to feel so damn unfulfilled."

"I understand more than you realize," Ryan's voice softened. But before we could dive in further, Josh summoned him to the pool table again.

I sipped my beer from my seat, swaying to the music as the guys finished their game and started a new one. Between plays, Josh would stand between my legs and kiss my forehead. It amazed me how similar he looked to his brother, yet they were vastly different in their mannerisms. Ryan was equally handsome but steadier, patient, and held an air of intelligence yet was still personable and funny. Josh bounced between stages of being goofy to quite serious, trigger-finger quick to anger while also seeking physical touch and attention. Josh was also without a doubt more impatient, which became more evident as the night continued.

"What the hell, dude? That was a shitty move," Josh called out to his brother, slamming his cue stick on the table, as though Ryan should help him win and not compete against him. Josh was used to being the best at everything, especially with me around since I lack any hand-eye coordination. He always dominated in bowling, air hockey, racing kayaks, or anything we played, and had no shame gloating about it.

I peeked over my phone. "I'm guessing Ryan won?"

A glare from Josh. "Obviously you're not paying attention so don't ask stupid fucking questions."

My cheeks heated but before I opened my mouth to comment, Ryan beat me to it.

"What would have been the right move?" Ryan asked calmly, with what must have been his school therapist voice. Josh was acting like a child, and Ryan was trained on how to handle them.

Josh didn't bite. "Don't pull that shit on me, dude. Rack up. Let's go again."

They started another game and Josh kept his back to me the entire time, as though I'd betrayed him. I sat back and observed, careful to keep my eyes on them and not my phone so I wouldn't piss off Josh again. I could tell it was going to be a short game because Ryan was on fire and Josh's frustration wasn't improving his game.

"I'm done." Josh threw his stick down on the table, upset that Ryan won yet again.

Ryan grabbed his cue and then reached for Josh's, sliding them back into the wall holster. As he considerately racked the balls again for the next drunken group to play, Josh downed the rest of his beer and reached for Ryan's, finishing it off.

My eyes widened, and I bit my lip. Josh was more of himself with one drink. At one and a half, he turned into one-hundred percent himself, all guards down and full of sweet intentions. He was optimistic, on top of the world, and everyone loved him. At two, he was every guy in the bar's best friend. An introvert turned extrovert and full of charm. However, drink three wiped out all the good vibes of the first two, replacing charisma with spite, jealousy, and defensiveness. Mix those together, and you've got a real asshole. I hated drink number three and beyond.

Ryan caught my look with a knowing nod. "I should head back to Downers Grove, anyway. I'll call for a Lyft."

"Don't do that," I put my hand on his arm. "I'll give you a ride. I barely had one beer, and it's not too far out of the way."

"You two figure it out. I've gotta piss." Josh weaved through the crowd to find the bathroom.

Ryan sat down in the chair next to me and whistled through his teeth. "That guy hates to lose."

"Clearly." I acknowledged, embarrassed by Josh as though it reflected me. But Ryan must be more accustomed to this than I am. He grew up with Josh.

"He's a good guy, Haleigh. I know he can say stupid things when he drinks, but I promise you, his heart comes from a good place."

I nodded, wondering if the doubts swarming through my head were painted on my face. "I grew up with an alcoholic dad, so episodes like this scare me a bit." The moment the words were out of my mouth, I wished I could suck them back in. "Your true superhero power must be getting people to confess things they don't normally say out loud because that's been happening all night."

"It's that therapist vibe. For good and bad. I'll be sitting on a bench at the mall while Lindsay shops and people will sit next to me and tell me their deepest secrets and stories. I always have to glance down to make sure I'm not dressed like a priest. But," he poked my knee with his finger, "you don't have to worry about telling me things. We also grew up with an alcoholic dad. Josh has a deep-rooted fear that he will turn into him so that's where his anger truly stems from. He says and does things that remind him of our dad and it makes him spiral."

I shook my head, processing Ryan's words. "Josh never told me that."

"Does he know your dad was the same way?"

I paused before responding carefully, "I told Josh some things about my life growing up, but my dad has changed, so I don't tend to use that word to describe him anymore."

"I get that," Ryan rubbed his chin with his hand while considering his next words. "Josh was careful not to drink for most of his life because he didn't want to end up like Dad. But when he joined the firm, drinking was the norm for social events. He started doing it more. He just needs to stop after two drinks, and he'll be fine. He's a better man than our dad was."

"Yeah, I get that." I kept my eyes on the pool table as another group took over.

"Just remember, only through forgiveness can you move on." Ryan tapped my knee again. "You have an affinity for rescued dogs and cats and any animal you can save, right?"

I looked at Ryan, confused whether I heard him right. "Um, yes? I'm guessing Josh told you about that?"

"Nope. When I met you tonight, I immediately thought, 'I bet she's the type that volunteers at the Humane Society and saves turtles from busy roads'."

It was such a strange comment that I couldn't help but giggle. "Is this your third superpower? I'm starting to believe you're a bona fide superhero." I teased.

Ryan leaned into the armrest closest to me with a wide grin spreading across his face. "It's just something I do. I was shy growing up, a total introvert lacking confidence. I was tall and lanky with thin arms and legs. *Twiggy.* That was my nickname for about two years in junior high."

I glanced at his arm and noted the muscles peeking out through his sleeve. There was no doubt those twigs had grown into trunks.

"Hard for me to imagine," I responded, half compliment, half flirtatious, but I didn't care to revise it. Anything can be said in a dingy bar and taken with a grain of salt.

His smile reached from his mouth to his eyes as he continued, "To force myself to talk to people, I would look at them and think, 'I bet they're the type of person who...' then fill in the blank. It became a game to find out if I was right. It worked to get me out of my shell and also fine-tuned my people-reading skills."

"Apparently it worked so well you never stopped doing it."

"You got it. But anyway, Haleigh, listen to me. Josh is like an abandoned puppy at the shelter. With the proper love, he will grow into a well-trained, amazing, best friend of a dog."

"Totally get what you're saying. But turning Josh into a dog in my mind may kill any chances he has for getting lucky tonight."

Ryan raised an eyebrow. "Didn't he kind of kill it already?"

"Cheers to that," I agreed, and we fake-clinked glasses we were no longer holding. Talking to Ryan was more like chatting with an old friend, and it felt like I had known him for years. Any filter was long gone.

Bumping my elbow with his, Ryan pointed to a man sitting on a stool at the corner edge of the bar. Shaggy, graying blonde hair poked out from under a cowboy hat and fell on the back of a gray cut off t-shirt worn with frayed jeans and white tennis shoes. "I bet he's the type of guy who likes omelets on Sundays but powdered donuts Monday through Friday."

I snorted because it caught me so off guard. This was dumb—and exactly the type of game I needed to lighten the mood. "And fasts on Saturdays."

Ryan lifted his arm for a high five and I met it perfectly in the air. "You got it!"

"Now you have to go find out, right?"

He laughed. "Yep, that's the next step."

I pointed to the girl two seats further down. Hiding her phone under the bar, she attempted to text while the guy next to her stared at the TV in a trance. "I bet she's the type of girl who can do more push-ups than any man. And I bet he's the type of guy who flosses in bed while leaving little food particles everywhere."

Ryan scrunched his nose and said, "Okay, that was brutal and gross. But you nailed it." He pointed to another innocent victim of our game. "I bet he's the type that has his political views, religion, and social media stances spread across fifteen bumper stickers on his car."

"I bet he's the type of guy who has a magic eight ball in his pocket at all times because he can't make a decision without it."

We continued the game until both of us were in tears from laughing so hard. No one in that bar was safe from our assumptions. Trying to catch my breath, I could barely get my next words out, "Okay, time to go meet them and find out!"

"Uh-oh. Looks like I'll be here all weekend now after all."

"Good," I encouraged without hesitation. Ryan removed the tension from what was building with Josh. This was the happiest I had been all night. I didn't want him to go.

He held my gaze for a moment before speaking, "You are seriously—" but was cut off mid-sentence.

"What the fuck? You haven't even moved?" I may have forgotten we were waiting for Josh to get back from the bathroom. Apparently, his needless anger had doubled since he left.

"Were we supposed to meet you somewhere?" Ryan stood cautiously.

"Were you smoking?" I asked incredulously as the cigarette smell radiating from his shirt filled my nostrils.

"It's your fault. I was waiting for you guys outside, and it's fucking cold. Someone had a cigarette, so I joined in to warm up."

Ryan stuck his hands in his pockets and rocked on his back heels. "You had a cigarette to warm up while waiting for us outside, instead of coming back inside, where it's warm, to find us?" I was grateful for Ryan's boldness; it was exactly what I was thinking.

"Don't put this on me. You're the one with a damn rail to catch."

Ryan looked at his watch. "Crap, I didn't realize how late it was. Haleigh, you don't mind, right?"

"Of course not. Let's go." I grabbed my purse and booked it to the door, anxious to get out in the cold air where some of it could blow the cigarette stench off Josh. Once we slipped into my car, I could still smell it. I had sensitive allergies to smoke. He knew that; we had talked about it multiple times. The more I thought about it, the angrier I became that he smoked a cigarette with me around. And he tried to turn it into my fault on top of it. I gripped the steering wheel tighter. The only noise was the wind whipping through the open windows and the heat pushing through the vents to offset the chilliness caused by more than just the outside air.

As soon as we arrived at the terminal, Josh rolled out of the car as though he was the one late for the train. I walked in step with Ryan as we tried to catch up with him.

"So, do you?"

"Do I what?"

"Volunteer at the Humane Society."

Laughing at his ability to ignore the tension and pick up our conversation where it left off, I answered, "Yes, twice a week."

"And once again, I win." He pumped his fist in the air. Ryan was a bit dorky, and I liked it. Sometimes Josh felt too cool for me with all his near-perfect skills, so it was a great balance that his brother was more of a nerd like me.

"I bet you're the type of guy who likes coffee in the morning but *loves* coffee in the evening."

He beamed. "You pegged me."

"I prefer it in the evenings as well."

"I could have guessed that one, too."

We made it right as the train arrived, just in time to quickly give hugs and say goodbye. As I followed Josh back to the car, I glanced over my shoulder to see if Ryan had boarded the train yet. He turned around at the same time and waved with a tilt of his head. I could almost hear him saying, "Good luck. You're going to need it." I drew in my breath and waved back, then hurried my steps to catch up to Josh. The unspoken encouragement from Ryan was spot-on. I would need a lot of luck mixed with a heavy dose of patience and grace. The echo of my car's passenger door slamming as I stepped into the parking garage foreshadowed what was to come.

Josh managed to stew in silence in the car, and I thought maybe he was working to get it under control, until we entered his house. Then he exploded like a lit piece of dynamite.

"If you were so fucking bored, you shouldn't have stayed."

Josh's cursing increased once the drinks kicked in. Another warning sign.

"I didn't say I was bored. I watched every game you played."

"It was written all over your face. It's not like I get to see my brother all the time, Ha-*leigh*," Josh enunciated my name like it was the biggest joke, throwing his jacket on the table which made the keys in the pocket clang loudly.

"Listen, I was excited that you and your brother were hanging out. You said you wanted me to be there, so I came."

"Yeah, I wanted you to meet my brother. Shouldn't that say something to you?"

"It does! That's why I came."

"So, it's my fault you wasted a night watching us play pool?"

"Josh, I never said I wasted a night or that I was bored. I don't know where you got this."

"Your face. Your face said it all and you were on your phone talking to God knows who the whole time."

"I was not on my phone. I was talking to your brother the whole time. I'm not sure what you're getting so worked up about."

"Because you were a total buzzkill during one of my few nights out! I shouldn't have asked you to come. Lesson learned." He threw himself on the couch with his arm draped over his eyes.

Speechless, I stood in his kitchen, choosing my next words carefully as I filled a glass with ice water. Setting it on the coffee table next to him, I declared, "I don't deserve you being a dick to me." Maybe those weren't the right choice of words.

"If you weren't such a bitch, then I wouldn't be a dick," he hissed back under his arm.

After glaring at him in stunned silence, I turned my back to hang up his coat and car keys on their respective hooks, steadying my hands. *It's just the alcohol talking, Haleigh.* To take the high road and salvage what was supposed to be a great night, I shifted the conversation with a calm tone, "I thought you said Ryan was going to stay all weekend?"

"He was. But once he saw how fucking boring you were, he left early."

Lies. Hurtful, purposeful lies. Everything out of Josh's mouth was bullshit. Nothing ever makes sense after three drinks, and I'm pretty sure he had double that tonight.

My fingers touched my temple as I squinted at him, partially expecting him to break into laughter and tell me it was all a joke and he was being a weird type of drunken funny. "Are you being serious right now?"

"*Are you serious right now?*" he mocked as he reached over the couch for his basketball, spinning it on one finger while laying back.

"Wow." With a rolling stomach, I grabbed my purse, pulling out two tablets of Aspirin and laying them on the table next to the glass of water. "Try drinking some water instead of more beer." I slammed the door behind me, fleeing before my tears could convert into more ammunition for him to use.

I sat in my car for a few moments as I collected myself, half-hoping Josh would come out and admit he was a jerk. My mind was spinning trying to make sense of it all. Ryan's words repeated in my mind: "He's a good guy with a good heart." *Was Ryan oblivious to this side of Josh? Maybe Josh was only like this with me.* My dad had told me multiple times while growing up that I have a knack for getting under people's skin, and it seemed to surface when Josh got like this.

Taking a deep breath and one last glance at the darkened windows of Josh's townhouse, I shifted my car in reverse and headed home, grateful for the fresh air to calm the heat radiating off my cheeks. What a miserable end to what started as a great night.

Chapter Two
Him

Some people inherit the confidence in their lives to know who they are, to boldly be that person, to change the world and to follow their dreams.

Other people take a little more time in life to figure it out.

My revelation didn't happen until later.

When I met you.

Suddenly, everything became clearer.

I wish I could say it happened before. That I was the man I could have always been. But it didn't happen that way for me. It took extra time. I'm more shaped by my mistakes than my accomplishments. I had to make a lot of mistakes to find what I needed the most, to meet you, and to know what was right in this life.

Fuck, I made so many mistakes. But they're all worth it. Every damn thing is worth it. Because it led me to you.

Chapter Three
Her

Brunch with my parents had been a Sunday morning ritual ever since I moved out of the house. They lived only thirty minutes away in Lake Barrington so we would meet at a place in the middle called The Family Restaurant, with yellow block letters in its sign that reminded me of a Waffle House. It was a much-too-large building filled with cafeteria-style tables and old metal chairs with stuffing poking out through the torn plastic seat covers, ruining any attempt at sitting comfortably. But they knew how to make the best pancakes. Blueberry or plain, those were the only options. They were addicting; fluffy and light, with the perfect amount of crispiness on the edges, and they kept us returning week after week.

My knees shook under the table. I could blame it on the coffee, but there was always something more when my body became jittery. I'm not an anxious person. Naturally composed in all situations, I probably should have become a surgeon. Not squeamish with blood, not nervous presenting in large groups, not afraid to skydive or climb a mountain. Very few things faze me. But Jessi was coming in from the city, and I knew between her and Mom, at least one of them would want to talk about Josh. My phone was still silent after last night's disaster, and he was the last thing I wanted to talk about. Especially since it would be drenched in boiling frustration mixed with a little heartache.

Ever since Jessi and I met, she had high hopes for me. She swore off men three years ago, investing herself in my dating life as though I needed a shareholder. Jessi's view on romantic relationships mirrored that of a rom-com. She wholly believed the best ones could play out exactly like a movie when you find who you're meant to be with. I, however, held a more cynical view, doubtful that real love could come that easily. Jessi kept waiting for me to change, but she would be waiting a long time.

I rarely dropped Josh's name to anyone, Jessi included, since my first date with him. Fortunately, she was distracted these past few months as her "Jess Knows Best" blog and social media platforms hit a million followers. Now she was launching a podcast. For once, Jessi was focused on her life, not mine. I preferred it that way.

My knees bounced up and down under the table until Jessi slid into the chair next to me with a quick hug.

"Okay, before your parents get here, give me the full scoop on Josh since clearly it's getting more serious," she started, glancing back at the door. How do you convince a starry-eyed romantic that not everything is hopelessly romantic? "This is the Freddie Prinze, Jr. back-in-his-prime look-alike you met at Starbucks, right?" Jessi only knows how to describe men by linking them to any rom-com leading man, with a specific preference for the '90s and early 2000s.

I stalled by flipping her coffee cup over so the waitress would fill it up, knowing I was about to shatter one of Jessi's many illusions of this "mystery man" I've been spending time with. Shaking my head, I wiped lipstick off my white mug with a napkin, smearing the red stain all over the glass and my fingers in the process. I never wear lipstick, but Jessi convinced me to try the Hot Damn Seducing Seductress at the Natural Balm Café when we were shopping in the city and I knew if I wasn't wearing it today, she'd paint it on me herself. It was out of my league, yet she enjoyed glamorizing me like I was her real-life doll.

"We met at a work conference. Much more boring."

"Love at first sight?"

"Not even love *now*, so definitely not at first sight," I added with an impatient sigh. Believe it or not, the first romantic movie I ever watched was with Jessi, and it was only because she said it was required to stay friends. Now in the three years since, I'm pretty sure we've seen every rom-com that exists. None of them made me change my view. I've seen what relationships can do in real life, how people can so easily lose themselves, which is why I never watched them before. My mom lost many years waiting around for my dad to finally treat us as though he actually valued us. I vowed I would never be like that.

"But you're starting to meet the family?"

"Is that not allowed if you're not in love? It's only been three months of dating. Besides, it was just his brother." I reached for the mini vanilla creamer, cracking it open to check for mold before pouring it into my coffee. A bad experience with creamer in the past left me forever scarred and paranoid. It's part of the reason I take my coffee black, except when I'm feeling anxious.

Jessi threw her hands in the air and cast her cat-like green eyes into mine. "Where's the passion at, Haleigh? Where's the excitement? Why aren't your eyes lighting up?" Josh said I had intense questioning skills, but he hadn't sat across Jessi yet. She could have been a damn good detective, grilling criminals for the truth, as a backup career if her lifestyle blog wasn't so successful. Jessi sat back against her chair with folded arms. "Your love story disappoints me."

"Maybe because it's not a love story. The word hasn't been dropped at all. It's not like we've known each other for long." I shifted my body in my seat, fighting memories of last night, ready to change the topic.

"What's your favorite thing about him?"

I sipped my coffee as a delay as I searched for the right answer.

I dated a lot through the years but to Jessi's point, I wasn't the type of girl who would become overly giddy about a boy. Dating felt like a joke half the time because most men's intentions were clearly not aligned with mine. I figured someday there'd be someone who'd grab my attention and things would naturally fall into place. Josh Claystone was the closest there had been. His beautiful blue eyes with long dark eyelashes and his big, strong hands, capable of anything. Even his non-existent nails chewed down due to a nervous tic was somehow endearing, a peek into a vulnerable side of him that he rarely expressed.

I finally responded, "There's no doubt we are supposed to be in each other's lives." That was a perfect summary of the undeniable draw. I knew that from the first time I heard Josh speak. It was like a voice I recognized from a dream and it immediately turned my ear to him. The first time I saw him laugh as he tilted his head back, the soundwaves floated through my body, generating butterflies.

Meeting Ryan last night and how immediately comfortable I felt with him all but confirmed it, like being a part of their family made sense. There are people you meet who you know you were destined to cross paths with, and I knew that from the moment I met both of them. And that's why my stomach was rolling. I realized in that moment that I was scared that Josh and I were done. How can you be so sure you're supposed to be in someone's life, but in the same breath know they could be gone in an instant?

Jessi bared all her teeth as she glorified my not-yet-a-love story into whatever she wanted it to be. "So, like, meant to be?"

I nodded to appease her. "Sure. Maybe some variation of that." A loud cry behind me got my attention. I turned my head just in time to watch a young mother lift her baby out of the stroller and cuddle her close to her breast. She rocked the infant, adjusting her tiny pink bow which was holding on to a few of her fine black hairs on top of her head. I turned back to Jessi. "Also, I know Josh is going to be an amazing dad. You should see the way he talks about his nephew. You would think it was his own son."

"It's not actually his, is it?" Jessi's eyes gleamed as she sipped her coffee spiked with Baileys from her rose-colored flask, a third arm attached to her body. You could always count on her to liven up a coffee date. "And Josh for sure wants kids?"

"His face lights up when he talks about being a father someday, Jess. He has a list of activities he wants to do with them and places he wants to take them. He said it's part of why he's working so hard now. He's hoping to be able to work part-time while the kids are young. I've never met a man who is so driven to have a family."

"How are you not in love with this guy yet? Are you out of your mind? You've been talking about finding a man who could be a great dad, and here you go. Hot and freshly delivered on a platter, yet you're still sticking your nose up as though he's not good enough."

The events of Josh's immature meltdown last night rushed through my mind. It was the third time I had witnessed Josh's personality change after drinking too much, and by far the worst occurrence. "Like I said, we're still getting to know each other."

Jessi glanced behind her to see if my parents were coming, then leaned over and grabbed my hand, her eyes narrowing with concern. "Haleigh, listen. If he's already this excited about having kids and has actually written down the type of father he wants to be, it's important to him. He's not your dad. I like your dad, he's grown on me. But I don't like that he hurt you for so many years."

I glanced out the window, fighting tears. This was the immediate response anytime anyone talked about a father-daughter relationship, even if it wasn't about the one I had. The door repeatedly slamming behind my dad and him being gone for weeks, even months, at a time, while I watched my mom stir his favorite sauces and soups on the stove in a daze as she waited for him to come back left a deep mark. The things he would say to me during those years were the worst. I never told Jessi or anyone about that, though.

I focused on the locust trees swaying in the wind, leaves falling off one by one, to get my mind off my dad. A perfect fall day in October. It sent electricity through the air, pressing the need to do something, anything, and not sit inside all day before it all disappeared in the inevitable cold.

Jessi's voice broke through my thoughts. "So, this brother of his... hot?"

Ryan's soulful eyes were burned into my mind. "Doesn't matter. Married. And with a kid."

"Damn. Probably a dad bod. I'd be down for that." Her dating hiatus was starting to affect her in more obvious ways.

"Definitely not a dad bod." I said, using my cup to hide my smile.

Jessi's eyebrows rose. "Ooh, tell me more."

Shaking my head with a laugh, I said, "Married. With a kid. Don't forget that part."

"Aren't they all?" Jessi sighed dramatically.

We were different in the best of ways. Jessi was the crazy I needed in my life, pushing me one step further and to be bolder than I've ever been. I grounded her when she needed it and was a regular sounding board for all her ideas.

Truth be told, I couldn't help but feel a bit jealous of her at times. She glided confidently through life, paving the path she wanted to make, not taking "no" for an answer if something stood in her way. With her petite frame and brunette hair painted with red streaks, Jessi was a captivating mix of a graceful swan and a hurling fireball.

We met at a bookstore only a few weeks after she made the trek to the big city from her small Wisconsin town. We grabbed for a book at the same time, our hands grazing. Jessi turned to me and said, "Figures. Your hand was too smooth to be a man's. This would have been the perfect meet-cute."

I held the book up. It was a new release contemporary romance recommended on the *New York Times* Best Sellers list. "Would you want a man buying this book? I'm pretty sure it would mean he was buying it for his girlfriend or wife."

"Or he could be *very* in touch with his feminine side, which I may be into, depending on the day of the week." She wiggled her eyebrows, eliciting the very beginning of endless laughter between us.

As it turned out, Jessi's best friend from her hometown, Autumn Goodfield, wrote the book, *Never in My Dreams*. Autumn had gifted a few copies to Jessi, yet Jessi would still buy new copies at every bookstore she passed and leave them behind at random locations for other people to read. She said it both supported Autumn and spread the word of a great novel to people who may otherwise not have heard of it. That little tidbit showing loyalty and support of her friends made me like her even more. We left the bookstore together to grab coffee afterward and talked for hours like we had known each other our whole lives. That feeling remained through the years. We didn't have to talk every day, and sometimes weeks would go by before we did, but we'd pick up right where we left off.

Jessi hummed to the background music while tapping her foot and scrolling through her phone. She looked up with a scowl on her face once she realized her energetic foot couldn't match the pace of the elevator music. "Since you're a regular here, you should convince them to play one of your playlists instead. That'd get more people in this joint and not just those looking like they're counting down to their next nap." She used her phone to gesture to the groups of senior citizens surrounding us.

Creating playlists for people was one of my love languages, and something I regularly dished out to those I love. I missed my calling to become a music supervisor for films in Hollywood, to use my natural knack for knowing what songs could make movie scenes more impactful, sometimes more so than the ones chosen. Sometimes I regretted not taking the risk to move out to Los Angeles after getting my degree in Music Business. Instead, I stayed the suburbs.

Despite my dad vowing he was a "new man" my senior year of high school and working hard to prove he turned over a leaf, a part of me never forgave Dad's abandonment streaks. Fearful he would do it again, I didn't stray far from my mom so I could be there if she needed me. Just like when I was a little girl, I was the only one who stayed by her when times were rough, even if she never acknowledged it.

Mom was a beauty, and everyone commented on how alike we looked, more so as we both aged. She gave up dyeing her hair long ago, transitioning from yellow blonde to a dirty blonde, which actually suited her better, especially since she miraculously kept gray hairs at bay. She wore it to her shoulders, bangs fluffy and covering her forehead, the same unchanging hairstyle since the early 90s. She could wake up in the mornings with her hair looking exactly the same as it did the day before, thanks to the hairspray that layered each strand.

The scent of White Rain hairspray always reminded me of her. I wasn't great at doing my hair, choosing to wear it back in a ponytail most often, so I admired the way Mom took the time to curl her hair, spray, curl, spray. She rarely wore her hair back. But when she did for special occasions, with her bangs swept to the side, she looked the prettiest. It highlighted her big hazel eyes and long eyelashes even more. Very few people knew that since her bangs regularly covered her forehead, hiding her most striking features.

Mom finally walked into the restaurant, nearly sprinting to reach our table because she hates feeling like she's making a scene when she enters places.

"Where's Dad?"

She reached down to hug me and then Jess before pulling out her chair. "He had a migraine, so I left him on the couch with an ice pack."

"Oh, that's too bad. Must be the change of the seasons."

"That's what I'm thinking, too. Did you ladies order yet?" Mom unwrapped her silverware and put the faded purple cloth napkin in her lap, patting it down carefully.

"Black coffee and plain pancakes with warm buttermilk syrup

for the whole table!" Jessie declared. Same thing we order every week.

"How've things been going, honey?" Mom asked, and I see Jessi out of the corner of my eye sit up straighter with a smirk on her face. She knows how this conversation is going to go.

"Well, work is work. Not so exciting."

"But you have a great job and you should be grateful for it." Mom was the person reminding *everyone* they need to be happy with the things they have since there were others less fortunate. She had been on that streak since my Dad came back permanently, citing the fact that she never gave up as the reason he came back, and claiming life was perfect again.

I tapped my cup to the beat of the music. "I know, I know. I do enjoy the paycheck part."

"And you met your boyfriend through it." Jessi said with a laugh. "Oh my God, you literally just flinched when I said 'boyfriend'!"

"One, I never called him a boyfriend. And two, meeting men at work is currently a debatable perk." I said, hoping the waitress placing the plates of pancakes in front of us would distract them long enough to change topics.

Mom didn't even wait for the waitress to leave before she asked, "Having problems?"

And this is exactly why I didn't want to talk about Josh today. "You could say that. Josh introduced me to his brother last night. It was going well, but we ended in a big fight and haven't talked since I left his place."

"Oh, Haleigh, what did you do?" Despite my mom's positivity toward most things in the world, she assumed I was the reason for the demise of any relationship in my life. Both her and my dad defaulted to that immediate suspicion whenever I said I stopped dating someone, which is why I stopped telling them when I was. It seemed easier for Mom to place her heartache from Dad's past on me, and my dad acted like I never do anything right, which is ironic considering he was never around because of all the things *he* was doing. I became the scapegoat for my parents' marriage, and I found a weird peace with that over the years because they seem happy now.

"I didn't do anything! He got angry at me for no reason." I left out the fact that it regularly happens when he drinks because I didn't want Mom to associate Josh with Dad. Dad drank every day and night when I was a kid. Josh didn't have the same problem. He only drank when he was social.

Jessi was the friend who knew the most about my dad leaving us over and over when I was a little girl. I finally told her after she grilled me about my disdain for romantic movies. Most of my friends believed I was incapable of becoming love-struck because my parents' relationship set the bar too high. Wherever my parents went, they held hands, which provoked remarks about how cute they were. That was all it took for people to think a relationship was solid. As long as the two people were touching. Even more incredible if doing so after decades together.

I didn't see my parents in that same light. Most of my memories of them from childhood were comprised of covering my ears while they fought, many nights where my dad lived elsewhere for extended periods of time, and when he was home, there was nothing but tension, strained communication, and empty bottles. My dad wasn't intentionally physical with my mom. Although, there was one time when she blocked him from leaving again and he pushed her out of the way. She fell back into the wall as a framed picture crashed on her head. Dad didn't even stick around to see if it hurt her. He left while she was crying on the floor, shards of glass surrounding her. I ran to Mom as soon as he was out of sight. "It's just the alcohol talking, Haleigh," she justified. Luckily, she didn't require a trip to the hospital or stitches. But I'll never forget that scene and the sounds of her screams as the door slammed shut behind him.

Mom never gave up on him though. "Others have it much worse," she said after every fight.

I'm not sure what changed. Mom didn't address it. But one

day, my dad stopped running. He stuck around. He stopped drinking. He was a parent once again. The atmosphere shifted the year I turned eighteen. Maybe Dad could never handle having kids. Some people aren't built for it. At least he discovered how to love better, or maybe learned what love really was. It's like Mom believed in him enough that he eventually became what she always saw, that few others did, in his worst moments.

Mom sipped her coffee, clearly doubting I could be innocent in the events that took place that night. "You're too hard on men sometimes, Haleigh."

"That's what I'm always telling her, too!" Jessi jumped in with a mouthful of pancakes.

"Hey! You're supposed to be on my side!"

"We both are, honey," my mom said. "We just want you to be happy."

"No, you're just waiting for me to have grandchildren." Her only daughter being unmarried with no prospects in sight at twenty-nine wasn't fitting into her life plan.

"Haleigh, you drag me into baby stores to look at the cute clothes," Jessi accused. "I don't know who is going to be more excited when you finally get knocked up, you or your mom."

Mom's eyes widened and her cheeks turned red as she all but buried her face into her napkin.

"You can't say knocked up in public, Jess. Mom's too innocent for those words."

"Just be proper, girls," my mom reprimanded us. She put her napkin back in her lap, sat up straighter, and followed up with the big question, "So are you still going to see this Josh guy, Haleigh?"

I must have been quiet for too long as I mulled this over because Mom grinned.

"If you even have to think about it for that long, it tells me you like him. You're not one to give someone a second shot."

Her insinuation struck me hard. I looked like my mom but my personality reflected more of my dad's, prone to run away and quick to cut ties. I had a clear trend in my relationship history.

Always craving a relationship but always the first one to leave. I didn't want to be like my dad. I could commit.

Mom patted my hand. "Give Josh a break. It could have been a bad night. People have a lot going on internally, and you need to give them more grace now and then." Satisfied with the bit of advice she could offer, she finally changed the subject. "Have you seen any housebroken dogs at the shelter you think I could convince your dad to adopt?"

———

During the workweek I was consumed with counting down to Sunday night where I spent time at Pet Angels, the Roselle non-profit animal rescue shelter, giving dogs baths and cleaning cages. It was dirty work, but I loved every single second. Nothing about accounting made me as excited as ensuring these animals were clean and fresh inside a sparkling facility. Each task helped boost weekly adoptions and was my small contribution to a passion that equaled my music one.

My "Doggy Be Gone" playlist blared through the speakers. I danced in the cages with dogs of all sizes, holding their paws as we moved. I belted out tunes while holding my broom like a microphone. Kristen's voice matched mine as she worked the cages across the divider, our voices reverberating around the tin walls.

Kristen was my constant companion on Sunday nights. We worked so well together that we made the joint commitment for these evenings without verbalizing it. We fed off each other's energy, and the animals seemed to, also. Kristen was one of those stunning women who made everyone do a double-take when she walked by. With one side of her head shaved in a pixie-style haircut, you could never guess the color it would be from one week to another. A sleeve of tattoos snaking down one arm and gorgeous almond-shaped eyes gave her both a good girl and a bad girl vibe.

As we finished cleaning, Kristen mentioned the dreaded reality of work the next day. We were employed at different companies but those companies occupied the same building, so it allowed us to get together for lunch frequently. She was the marketing assistant for a boss who rose to his position in spite of a lack of talent, so she was doing his job on top of hers, with little credit ever thrown her way.

"Do you think about saying 'screw it all' and walking away? Or having some big *Jerry Maguire*-style epic breakdown that would likely result in complete humiliation, but at least it'd be a funny story for people to share for a while?"

Kristen grunted as she mopped the aisle. "You really don't care what people think of you, huh?"

I've had my fair share of not fitting in, and the best part about getting older was learning I can't please everybody. Yet there were two people I *always* wanted to win over, no matter how hard I tried to fight it. "Sadly, I'm still trying to convince my parents I'm no longer the thirteen-year-old girl they think I am. Maybe I'm too consumed by that to care about anyone else's opinion."

"Ha, I feel you there." We've shared our parental woes before, bonding over dads that didn't seem to want to be dads, and a shared history of dating the wrong type of men to make up for it.

"So... 'no' to supporting my *Jerry Maguire* escape?"

"Are you really thinking about quitting?"

"I dream about it every day. Doing this on Sundays once gave me the strength to get through the week, but now it's a reminder I'd much rather be doing something else."

Kristen wiped off her shoes from the mess of the last dog pen. The food had not settled in that poor beagle's stomach. "What would you do? Work here?"

"I don't know. I mean... it sounds better. Although I wonder if doing this full-time would turn me restless after a few months. Sometimes I think about packing everything up and heading to Cali. At least out there I could make connections while figuring it out. There's nothing happening here to get me closer to becoming a music supervisor." My mind was officially in full dreaming mode, and it all sounded better than the surrounding reality.

"Well, why not do that now? A move to LA sounds pretty damn good, especially as the weather gets colder."

I shrugged and leaned my chin on the broom handle. "I can't let go of this idea that my parents may need me. It's like I'm locked into some elusive fear that once I leave, something bad will happen."

"Yeah, I get that." Kristen threw my jacket at me as she reached for hers. "But you're also not your parents' keepers. You gotta live your own life. You let me know if you quit, and I'll do it, too. I'll be the one to grab the fish from the tank. We can hitchhike to the coast together. You, me, and the office fishies."

Maybe now *was* the time to take chances. Outside of Jessi and my parents, there wasn't much here that I would be leaving behind since Kristen would come with me. Heck, maybe Jessi would, too.

For all I knew, Josh was already out of my life. Almost a full day had gone by and still no call or text from him. Maybe I didn't pass whatever test he was trying to put me through by meeting his brother and he was disappointed by me.

Or maybe, like Jessi and my mom always said about me, Josh just couldn't see when there was something good standing right in front of him.

Chapter Four
Him

I didn't have passions in life. Until you. I didn't know what passion was. Until you.

I thought life was full of decisions, all head, no heart. I didn't know how to touch my heart at all. Sure, I had glimpses of it before. Maybe a few close-calls. But you can't touch your heart and then rebound back to cold and closed off. It doesn't work that way.

I wasn't in the right state of mind to meet you.

Sometimes it takes being an asshole to realize I found someone special. Anger was my default. I knew it, but I didn't know how to change it, or if I wanted to change it, for that matter.

Until you.

You make me a better man.

Chapter Five
Her

Determined to start fresh, I slid into my desk Monday morning, convinced I could finish the stack of ledgers early to spend the rest of the day planning my getaway to the West Coast. The conversation last night with Kristen had reignited my passion and belief that maybe it wasn't too late to start over.

After working on a few documents, I stretched back in my chair to give my eyes a break. Lately, the idea that my time with Gungston and Associates should come to an end had been weighing on me. It was time to move on to the next adventure. I'd saved frugally over the past nine years, so I felt comfortable enough to walk away from it and do something I was more passionate about than accounting.

I was approached by Angela, the Pet Angels Executive Director, about joining the team since I shouted my love for the organization every chance I got. They were the most caring folks and traveled all over the U.S. to rescue animals anytime there was a natural disaster. It would be a significant pay cut and only part-time, so I'd have to pick up another job on the side, but my heart felt more called these days to take that risk to be more fulfilled.

I shared that desire with Josh a month after we started dating, apprehensive of his judgment since he was one hundred percent made for the corporate world, down to the perfectly-pressed suits and shiny shoes more expensive than my car. But he simply smiled, grabbed my hand, and said, "One of my favorite things about you is your passion for animals. You care about each living thing's life. I admire it." After a pause as he played with my fingers, he added, "Maybe someday I could be the one to help you pursue those passions. You know, take away the pressure to do things that don't make you happy to stay afloat." I was taken aback by his reference to a long-term future together, one that most guys like him actively avoid. It further fueled the visions I already had about creating a family with him.

By mid-morning at work, an older gentleman, sporting a ballcap pulled over his eyes and a gray name badge with EARL stamped on it, put a green vase filled with a dozen red roses on my desk with two shaky hands. There wasn't a card, but I knew they were from Josh. It seemed to be his go-to way of apologizing, but I hated flowers. They died too quickly, and it made me feel guilty, as though I was intentionally murdering this life form. We didn't cover that before he started sending them, and now it was too late to bring it up.

All my female coworkers gushed about Josh like he was the greatest man in the world, all based on the number of bouquets he sent me in our short time of dating. I didn't tell them he sent the flowers because he was being a total asshole.

I stared at the red petals all day, contemplating texting Josh. Usually I would do it right away, quick to forgive him despite my reluctance to do so with most people. But Saturday night hurt more than the other times. It was a milestone for us, with him opening up enough to let me meet the family member he was closest to. Josh could have followed up yesterday and said sorry. But he stayed silent. Until now. Was it a last minute thought this morning to finally do something to apologize? Or did he spend all weekend regretting his words?

I wanted to hate him. Few people would argue against the

reasons I collected to harbor such a feeling. But when Josh was on point, he was fantastic. Sweet, thoughtful, loving, and insanely good in bed. He was quiet yet adventurous, loved to travel, and was always on the hunt for a new challenge. I loved that he forced me out of my comfort zone to try new things. Since he rarely laughed, it was the best feeling in the world when I could make it happen. Josh would wrap his arms around my waist and nuzzle his face in my neck as though he was equally grateful I could elicit that reaction out of him.

With an hour to spare in the workday and boredom serving as an advantage for him, I texted Josh,

> Thank you for the flowers, they're beautiful.

His reply didn't come until four hours later. Enough time for me to get home and drink two glasses of wine while sprawled out on the couch reading a historical romance book Jessi had recommended. By then, I had convinced myself to redirect my mind and set out to find Prince Charming. Screw this mediocre stuff. Maybe it was time to believe in fairy tales. Jessi would be proud if I could get my heart there.

The long-awaited beep on my phone aborted that mission as Josh's text appeared,

> The flowers aren't enough to make up for it.
> Go to your doorstep.

Bouncing off the couch, I glanced in the mirror to check for wine-stained lips. Tucking messy strands of hair in my bun and pulling at my loose wool socks, I tried to look somewhat sexy enough in a casual manner.

My shoulders slumped when I opened the door and didn't see Josh standing on the porch. Instead, a CD case rested on the mat marked, "Something About a Girl."

I stood on the doorstep, clutching my arms to stay warm,

searching for any sign of him. Returning inside, I flipped on the electric fireplace, refilled my wineglass, stuck the CD in the stereo, and hit the play button.

As I settled on the couch to listen, I immediately realized a deeper reason I was so drawn to Josh. He was the first guy I met who could challenge my playlist-making skills. Josh knew how to talk to me through my language—music, reminiscing on key moments (first kiss, first date, first concert) in our relationship by choosing songs that were playing in the background at the time. Most of what I gathered about his feelings for me came through songs as he'd lean over and whisper in my ear, "This one makes me think of you."

After an hour of listening, I sent him a text,

Good choices.

Josh's response was immediate, like he had been sitting around waiting for me to text,

You like? A lot? A little? More than a lot?

Assuming he was hinting at my feelings about him more than the CD, I thought carefully, my cheeks heated from the bottle of wine consumed, and replied with,

More than a lot.

Good. Same.

I placed the phone back on the table, unable to hide the smile creeping on my face. Josh kept winning me over. No matter how hard I tried, I couldn't shake him.

A few minutes later, my phone dinged with another text from him,

> Goodnight, beautiful. I want to take you on a
> proper date tomorrow to make up for it all.

And he did. A proper date, followed by an improper night at his place. It was perfect.

As I laid in bed with his arms wrapped tightly around me, I knew the truth. I was hooked on him. Josh knew it, too.

————

For what would have been our five month anniversary, Josh invited me to meet him at Starter's Lounge for a drink. Somehow, we had fallen into another black hole of silence–three days, to be exact. He wasn't calling or responding to my text messages. A part of me was saying, *Yep, I expected this. It's just what guys like him do when it gets too serious.* And the other side wondered if he had been spending time with someone else. Either way, I almost told him "just text me that you're done with this instead of me wasting my time by meeting you somewhere." But instead, I erased the message I had typed out, and put on what I knew were his favorite black jeans because they make my butt look good, just to show him that I'm alright without him.

Besides, the night was an unusual December evening, a welcoming weather pattern resulting in a perfect sixty-five degrees, uncommon for northern Illinois. Everyone was flocking to any available outdoor setting, already tapped out of winter even though it had just begun. So, it spurred my willingness to meet with Josh and hear him out: a final pre-winter drink in a cozy outdoor setting with live music. Starter's Lounge had one of the best beer gardens, intimate and tranquil, an idyllic location for an easy goodbye.

In a way, it already felt like we mutually called it quits through our silence over the past few days. Josh didn't send me flowers this time, which was his standard apologetic move. I squared my shoulders as I walked toward him, wondering if we would do small talk first or get straight to the point.

"I'm so sorry," Josh's surprising words tumbled out as soon as I sat down at the table. He slid a beer to me, a reconciliation gift to make his excuse easier to accept. This was something different. Him actually apologizing... with *words*.

The sun settled behind the clouds as it lowered back to the horizon. White tube lights wrapped around the trees in the fenced-in beer garden. A musician strummed acoustic covers on the makeshift stage, a simple pallet in the corner of the yard. It was one of the last evenings Starter's Lounge would be open for the year. The air was filled with the type of energy that only comes from moments like these, when people know it's the end and they're maximizing every possible minute as though they're invincible, like New Year's Eve.

Josh's midnight blue mock-neck sweater intensified the remorse in his eyes. I had yet to see him look anything close to regretful, and the sight pulled at my heartstrings.

"I also got you those onion rings you like and requested extra sauce since you always seem to run out." Josh breathed deeply and put his palms on the table, as though preparing for his defense statement in court. "Listen Haleigh, I can be a real dick, and I know that. I have trust issues. I don't believe things will last, so it's easier for me to push someone away than be surprised when they're gone the next day."

"But why are you still pushing me away after five months of dating?"

He grumbled while wiping the condensation off his beer glass with his thumb, "I don't know, Haleigh. I care about you. A lot. You're good for me. Ryan agrees. You're not like other girls I know. Dating you is hard for that reason. You make me want to be better, and I get pissed that you make me want to change."

"I never asked you to change."

"I know. But you make me *want* to. That feeling is new to me.

You make me constantly think about the future. Like I need to get my life in order so we can have a shot at one, otherwise I won't be good enough for you."

I sit back in my chair, letting the surprise wash over me. I wouldn't have thought Josh would be the type that didn't think he was good enough for any girl, let alone for me. His arrogance blended with his charisma and it was hard to see one for the other. Self-esteem issues would not have been something I expected he'd struggled with. There was still a lot I was learning about him, and it kept me intrigued.

"And I wanted to give you this..." Josh slid a white envelope across the table like a business exchange, as though he had written my new salary down on a piece of paper, a raise to come back to work for him.

I raised my eyebrows as I tapped the envelope with my fingertips.

"Go ahead, open it," he encouraged with a smile full of hope.

I lifted the flap and peeked inside to see a piece of paper folded in half. Carefully, I slipped it out of the envelope, unfolded it and read the contents.

"You booked me a trip to Jamaica?"

"I booked *us* a trip." Josh reached across the table and put his hands over mine. "You said you wanted to go because of that Beach Boys song that was stuck in your head ever since you were a little girl." I shook my head in awe. I told him that random fact on our second date during a hockey game, where I was pretty sure he didn't hear a thing I said the whole time since it was so loud and his eyes never left the ice. Clearly, I underestimated him. "I'm aware I've been distracted and spending a lot of hours at the office. Right around the time we met, I found out that several execs are retiring in my division. I had been working my ass off for years as is and I wanted first dibs at their jobs. This promotion sets me up for exactly what I want for my future. I should have explained it to you, but..."

"You couldn't handle somebody asking you about it because it would have stressed you out more," I finished the sentence for him.

He smiled. "Exactly. You get me. I couldn't handle the extra pressure. If I didn't get it, it would have been embarrassing."

I kept my arms folded on the table and nodded. I was glad he shared more, but I didn't feel at peace inside. "Did you get the job?"

"I did! Just found out today!" He cleared his throat, realizing my excitement didn't match his, nor was it a time to celebrate. "Listen, it wasn't fair to ghost you, Haleigh, and I'm sorry. You have every reason to hate me. I wasn't prepared for someone like you to come along. Especially during this time. I needed to get this job because it'll change everything for me. I'm taking a much-needed vacation to get away and reset before it starts. I want you to come with me. Please." His voice matched his eyes, both pleading with me. I doubted Josh asked anyone for anything. For once it felt as though I had more power to hurt him than he had to hurt me.

Jessi would have been thrilled over the idea of Josh whisking me away on a trip since something between us finally aligned with her romantic ideals. Although flattering, my annoyance was fiercer than his arrogance that he was so sure I'd say yes after the questionable past few days. "So, you went ahead and booked the ticket?"

"I figured you were worth the risk."

Avoiding my initial reaction to call him crazy, I paused to think it through. "I need to run to the bathroom." I shoved back my chair, crossed the beer garden, and climbed the concrete block stairs to the single stall. With each step, I cursed myself for agreeing to come out with him tonight. My car beckoned behind the fence, offering an escape route. *What in the world was he thinking? A trip is insane.* I could only imagine the issues that would arise once we were stuck on an island with no available plane to rescue us when we needed it. We were both damn good at running away.

Looking in the mirror, pulling my hair away from my face and fanning myself, I coached, *You are better than this, Haleigh. You deserve something more. You hate drama. It's been nothing but drama since the beginning. Run. Run. Run.*

But then there was the voice repeating Josh's confession, his apology, the reasons for his unprovoked actions. Those imploring puppy eyes. A vulnerable Josh. *He did it all for you. Don't you see that?*

By the time the bathroom door slammed behind me, I had drowned the voice advocating for him, and resolved I wouldn't go on the trip.

As I walked back to the table, preparing my speech to refuse Josh's offer, everything around me suddenly played out like one of Jessi's favorite early 2000s chick flicks. The guitarist in the corner strummed Dave Matthews Band's "Where Are You Going?" while the white lights tinted a faint romantic glow. Josh looked up from his drink and sat back in his chair with rapt attention and parted lips; even from a distance, I could hear his exhale. His eyes narrowed in on me with a smile brighter than the moon, transforming me into the most gorgeous woman in the world. As his eyes glistened, I could hear him say, "You're the woman I will marry." Once I arrived at the table, he all but confirmed it. "You are perfect for me. I *need* you in my life, and I want you as my girlfriend."

"Ok, I'll go," the words trickled out before I could catch them. That's not what I had planned. That's not what I wanted to say. *Damn you, Dave Matthews Band cover guitarist. Damn you, tube lights. Damn the first romantic scene I've ever acknowledged before in my life.*

Josh pulled my chair toward him, the metal legs scraping against the concrete until it connected with his. "Did you really just call me your girlfriend?" I asked. He put his arms around my shoulders and pulled me in close.

"Hi, girlfriend," he whispered in my ear, lifting my chin with his thumb and kissing me on the nose. I wouldn't forget that look for as long as I lived. It was the day I believed Josh fell in love with me, and maybe a part of me confessed I was falling for him as well.

———

The trip to Jamaica was a pinnacle in our relationship. Josh turned into a different guy, or maybe the man he always was.

We completely let loose, a term I never would have associated with Josh. He had been uptight since the day I met him. Maybe it was all for his job and now with the promotion, he could relax, a sight that proved to be enthralling and sexy. Josh's hands didn't stop touching some part of my body, no matter where we were, no matter how sweaty I was from the Jamaican sun. We drank a lot, but drink number three and beyond didn't surface his "other side" that I had once dreaded. Drink one and drink twenty-two all produced a happy Josh. We turned off our phones and locked them in the safe, determined to savor the few days we had without the demands of the world calling on us.

Seeing him unwind was a sight I felt privy to witness. Josh laughed more than I thought I'd hear him laugh in a lifetime. I watched, awestruck, as he angled his head back, his lips parting with perfect teeth flashing, the laughter coming from deep within. The same laugh that captivated me the first day I met him. His laugh was majestic, something I wanted to bottle and forever keep, remembering him just as he was in those moments.

Everything was magical, from the gorgeous blue waters to the crazy dancing we got sucked into at night because we had nothing else to lose. No one knew us; we could be whoever we wanted.

On the third day, Josh held my hand as we sat side-by-side on our strategically-placed lounge chairs, only a few feet from the cool breeze of the ocean.

"I am so happy you're here."

I turned to him, pushing my sunglasses to the top of my head so I could better see the look in his eyes. "It'd be pretty lonely sitting here with your hand outstretched and no one to hold it."

He smiled, the rare genuine one that manufactured a dimple out of the blue. I wanted to reach out to trace it, to embed the image in my mind.

"I'd have this guy to hang out with," Josh thrust his thumb toward the ocean. Every day, a man with a straw sunhat and a tray of goods hanging around his neck walked up and down the beach, his feet dipped in the water, yelling, "Cig-as, Cig-as." It was the start of an inside joke, a special trip recalled by the cigar salesman walking the shore.

On our fourth day, Josh gave in and bought two cigars off the man. One was stale, but one was the "best damn cigar I've ever had." We wondered if there wasn't a little something more in that second one. For the rest of the night, Josh was on a high, bois-terous and child-like, running in and out of the water, on a frantic search for seashells, ordering just about everything on the menu so the waiter had to bring a second table to hold all the plates. He was *free*. Damn, I couldn't stop smiling. *I. Could. Not. Stop. Smiling.*

Each Jamaican night, Josh put his hands on my hips, his fingers sliding under my shirt. It was his code, a battle cry of his intentions for what was to come next. He kept me guessing whether he'd travel up or down from my hips, and somehow that simple question made it thrilling.

On our sixth and final night, Josh's hands lanced on my hips as we watched the ocean from our private balcony. His body pressed into my back as he kissed my neck, forcing me to arch into him. His right hand moved from my hips to my stomach, his palm pressing me back into him where I could feel his entire being, nothing left to the imagination. As I reached behind to grab on to him, he was already naked. Josh had walked straight from the shower to the balcony, a bold move for someone so modest. He was finally uninhibited with me. I liked him that way the most.

We kept our phones off until we were back at our own houses, ending the flawless trip as we hugged and kissed goodbye like we couldn't get enough of each other, despite spending every waking minute of the previous week together. Josh didn't sleep at all the first night home as he returned voicemails, texts, and emails he missed from work. That's when I knew his feelings for me were genuine. Putting the rest of the world on hold was his way of fighting for me, to make things better than they had been.

Those facts weren't lost on me. It made me fall more for Josh, like winning over the man who couldn't otherwise be changed, who was once too set in his ways. I don't care what a woman says, there's an ingrained part of us with some profound hope, even for the unromantic ones like me, that wants to be *the one* a man realizes is worth fighting for. It may not have been in this super obvious made-for-movies-sort of way, but it was Josh investing himself in *us*, which meant more than words ever could.

———

Jamaica catapulted many more trips over the following two years. We proved we traveled well together, an important value for both of us. Josh's new role sent him to meetings and conferences all over the States. I went with him on the majority of his trips as we explored new cities, restaurants, and experiences. Josh was happier when we were somewhere else. He liked that he could be anyone he wanted to be, not held down by expectations of people who already knew him, and I enjoyed that side of him. Every time we were someplace new, I would look at him and think, *this is my guy*. Even after three drinks, he wasn't all that bad, as long as we were any place other than home.

When we were back in the suburbs, things were different. I had to force myself to think of Josh in terms of Ryan's dog reference. A dog that would get agitated and aggressive if cooped up in the house for too long. Once the door opened and he was set free, he was happy and wagging his tail all over again. I took pride in understanding his idiosyncrasies and catering to what Josh needed to thrive. More outings, more trips, more interactions with the world around us. He didn't like the places he already knew. He was an explorer. And I'd take him being an explorer over running away from me any day of the week.

Chapter Six
Him

My fears were unknown to you at first. Improperly directed anger would become my reaction as I struggled to work through those fears. Eventually, you caught on. Although I could see the pain cross your face, knowing full well that I hurt you, you remained selfless. You would suck down your own rage as a reaction, and instead, cup my face and kiss me. You were proving to me you would stay, you would try to understand the mess beneath the surface, and you would love me no matter what.

That's when I knew I had found someone special. Someone I couldn't let go of. No matter what.

Chapter Seven
Her

Dad was the one who first alerted me that Josh was preparing to take things to the next level. He let it slip while I was eating dinner at my parents' house, clearly unabashed by ruining people's surprises.

I noticed Dad's forehead wrinkling with deep lines as he listened to updates on all areas of my life, including Josh, work, volunteering, traveling, and friends. I knew something was up when he asked if I wanted to have a drink with him on the porch while Mom cleaned up from dinner. He poured us sweet tea and we sat on the back deck in their wooden rocking chairs, watching the lights in the neighbor's house turn on and off and listening to the faint howls of coyotes.

"Are you getting serious with Josh?" That was not what I expected from my dad, a man prone to immediately exiting the room when any topic that resembled romance was spoken about.

I shrugged and pulled my hair into a ponytail, surprised with how warm I felt from Dad mentioning his name, as though the two colliding created deep unease within me. Josh and I recently hit our two-year anniversary, although we both refused to celebrate it, which only convinced me more that we were good for each other.

"I love him. I could see life with him. We balance each other. I wouldn't be opposed to marrying him."

"That doesn't sound like you're excited about it, though."

"To be fair, Dad, when have you ever cared enough to hear me be excited about a relationship?"

He swirled the ice cubes in his glass. "Josh stopped by the other night to ask my permission to marry you."

I stopped rocking, sat up straighter, and closed my mouth when I noticed it was agape. Josh had been asking questions about what sort of ring I like, but I didn't once consider he was truly prepared to ask. I pushed it off as mere curiosity caused by the spike of recent engagements among our social circles. We were constantly flying to weddings everywhere. "What did you say?"

"I asked him if he was sure he wanted to marry you, that you can be tough to please."

My hands gripped the armrests on the chair. These were the things said casually by my dad that made me think I would never be good enough for him. Shouldn't fathers be protective of their daughters, not trying to warn a guy that their daughter is imperfect?

"Well, that's not the way I pictured it would go," I muttered, disheartened.

"Would you say yes if he asked you?"

I threw up my hands. "Well, who knows if he will even ask now! I mean, holy hell, Dad." I shook my head, unable to articulate what I wish he could know. If only my parents could realize the negative impact their harsh words had on how I view myself.

I bit the inside of my cheek and answered, "Yeah, if he thinks I'm *worthy* enough to marry, then I probably would say yes." Bitterness doused each word.

My dad missed the point of my tone. "Okay, then. I wanted to make sure you were ready. Marriage is hard, you know. You gotta stick through it even when you don't want to sometimes." He cleared his throat, a struggle for him to say more than a few words at a time. "You choose the person you marry, and you vow to love them, and you learn to love them even when it's hard as hell. And in the end, there are good rewards. Good eventually comes out of it, even if it takes a few years to surface."

He was summarizing his own marriage, similar to my mom's interpretation, more than giving the advice he *thought* he was giving. With the poor examples set by his own parents and other marriages in his family, the one he and my mom had was the most successful by far. That made Dad an authority figure on marriage in his eyes. I wondered if he knew how lucky he was that Mom stuck it through, and it wasn't because of his own doing. I hoped tips about raising children weren't next because I'd have a really hard time swallowing that from him.

"Thanks for the advice."

"Sure, sure." He finished the last of his drink. "Let's go back in and see what your mom made for dessert."

———

Josh and I succeeded in being argument-free for five whole months, producing my second engagement alert. In fact, he didn't drink at all around me during that time. No apologies were necessary for once. There was nothing but pure sweetness and consideration from both sides. It gave me hope that this is the way it could be when two people put each other first with honor and love. Josh was finally coming around. Maybe I was, too.

The third alert happened the day Ryan came to town for a baseball game. Josh all but begged me to join them for lunch. I had refused to join a boys' outing since the first night I met Ryan, a decision that was intentional so as to not repeat history. Although that terrible night happened almost two years ago, some wounds take more time to heal. Because of Josh's persistence, I gave it another shot.

"Haleigh!" Ryan's magnetic smile lit up the dining area of Capodice's, our favorite Italian restaurant. Josh and I ate dinner there weekly and visited the bar for coffee and dessert at least one other time throughout the week. It was a convenient half mile from his house.

Ryan had spotted me before Josh, who was invested in the menu even though he knew it inside and out. Ryan immediately stood up, smacked Josh on the arm, and embraced me in a tight hug. "Great to see you again."

His scent was far more rugged than Josh's. It was the first time I noticed it. Josh wore the fanciest new cologne, whatever his men's magazine said was the hot scent. Two squirts, one on each side of his neck, and then one on his crotch. It would drive me nuts. "Why are you spraying your crotch?" I'd ask in bewilderment. He never gave me a straight answer. I could only assume it came from some of the stupid suggestions in those men's magazines he read.

Ryan had a woodsy scent, more citrusy. Maybe it wasn't even a cologne. It could have been the way he naturally smelled.

"It's great to see you, too."

Josh apparently made his selection because he finally put down the menu and stood to kiss me on the cheek. "Hey, hon. Glad you made it." Ryan pulled the chair out between them so that's where I sat, a brother on both sides.

A waiter took our orders, and we sat in uncomfortable silence for a moment after he left. Josh and Ryan were having a silent exchange of words over my head. Evidently there was a specific reason why I was invited to join them.

"How's work going?" Ryan broke the quiet with what may be one of my least favorite questions to be asked. I was terrible with small talk, making conversations awkward at times because I didn't want to provide an answer that wasn't true just for the sake of responding.

"Well, it's a job, and it provides a paycheck."

"That's her response every time someone asks that, so you can bypass that question," Josh interjected.

Ryan ignored him. "So going quite well, huh?"

I grinned, "I thought you were supposed to be great at reading people. How's your little man?"

Ryan leaned in for our own private conversation. Disengaged, Josh focused on his phone, which was unnerving.

"Adam." Ryan smiled at the thought of him. "He's amazing. Every week he's doing something new, and it's fascinating to watch. It's crazy he will be three soon."

"Do you read all those baby books and make sure he's up to par with where he should be?"

"Oh, God, no. Those books are terrible. Same thing with internet searches. Endless abyss of bad information. Chat boards, even worse. People provide advice that contradicts common sense, yet are ready to judge the hell out of you the moment you do something they don't do. Like there's only one way and they know best. Trolls live for attacking new parents."

"Oh my gosh, you make parenthood sound awful." I laughed at the thought, glancing at Josh, expecting him to join in. But he scrolled through his phone, ignoring us. "So basically, there's no good place to go for advice? You're in it, and every day you just hope your child comes out alive?"

"Basically. Parenthood is great, don't get me wrong. It's trial and error. You have to trust your intuition. And if you don't have intuition, pray your partner does." Ryan paused as he pointedly stared at Josh. "We're actually expecting baby number two come December."

"That's awesome! Congratulations!" I briefly hugged Ryan as Josh looked up from his phone long enough to smile at me. I could tell he was pumped to be an uncle to another little baby, and I was surprised he didn't tell me himself already.

Ryan reached for a piece of bread and dipped it in a plate of oil and parmesan cheese. "Are you wanting kids someday?"

"A thousand percent, yes. I'd love to have two or three if that's the way life plays out. I'm open. Except I don't think I could go over five. I couldn't handle being that outnumbered. I don't have it in me."

Grunting, Ryan responded, "I feel the same way since I come from a two-child family. Lindsay wants eight or nine. I told her we may have to agree to a polygamous relationship instead so she can get that with other men."

"I'm hitting the restroom. I'll be back," Josh's nervous energy was resounding.

I caught the look Ryan gave him before he left.

"Okay, what gives? These secret exchanges aren't lost on me. Is Josh having another bad day? Are you here to break up with me on Josh's behalf?"

Ryan smirked while twisting the silver wedding band on his finger. "How awful would that be? Nah, he's fine. And no, he's not breaking up with you, or I'm not, however you want to put it."

"I'll be dissecting these looks between you two until someone speaks up. My pasta won't be touched until I get answers."

"Well, we can't have the pasta punished now, can we?" Ryan deliberately chewed a bite of bread to stall. "I just wanted the chance to see you again without everyone else around. I know you and Josh are a bit more serious since the last time the three of us hung out alone. It's sensible for the big brother to check in on things."

I winced at Ryan's reminder of our first meeting. "I'm happy to announce that he has graduated from 'puppy,' as you warned me about. It was a tough housebreaking period but he seems to be adjusting well."

"Shock collars can do wonders."

"Amen to that." I tilted my wineglass to him.

"So, you're happy?" He turned serious, surprising me since it seemed to be the type of question he should ask the person closest to him, his brother, and not his brother's girlfriend.

I pondered it before answering. Maybe it was Ryan's therapy background, but he solicited the rawest urges to be unreservedly honest in every word I spoke. I felt like if I weren't, he'd know anyway. "Yeah. We're getting where we need to be.

Finally. Even if it was rockier than it should have been in the beginning."

"That's good. Makes me happy to hear."

"Makes you happy to know I'm happy?"

"That it does."

"Is he happy?" I nodded toward Josh who was snaking his way through the tables back to ours.

Ryan smiled. "As happy as Josh gets, and that's saying a lot."

"You guys have a good conversation while I was gone?" Josh directed the question to Ryan.

Ryan rested his arm on the back of my chair. "She passes the test. Apparently, we weren't too stealthy because she figured out our intention right away."

"She's a smart one, my girl." Josh kissed my cheek, startling me since he had been so standoffish in the beginning.

With the tension gone, the rest of our lunch date was filled with laughter and great discussions. Sharing pasta dishes, acting like we were all the best of friends; it restored my desire to have a future with Josh. Ryan was the final assurance, the guarantee that Josh and I were made to make this work, despite the doubts that may have existed in the beginning. I couldn't imagine anywhere else where I could fit more than right here between them, the start of a new family. When Josh announced they needed to get on the road to make it to the game on time, I was bummed lunch had ended.

As Josh paid the bill, Ryan leaned his head closer to mine to utter, "Our waiter is the type of guy who marinates his beef, but eats his poultry raw."

I snorted while holding a napkin to my nose, convinced the water stinging my nostrils would shoot out. "What does that even *mean*? That has to be the worst one you've come up with."

Ryan held out his hands in a shrug, "I don't plan on sticking around to find out more about him, so that's all I had."

In the parking lot, Ryan wrapped his arms around me and whispered in my ear, "Seriously, so glad you stuck it through."

When we pulled apart, he gave me a knowing look and said, "Hopefully it won't be long until the next time I see you."

Josh ran his hands through my hair and passionately kissed me on the lips, the most affectionate he's been in front of his brother —or anyone. Ryan's consent clearly meant a lot to him. Ryan and I got along effortlessly though. We naturally understood each other. Maybe that's why Josh fell for me; I reminded him of the person he was closest to. If so, I was honored to be tied to Ryan like that.

"Have fun tonight!" I called out to both of them once Josh pulled away, his surprising kiss warming my entire body, leaving my toes tingling.

Ryan waved as he closed the driver's door.

"We will." Josh kissed me again like he couldn't stand to leave me. "Tomorrow night I want you at my place. Feel free to show up with little on. Clothes won't be necessary."

"Like nothing but a trench coat?"

"Would you do that?"

I lowered my eyes and lifted them again slowly, batting my lashes and biting my lower lip, a look I knew he loved. "You'll just have to find out tomorrow night."

His eyes shone with excitement. I knew he would wonder how serious I was.

The next night, I followed through with my words as soon as it was dark enough to be discreet from the neighbors. I showed up on Josh's doorstep in a tan trench coat, black heels, and nothing underneath.

———

While exploring a black rock beach in Hawaii four months later, Josh sunk down to one knee, pulled out a ring box from his blue shark swim trunks, and asked if I would marry him. It was exactly how I would have described my perfect engagement. I wasn't crazy about the big elaborate scenes, the setups, the planning of what to say; I preferred the in-the-moment, say-what-you-want proposal, exactly as he did it. Even though others (especially Jessi) seemed disappointed in the lack of a great romantic story, I appreciated his technique.

Josh was genuine, earnest, and waiting intently for my reply as he held out a stunning staggered row, princess cut diamond ring. At two karats, it was a bigger than I would have liked, and it made me pause, wondering if he wanted me to be more than what I am.

My dad's words rode on the breeze, *Who else would put up with you, Haleigh?*

"Yes," leaked from my mouth before I could consider why a part of me was whispering *no*. But I knew Josh would be the perfect dad, and I already fit into his family. We had worked so hard over the past couple of years to get here together. We were making it work. There was nothing else I could want than someone who was willing to show up and stay, even when things got hard. We celebrated by finding a little bakery in Hanapepe for dessert, carrot cake for him, chocolate coconut pie for me.

Funny how the future of a relationship can be reflected in the early days. If only hindsight could be a superpower in the present and not clarity that comes when it's much too late to change what's happened. No one knows that during our eight-month engagement, we almost called it off twice and actually did break up for twenty-four hours. Both of us kept our mouths sealed, which was a relief when we reconciled.

As confident as I was that Josh was supposed to be in my life, the engagement itself felt forced at times. Almost as though someone was holding a gun to our backs and forcing us to the altar. But we made it to our wedding day, purposely maintaining a low-key celebration with only seventy-five guests and minimal decorations.

My name changed to Mrs. Haleigh Claystone almost three years to the day from our first date. After the wedding, our relationship remarkably improved even more, providing the reassurance I deeply craved that it was indeed the right decision to make.

We cruised through the Caribbean (in part to reminisce on our first trip together) in honeymoon elation. Josh didn't stop holding my hand wherever we went, even when at home on the couch.

He texted me several times a day that he loved me and left me sweet notes all over the house and my car expressing what he loved the most about me. The unpredictable Josh I dated disappeared; this was a new Josh, the best version of him and the one I think he always wanted to be. I was in love and grateful that I stuck through the rough periods to arrive at this place of bliss.

We continued traveling. My friends and coworkers regularly reminded me we were the couple others wished they could be. Happy, carefree, and experiencing as much of the world as we could.

The unshakeable feeling we were meant to be in each other's lives seized my heart. All the reasons to run never held the weight they should have; all the reasons to stay became less about him.

Chapter Eight
Him

Traveling brought out a different side of me. I was my best self. I know it makes little sense to anyone else. "You have the perfect family and the perfect life," people say. But that doesn't mean I can't struggle. It doesn't mean I have to know who I am.

They always expected me to be someone else. Ryan was the perfect child. My mom loved the most on him. My dad gave him the most accolades. I was told I could be better. I spent my entire childhood keeping up with Ryan until finally, I surpassed him in every way I could.

I loved traveling. It's why I wanted that promotion so damn badly. I needed to travel. I needed to go where no one expected more than what they received from me.

You fell in love with me when I was traveling. That scared the shit out of me. I wasn't sure you'd love me when I wasn't on the road. I was still unsure of who I was.

You changed that though. You changed me. You helped me find the core of who I'll be from now on.

CHAPTER NINE
HER

Early Sunday morning, my phone dinged with a text from Kristen asking if we could grab coffee after our Pet Angels shift later that night. Before I left the house, I grabbed my jacket and kissed Josh goodbye, telling him I'd be late getting back home. He saluted me with a beer.

Kristen was quiet the entire shift at the shelter and even declined to dance to my newest playlist, which was unusual since it contained many of her favorites. Once we locked up, we walked a block in chilly silence to the Spotted Owl Café, a regular stop we would make to devour their delicious pour-over coffee and blueberry scones, no matter the time of day since they were open until 1:00 a.m.

Normally very chatty, Kristen's withdrawn demeanor was disconcerting. I did my best to not pry and to wait patiently for her to speak. By the time we placed our orders, I was thoroughly concerned something serious had happened.

As I watched the clock behind her strike 9:00 a.m., I couldn't stop tapping my steaming mug of decaf coffee, pouring in two creamers to calm my anxiety. She stirred in a dash of sugar before taking a deep breath and getting right to the point.

"Has Josh ever mentioned me?"

Josh was not the person I expected to be brought up in this conversation. The tension hunched her shoulders. My muscles tightened, and I slowly responded, "No... should he have?"

"Does he know we volunteer together?"

"Yeah, of course. I talk about you all the time." My stomach flipped as I retraced all my conversations with Josh, analyzing anything that would have stood out regarding Kristen.

"Okay..."

"Kristen, tell me what's going on." Dread poured into my nerves.

"Yeah, I don't know. I'm regretful I didn't say anything earlier. I guess I didn't think you and Josh would last." She paused as I grimaced. "I know that's shitty to say, but it's true." Kristen never cursed so that one word screamed how on edge she was. "But you're married to him now. It changes things."

"Kristen, what *is* it? Please get to the point." Frustration, anxiety, and nausea were boiling inside, unsure of why or for what, just waiting to explode. Kristen was one of my favorite people, relating more to me than most of my other friends. The anticipation filled me with fear, yet I was desperate to pull the words from her mouth.

"Josh and I were dating when you guys first started dating."

There it was.

It was almost as bad as I was dreading. Although the worst of many scenarios zooming through my head would have been if her statement was present-tense, not past-tense. Josh didn't mention anyone else. I wouldn't have thought it was possible with him spending so much time at work. "Dating or sleeping together?"

Kristen's shoulders curled over her chest, her shameful eyes focused on her mug, speaking the truth before her words did. "I guess it depends on your definition. But... both."

I rubbed my face with my hands, repeating her words in my mind, digesting, debating if I wanted to hear more.

She continued without a word from me, "We started volunteering together around the same time I was dating him. I knew about you and him, so I assumed you knew about me. I thought it was strange you talked so openly, but you were confident. I admired you. And then," she cleared her throat as she shredded her napkin into tiny pieces. "One day, you asked if I was dating anyone. I realized then you had no clue. Josh only told *me* about *you*. He gave me a reason to walk away, but I was too foolish to pick up on it. I should have figured it out earlier."

I shook my pounding head, unable to make eye contact with her. "So why tell me now? Why after I married him? Why not before?" I felt frantic for answers, although more from Josh than from Kristen. But she was the one sitting in front of me as I fought to process her words.

Tears dotted her dark eyelashes. "I don't make many girl-friends. You were like the sister I always wanted. It never felt like the right time since you rarely brought him up.. " At least that part was true. I didn't share my relationship with too many people, not in detail at least. Kristen knew the big things with Josh though. Like when we were going on trips together, when we got engaged, when we got married... *Why the hell didn't she tell me before all of that happened?*

I gripped the table tighter, my knuckles white as I struggled to control the rage inside and the quaking of my voice. "Why did it end?"

"He chose you. He sent me an email saying it was over between us."

"He sent you *an email*?" Appalled, I shook my head in disgust. "That's pretty shitty."

Her lips twitched. "Yeah, I thought so, too. But, Haleigh, I'm *glad* he chose you. He seems like he's changed. It takes the right person for that to happen and clearly you two have something special."

I ignored her attempt to compliment me. to praise my relationship with Josh after admitting mere moments ago that she didn't think it would last. Kristen never expected us to get married.

"When did it end? When did he send that email?" My thoughts traveled back to the beginning of our relationship, wondering at what point Josh thought I was actually good enough to give up his side action.

Kristen's face flushed a bright red. I asked the one question she didn't want me to ask. The timeline question. No guilty person enjoys answering that one. "I don't remember the exact date or anything… but sometime in October, I'd say."

I didn't need to pause to do the math. It's when I met Ryan. Three fucking months into our relationship. It took Josh three months, well after we had already had sex, to give up Kristen on the side. Now it made sense why he could go so many days without texting or calling or seeing me when we had a fight.

A laugh escaped my lips. I couldn't help it. So sick, so confused, so floored that I let out an insane laugh—loud, curt— and repeated it like I was drunk, generating fear in Kristen's eyes.

"We slept with the same damn man for months. For *months* we were in his bed. We *shared* his bed." I wanted to rip his throat out. "I have to go." I pushed my chair back, its screech across the floor ringing in the tiny cafe.

Kristen reached out, grabbing my arms. I glared at her, imagining ripping my limbs away from those fingers that touched Josh's naked body, and her falling on her face. She released her grip when she saw the fire in my eyes.

"Please, sit, please. There's something else I need to say."

My wobbly legs were the only reason I sat back down. There was no way I could have walked back to the shelter yet. The world tilted under my feet. Yes, it had been years since it all took place, but to think about a time that my life wasn't as I once viewed it was a hard pill to swallow, especially when it involved two people closest to me.

"I finally quit my job Friday. Put in my two weeks' notice." Kristen hesitated, expecting me to show signs of happiness for her. I would have been over-the-moon excited if it wasn't for the vile news beforehand.

"Okay," I responded as steadily as possible.

Kristen's hands shook, and deep inside, I felt terrible for her. We were friends, seemingly *good* friends who volunteered together for years, and yet it was all crashing down in pieces because of what happened almost three years ago. Maybe it was a part of her past, but it profoundly affected my present. I questioned how many other women were involved with Josh. Who was to say it was only Kristen and me competing for the left spot of his bed? The side of the crappy mattress that sank down when I lied on it. I made him throw it away when we moved in together. The one I joked was my sign to lose weight since it was curving from my body. Yet it wasn't my body it was reacting to, but the random weights of other women throughout time.

Kristen mumbled the next part, disenchantment thick in the air. She knew her words wouldn't be met with the expected excitement from me. Not any longer. If only she had shared her news before the bombshell.

"I'm moving to San Francisco. Found an art gallery to work at, and I'm waiting to hear on working part-time at one of the animal shelters." She couldn't come to our wedding because she spent a month out in San Francisco. Now I wondered if her relationship with Josh was part of what propelled her out there. I refused to ask.

"A dream come true for you..." My response was half-hearted, but I tried my damnedest to put aside my hurt feelings enough to acknowledge what was so important to her.

"Yes. It really is. You were my inspiration. All of our talks, all the things you said about living passionately finally helped me realize I wanted to live life only in that way. So outside of the crappy start to this conversation, it's why I wanted to talk to you, to thank you. I guess a part of me still hoped we could go together like we've talked about, but... I think I know your answer."

I nodded, astonishingly disappointed in the timing of it all. I would have gone with her in a heartbeat, if only it was before I married a cheater.

"Maybe if you warned me that I was pledging a lifetime to a guy who slept with both of us simultaneously, I wouldn't be stuck here or in this situation," I sneered, despite my best efforts. Kristen wasn't to blame for Josh's actions, but I was livid at her poor timing in revealing the news. *Why did she wait until we were married, after I had said "I do" for the rest of my life to a complete liar?* Now I didn't know if he *was* a liar or if he was just a liar *in the beginning*. And was he even a liar? Did I actually ask him if he was dating anyone else at the time?

I was going out of my mind.

"Did you ever meet his brother?"

Surprised by my peculiar question, any remaining hope of a reconciled friendship drained from Kristen once I rerouted the conversation back in that direction. "No. They were doing something once, and I offered to meet up with them. But Josh shut that down. He said he takes meeting family members seriously, and we weren't at that point."

I breathed out a sigh of relief. Ryan hadn't met her. Maybe he didn't know about her. I couldn't handle Josh and Ryan both lying. Or worse: putting Kristen and me together in a lineup of dumbly-smitten-over-Josh girls for Ryan to pick out which one he liked most. Although there could be many others for all I knew. I hadn't thought about Josh cheating on me. That wasn't an option in my mind. He was too consumed by work, and he told me he was working hard because *I* made him want a solid future. And now, I felt foolish for trusting him more than I should have.

"Can I ask you a question? I know you're super angry, but on the chance that this may be the last time we speak, which I hope it's not because I don't want our friendship to end... but if it is, I need to know... has Josh ever hit you? Or threatened to?"

Aghast at the question, my mouth dropped open. I studied Kristen's tiny nose, the tears in her eyes, the quiver of her lips as she pursed them together. I wanted to scream at her for asking something so horrific. *What was she trying to do to us?*

"No, he would never do something like that," I replied coldly.

Images of my dad pushing my mom came to my mind, but that wasn't Josh. He's *not* my dad.

"Not even when he drinks? I would hate myself forever if I didn't ask and something happened." She knew how Josh could be when he drinks. Kristen knew more about Josh than she ever let on, hiding the intimacy they once shared. Maybe they'd talk for hours in bed while cuddling after sex. Maybe she knew him better than me.

I rubbed my eyes, exhausted, shattered, queasy. "No. Never has." Then a terrible thought struck. "Did he hit you?"

Kristen shook her head quickly, and I exhaled, loathing she even made me consider that. "No, but he reminded me of a guy I dated in the past who did. And I've worried about you a lot. It happens before you can realize what's taking place."

What the hell? "Okay, that's enough." I stood up again, my voice rising, "Thank you for finally telling me the truth, which you should have confessed three years ago. But for you to sit here and speculate something so appalling about my husband on top of it? I will not let you do that. Good luck with your move." I couldn't even look at Kristen one last time.

She was a face I didn't expect to say goodbye to in this fashion, a moment bursting with intense betrayal and hurt. Yet here we were. A crumbled friendship ending over a man, of all things. How petty. But it was more layered than a juvenile argument over a crush. My perspective on Kristen and Josh shifted radically in a ten-minute conversation. Two people I thought I knew well, I suddenly questioned.

When the sharp, cold air hit my face, tears threatened to spill from my eyes. Sprinting to the Pet Angels parking lot, I rushed to leave before Kristen got to her car so my anger wouldn't succumb to the sadness of our ruined friendship with the sight of her. I couldn't decipher what I was most upset about; everything was loaded and complicated.

I didn't cry. I didn't allow myself to completely believe Kristen's words. Not yet. It was only fair to get Josh's side first. It was

only fair to try to understand what happened at the beginning of
our relationship before accusing him of anything.

I recalled how much of a jerk he could be in those early days.
How he'd disappear for days when we had a fight. Kristen must
have been that reason. She must have been what he fell back on
anytime things got too serious or crappy with us.

Maybe it wasn't worth bringing up. But if I didn't, would it
forever haunt me, sitting in the back of my mind, waiting to boil
with something entirely unrelated? I couldn't risk that either.

A football game on TV halted my march to him. It was point-
less to bring up anything when there was a game on. I could have
yelled "Fire!" and Josh would sit on the couch in his man cave
until a commercial break. A die-hard sports fan, everything else
became second place.

The game presented time to determine the best approach.
Regardless of how much Josh had changed and matured over the
course of our relationship, defensiveness remained his default
reaction.

The game ended with his team winning, so a positive founda-
tion was set. Or so I thought.

"Hey, can we talk?"

"Can it wait until tomorrow? It's late, and I need to get rest
before the morning."

"I'm hoping it'll be brief." All I needed for him to say is
"nope, it didn't happen that way" and that would be it. End of
conversation. Simple.

Josh stood to stretch and groaned, "Chats with you are never
brief." He left the room, calling back at me, "You can talk while I
get ready for bed."

I flicked off the TV, despising how he made me turn it off
even though he was the last one watching it. With my current
state of irritation inflamed, I didn't bother grabbing his empty
beer bottles. I wasn't his maid. Maybe Kristen would have. Maybe
she did other things better than I did.

My legs were heavy, suddenly titanium-filled as I took each

step to our bedroom and stood in the bathroom doorway, like a little kid waiting for her parents to pay attention to her. Josh peed while brushing his teeth. Once he walked back to the sink, he gave me a silent look over his shoulder that implied *okay, get on with it.*

I braced myself in the doorway and spit the acidic words out of my mouth, "Were you dating Kristen the same time you were dating me?"

He paused with the toothbrush in his mouth, then leaned over to spit again. Without looking back up, he said, "Yeah, you knew that. I told you both."

"No. No, you told *her*, but you didn't tell *me*. I didn't know about it at all until tonight."

"Oh." Josh straightened and wiped his mouth with the back of his hand. "Well, it doesn't matter, anyway. I married you, not her."

I cleared my throat. "Okay, but don't you think I should have known you were sleeping with both of us? A friend of mine? For the first three months of our relationship?" My stomach knotted as I realized I only assumed it was three months. That was only with Kristen and I haven't confirmed there weren't others. "Or was it longer than that? How long were you sleeping with other people while with me?"

Josh flipped off the bathroom light, sliding past me to get to bed, nonchalant, like none of this was a big deal. "I thought you said this would be a short conversation. She's your friend. It's just as much her responsibility. Yell at her, not me."

"If you gave straight answers, this could have been over with already."

"Well, I don't know what to tell you, Haleigh. Was I sleeping with both of you at the same time? Yes. Did I think it mattered? No, because we didn't talk about being monogamous. Did I eventually put a stop to it when I asked you to be my girlfriend? Yes. I realized you and I had the potential for long-term, which I didn't feel with her. I did nothing wrong. I didn't lie to you. I didn't break any vows."

I rubbed my face with my hand, nauseous. Kristen said it ended in October, after three months, but Josh implied it stopped when we became exclusive which was five months in. *Was there someone else, too?* I wanted to vomit.

"I didn't sleep with anyone else from day one, Josh."

He shrugged as he slid out of his boxers and into the bed naked. "That was your decision. Not mine. And not one we talked about having to agree to."

His arguments were shit. But he knew how to word things to make it near impossible to disagree with him. Hatred seeped throughout my body.

Josh reached to turn out the lamp, pausing to finally look me in the eyes, and asked, "Are we done talking? You're my wife, Haleigh. You won, not her. This is a stupid thing to argue about. Get some rest."

"I *won*?" I shot back with a huff. He rolled his eyes as I stood awkwardly before him, unable to form another sentence, shocked by his response and the ease of him admitting the truth that was hidden for so long. So instead, my shoulders slumped in defeat as I realized this topic would only get swept under the rug, like he intended it to be from the beginning.

The lights clicked off.

I couldn't bring myself to say goodbye to Kristen. I didn't know who I was more pissed at, her or him. But marriage prevented me from walking away from one, so that was who I forgave first. Although according to Josh, I had nothing to forgive, an automatic snarl escaping my lips anytime I thought about it.

Time eventually forced me to move on. I had to relent to the fact that it happened a long time ago, it wasn't in the present, and I would probably never know the whole truth. I tried to burn the memory, but the ashes just got swept into a vase for storage, along with Kristen's added concerns about Josh's temperament and my tears mourning a friendship that once was very special to me.

CHAPTER TEN
HIM

Few people know this, but I've fallen in love a lot. No one takes me for that type of man. I wanted the love that my parents had. So badly at times, I would force it when it wasn't there. I gave every good woman a chance. I didn't want to miss out on the right one. I got so damn tired of waiting. So exhausted with the self-consciousness that came from it all. I was never as confident as everyone assumed.

Ryan had found the perfect woman. He found someone that was exactly like my mom. My parents couldn't stop raving about Lindsay. Ryan started building a family when I wasn't even close.

I had to move. Fast. I couldn't let Ryan get too far ahead. I had to keep up.

The wrong reasons can replace the right reasons before you even know what's happening.

You were my wake-up call to everything I had done wrong in my life. You are my right. I know I need to fix it all to give you the lifetime of happiness you deserve.

Some people would say it's too late. I refuse to give up. I refuse to give you up.

CHAPTER ELEVEN
HER

Six months into our marriage, Josh woke me up in the morning before my alarm went off with a kiss. "Hey, sleepyhead."

"Hey," I said, trying to find my bearings and remember what day it was. "Did I oversleep?" I sat up, leaning on my forearms to try to see the clock.

"No, I was thinking about something and wanted to talk to you about it."

I wiped the sleep from my eyes and got my first non-blurry view of him. His eyes were a little red in the sides and his hair was standing up as though he was running his hand through it all night.

"Are you okay?"

He smiled, that million-dollar Claystone smile. "Yes, everything is fine, and will be even better. I want to start a family. I want to have kids."

My stomach rolled in surprise and made a sound that left us both laughing. *Was this finally happening?* "Are you sure? You said you wanted to save up enough so you can work part-time when we have kids."

He leaned over to the other side of the bed and grabbed a black notebook. "I know. That's what I thought I wanted, and I still do a little bit. But that was also before I knew you were going to be my wife. You are amazing with kids. I don't need to work part time when I know they're going to be in your hands."

"But I work the same schedule as you do. If we start a family now, we'll need to look at hiring a nanny or find a daycare."

"No," he said excitedly as he flipped through the pages that had his handwriting scrawled across line after line. "I've been up crunching the numbers all night and writing lists. You love Pet Angels. You light up every time you talk about it. If they'll still hire you on part time, you should do it. We'll make it work and then you'll be able to be with the kids when it's time."

I caught a peek at one of his lists in his notebook when he was talking. "Josh... is this about the money, the fact that you know I hate my job or... for some other reason?"

He quickly closed his notebook. "Haleigh, babe, you are way too talented for Gungston and any place that doesn't let your passion shine through. Happy wife, happy life, right? And I want my wife and kids to have the happiest life possible."

"You won't feel like you're giving up your dream to be a part-time stay-at-home dad?"

I thought for a moment I saw a brief look of sadness cross his eyes but it vanished by the time he grabbed my hands. "This will make you happy, and I want that more than anything else. Besides, if I play my cards right at work, we'll both be part-timers, and we'll raise our kids by being the most present parents in the world."

I sighed and leaned into his arms. "This was the sweetest way to wake up."

"Let's make it sweeter, shall we?" He threw his notebook off the bed and crawled on top of me with a laugh. His left hand traveled up my right leg slowly. "Ready to start baby-making?"

All I could do was reply with a moan.

———

Hunter James, eight pounds and eleven ounces with a head full of dark hair and Josh's bright blue eyes, entered the world fifteen months after Josh and I said, "I do." We finally had the baby we always wanted to start our family. Our love grew in shocking ways, for good and bad.

Josh made me a mom, and I couldn't be more appreciative of our relationship for that one reason. Blissfully happy when rocking Hunter in my arms, I couldn't imagine a life without him. This baby was mine; he was a part of me. It was the most terrifying and altogether wonderful feeling that could exist. Being a mom changed me. I became more confident in who I was, bolder in my decisions, and more certain of the elements I surrounded myself with.

However, a rollercoaster of emotions followed once we grasped the shifting dynamic between us with a baby joining our everyday life. Everything became cyclical. *Everything.* Even the way Josh and I felt about each other.

For the first three weeks, I fell more in love with Josh. He was attentive, sweet, forgiving, patient, and loving—everything I could have hoped for in a partner in life and as the father of my child. *I loved him so much.* I couldn't stop saying that to him as I kissed Hunter's cheeks, eternally grateful for our little family we created.

After three weeks, we despised each other. Both of us were doing one (or several) parenting responsibilities more or better than the other, or so we would accuse each other through snide remarks.

"I clean way more than you do."

"That's because you like it! And if I were to do it, you would just do it all over again, so what's the point? I'm the one that changes his diapers all day, every day. When was the last time you changed his diaper? When was the last time you got up in the middle of the night?"

"That's because you don't know how to only focus on what

he actually needs. Instead, you baby the hell out of him, reacting to every little thing as though it's a major crisis."

"That's because he's a *baby*! He's not self-sufficient yet!"

Josh took out his frustrations by going to the gym more. I took out mine by crying each time I could sneak in a five-minute shower. Otherwise, the outpour transpired while reading books to Hunter about bears with lost blankets and turtles that hated snow. Hunter would grow up crying every time he read a book if I couldn't get it under control.

Three months postpartum, Josh and I loved each other again and were on top of the world. We hugged and held onto each other, acknowledging the challenges we overcame so far as parents, elated about our accomplishments. Hunter was turning into an easygoing baby, and we took a lot of pride in that. We had dinner together nightly at the table, attempting to set a great example for Hunter early on. We didn't turn on the TV as much. Instead, we sat on the floor as a family, playing with Hunter, and having actual conversations about our days.

"Cig-as, cig-as," Josh repeated in his attempted Jamaican accent as we erupted into laughter, reminiscing about our first vacation together. Even Hunter learned to giggle as soon as Josh said those words.

"We'll get out again soon." I rubbed Josh's knee to console him, knowing that travel bone was twitching inside him.

Josh pulled his fingers through my hair, relaxing my body. He brushed my long bangs from my forehead and kissed it gently. "I know. We have a lifetime to travel. It's smart to wait until Hunter is older. Then we'll make him a world traveler."

"Ooh, and multilingual."

"Definitely. He'll be able to order us a drink in any language around the world."

I clapped Hunter's hands together. "I can't wait to mold our child into our own personal drink orderer."

Josh leaned over to rub his nose on Hunter's cheek. "He will be the best damn drink orderer in the world. He will be the best at everything."

Josh's blue eyes sparkled with adoration for both me and Hunter. It made me fall more in love with him. For the first time, I referred to Josh as my best friend. He finally felt like it.

Cyclical. Everything was cyclical.

At six months, we couldn't stand each other again. The divide had grown with a river of jealousy. I was envious that Josh could escape and have his "me time," even if it was only on the commute to and from work or when he disappeared in his man cave to watch all fifty of his favorite sports teams. Josh didn't have a child constantly latched to him, incessantly demanding his time and attention, making it impossible to do anything around the house or go to the bathroom freely.

Josh was jealous I got to spend more time with Hunter and be at home. He thought he could do it better than me. Meals would be cooked each night, and the house would be spotless if the roles were reversed. He also didn't have breasts that either needed to be fed on or pumped multiple times throughout the day, reducing my ability to get much else done.

At nine months, I was once again grateful to have Josh as a partner. We fell into a groove, balancing the daily demands. We gave each other credit for our strengths, the things we were good at that made our tiny family run successfully and recognized the contributions provided by both people. We also got out of the house together for date nights and sex became fun again.

After returning from a night out at a Blackhawks game, followed by Chicago-style pizza, we quickly checked Hunter was still asleep after Jessi left, then fell into our bed, tearing at each other's bodies, peeling clothes off as fast as possible. Our sleeping infant was a ticking time bomb with an internal alarm for whenever his parents wanted to get a little frisky, fully intending to be the only child.

Josh unexpectedly slowed us down though. He held my hands by my side as he intensified his kisses, dragging his warm lips to my earlobe, all the way to the base of my neck. He worked his way down, tugging at the v-neck of my cami with his teeth, sliding the spaghetti straps off my shoulders, and pulling it to my hips. My jeans had already been tossed aside in our frenzy, leaving only my cheeky panties. His hands stayed on my hips, his fingers clutching the cami, while his thumbs moved in circles on my panty line, stirring tremors through my body.

Josh's lips followed his thumbs, pushing through the mauve silk with his tongue, my knees weakening. I grabbed his hair to steady myself, desperate to melt into the bed sheets. He lifted his mouth to use his teeth to pull my panties down, over my knees, to the floor. Josh kept the cami on my hips, using it as a rope to tug my body closer to him, to pull my body further into his mouth as he went back on his knees, sinking his tongue deep inside of me, following with the flick of his fingers in and out.

Right as I covered my mouth to stifle moans, Josh stood, gently tugging on the cami, guiding my body further back on the bed until my head was on the pillows. I grabbed for him, pleading for him to enter me, to fulfill me, to bring me to an end. But he removed my hands and lifted them above my head and demanded, "Hold the bed frame." Josh continued to kiss every part of my body. There wasn't an inch left.

All I could think was, *This is love, this is what it's all about*, because my body was far from where it was pre-pregnancy. Fifteen pounds heavier, stretch marks that didn't exist only months before now streaked my sides, and I didn't know what down below looked like anymore because I was too scared to look. But Josh didn't seem to mind. In fact, he relished it all. I realized at that moment I had falsely considered myself unattractive since giving birth.

Self-consciousness sneaks up without awareness at times. All my attention went toward Hunter; rarely did any get applied to my needs or self-care. And for the first time in nine months, Josh made me feel like I was in fact still beautiful, the person he wanted to be with. It became my favorite moment in our bed, my favorite moment of us together, naked and raw.

Josh eventually did enter me, did take his own pleasure. We both lost it, holding onto each other, tearing at each other, squeezing each other, dissolving into each other's bodies. Sometimes our bodies together felt disproportionate, with his extra five inches in height on me, combined with my short torso and his long torso, we never had the perfect fit. But this time, we somehow found we could fit perfectly enough.

It was the first time since Hunter had been born that we didn't act as though we were in high school again, trying to get everything stuffed into a five-minute period before our parents got home. Slow can be so good, so satisfying, teetering more into the making love territory instead of just having sex.

"I love you so much, Haleigh," Josh whispered in my ear when I was on the verge of falling asleep.

I pulled his arms securely around my waist. His breath tickled my ear, but I didn't dare move from this newfound perfection. "I love you, too."

If only we could have stayed like that forever.

———

When we reached the one-year-post-baby mark, the atmosphere shifted. The cycles stopped. There weren't any more highs and lows, just even-keeled everyday happenings. Sometimes, that alone was worth being grateful. Other times, I wanted something more.

"This is why I don't plan to have kids." Jessi stretched her legs across my couch as she adjusted her body. I stiffened at the sight of the red wine splashing in her glass, knowing Josh would ban her from the house if she spilled on the polyester upholstery. "Don't get me wrong, Hunter is adorable. You know I love him, right? But kids are a guaranteed sex block for the next eighteen years. I like sex too much."

"I remember liking sex. But if I wait only a few more years, I'm sure the memory will be long gone."

"See? That's what I'm talking about!"

I laughed, purposefully playing into her fears, ignoring the harsh reality in between the words.

"But this is *our* situation. Other couples could be different. I'm sure some can pull off a killer sex life, even with kids. We haven't figured out how to do that frequently. We have some bouts that are great, but it's far from consistent." I let my mind wander to only a few months before when I thought we finally returned to the ease of love-making, but it turned out to be a one-time deal. I tried to emulate the memory with him, only to fail terribly and make it more awkward than it was already turning out to be. "To be fair, it's not like we've set the example of an ideal relationship."

Jessi sat up suddenly, leaned in closer with a wrinkled nose, and in a hushed voice asked, "But why? What could be better?"

Some people are put off by Jessi's candor but it's one of the traits I loved most about her. I wished more people would be as transparent. Josh, for example.

I glanced upstairs, expecting Josh to be listening. But he was on a work trip as usual, and Hunter was already in bed. A sip of wine trickled down my throat before I responded, "We've been through a lot. But we choose to do it together, and that's more than some people can ask for, you know? I know he loves me. I love him. That's pretty successful for marriage."

"So, why is it not enough?"

I replied with a thirty-year-ache in my heart, "Sometimes I wonder if we both truly trust each other. I'm not sure I'm built to believe someone can stay. Every time he goes on a trip, I wonder if he'll come back." I have to choke back a sob in admittance. "And I don't think he fully trusts me. When he asked me to quit working at the accounting firm, he said it was because he knew I wasn't happy there. But I caught a glimpse of a list he had written in his notebook of pros and cons. And one of the pros was that I wouldn't be surrounded by men he doesn't know. It's like he doesn't trust me when I'm the one who's been faithful to him since the day we met."

Inside I despised my concession. Saying it out loud for the first time was like a personal breakthrough, and it was one I hated because there wasn't much I could do to change it. I was married, with a son. And Josh was a great dad to him. I would do nothing to jeopardize that. I refused to let Hunter grow up in a split household. I made that clear to Josh during our twenty-four hour engagement breakup. When we had reconciled and decided we would move forward with the wedding, I told him he had from the time we get married to the time we got pregnant with our first kid to back out again. I would give him the grace for that. But there was no way in hell he could decide otherwise once kids were in the picture. He would be stuck with me then.

Josh was surprised to see that side of me, but he agreed. It helped set boundaries for his fickle personality, his tendency to run instead of fighting for what we have. Maybe it helped me, too.

Jessi shook her head and grumbled, "There is absolutely no reason for him to not trust you. That's bullshit. But Haleigh, like-wise, you have to stop holding your dad's sins over Josh's head. Josh could have quit his job like he wanted to but he chose to let you do it. He has to travel; it's not like it's his choice. He's not going anywhere. You're the best thing that's ever happened to him, and look at this beautiful family you've made! It's what you both wanted."

I swirled my wine in the glass. "We do make damn cute kids. If we have a daughter someday, I'll make sure she's raised better than I was. That's all I can do. Try to break the cycle and correct the trend for future generations."

Jessi nodded in agreement. After a few moments of silence, she spoke up again. "Marriage is some complicated shit, huh?"

"It can be."

"I don't know if I'll ever be ready for it."

"You will be someday. Or at least ready to commit to someone. Just listen to the mistakes your friends made. You'll find a guy that makes the rest of us envious and show us what being married really could have looked like if we waited around for the right one." I placed my wineglass on the table, blaming the alcohol for my unfiltered truths.

"How am I supposed to know what that is? There are so many damn men. The longer I'm out of the dating scene, the more overwhelming it becomes." She leaned her head on the back of the couch, pinching the bridge of her nose. Characteristically exuding confidence, it was the first time I'd heard uncertainty in Jessi's voice.

"What I've learned above all else is to find someone who loves you, is willing to fight for you, respects the crap out of you, and thinks you're the greatest woman on the planet. Everything else is extra." It's advice I wish someone had given me before Josh entered my life.

"Great. He will be as ugly as can be," Jessi huffed. The interviewer in her fired a question right back at me, "Do you regret marrying him?"

I didn't let myself hesitate. "No. How can I? We have Hunter. I've said it from the beginning: we are meant to be in each other's lives. I never doubted that. Granted, I didn't know what that entailed when we fought so much. But now that Hunter is here, it's clear."

Jessi smiled at the thought. "Maybe I'll have kids, just without the man. Pick out a good one via sperm donation and roll the dice." She sighed. "Yeah, thanks, Haleigh. You've set me on a new mission. Now there's no reason to date again!"

I laughed, knowing she was being sarcastic. At least for now. Once an idea gets planted in Jessi's mind, it'll grow until she decides whether to prune it or burn it. She lived a life that resembled my favorite reality show; I was always eager to find out what would happen next.

"Okay, enough about me. Fill me in on what I should be in

the know about with all things cool. Hip? Bussin'? Crap, what's even the right word these days? I am so old."

Jessi shook her head at me. "Why the hell do you think I do this blog? It forces me to stay in tune with society and updated on all the trends. This way I can blend in with the twenties well into my fifties."

"I never thought I'd be sitting around in my thirties talking about feeling old."

"Kind of sneaks up on you, huh?"

"That's what wine is for." We clinked our glasses and found a romantic comedy to lose ourselves in, as I tried not to think about how different life would be if I hadn't met Josh.

Chapter Twelve
Him

I won't say I regret having a child.

I just wish the timing was better.

But Hunter stole my heart. He also scares me more than anything else in this world could. The moment I first held him, I sensed the weight of the responsibility I now carried. Providing for him, taking care of him, and influencing him the best I can.

My relationship with my dad is always in the front of my mind. I don't want Hunter to feel like he isn't good enough. I don't want him to carry resentment toward me.

That kid broke me. I didn't know what to do. So, I stopped doing anything that felt outside the norm of what I had already been doing for years. I stay focused on work. It is easier that way. It is the one thing I can do impeccably that will provide him with everything he needs.

I know he will appreciate that one part of me. I don't know how to do the rest. That's why I need you.

CHAPTER THIRTEEN
HER

It's a little too easy to fall into a state of contentment, and once you catch yourself there, it's terrifying, especially if you recognize pieces of yourself who always chased the stars. Being content seems reasonable enough at first. It wouldn't have been once before, but suddenly it is. Then it drips over into mere survival. Sometimes a person doesn't realize that day in and day out turns into that. Surviving to get things done, enduring to make it to the end of the day with exactly what the day started with, no energy for additions, only trying to protect what's left, whether that's physical possessions, people, or sanity.

Survival mode was where we found ourselves. Time went on, and we did what we had to do to simply live with as little misery as possible from sunrise to sunset. Usually, that resulted in very few conversations and utilizing the TV to provide the missing noise. Somehow it went from us all playing together as a family to an obvious divide: me and Hunter on one side, Josh on the other.

"Thank God," I muttered under my breath. I opened an invitation from Lindsay and Ryan for Grace's third birthday party. They were late sending out details, so the party was happening the upcoming weekend. We were given a head's up and had marked it on our calendar, but I was adjusting to being a mom still and took each day as it came instead of looking too far out in the future. It was all I could do to survive on most days.

"What's that?" Josh was typing away on his computer, working on what I assumed was a work email as usual.

"Invitation to Grace's birthday party."

"Oh, cool. It'll be good to see everyone again."

These days we only saw family for a few holidays and birthdays. No one had time for additional trips unless there was a special purpose behind them. Life was too busy.

"Yeah, I'm excited. Hunter can get some cousin time in." Although that wasn't my primary reason for being so relieved about it. My favorite version of Josh used to appear while we were traveling. With the addition of Hunter to our family, our trips together stopped. Now my favorite version of Josh showed up when we were with his family. He always put on his best face anytime his mom was around. In those moments his touch didn't stray, whether it was an arm draped over my shoulder, a hand on my leg, or his fingers running through the ends of my hair. We became unified once again. I never understood the reason why, but it was as though Josh was actually proud to have me next to him, something rarely shown in our home.

I didn't realize how much I craved a connection with Josh again until the thought of being with his family energized me after a string of lackluster weeks. I missed feeling wanted. I missed being touched. I missed feeling like I was somebody other than just a mother; I was a woman again. A desirable woman.

Being a mother had become my greatest joy; Hunter was my greatest joy. As complacent as life had become, I couldn't imagine laughing or smiling as much in this life if it wasn't for Hunter being in it. Every two weeks seemed to bring new challenges or new accomplishments and I looked forward to seeing what he would do next.

Hunter was a much-needed distraction on the numerous days Josh was traveling, and on the tense days he wasn't.

From the first time I met them, I blended in seamlessly with Josh's family. For the most part, anyway. Lindsay and I struggled to get along. She didn't quite fit my vision of the woman Ryan would have married. We were two different women, to put it mildly. I dressed in second-hand tees, jeans, and flats for most of my wardrobe with limited, if any, makeup. Lindsay, however, wore polished athleisure since she was constantly doing something at the gym, yet consistently flawless, every single hair perfectly in place, with glowy makeup and hoop earrings. Honestly, I was in awe she could look like that. Josh's eyes would drift up and down her body when she walked into the room. I wondered if he wished I was more like her.

The second time I met Lindsay, Adam was hysterical, refusing to calm down. I asked if I could hold him and she all but threw him in my hands. He stopped crying immediately. His big brown eyes locked with mine as his tiny hands grasped for strands of my hair. I was smitten, which kick-started my baby fever. Soon, Adam drifted into sleep in my arms. Wrongly thinking I helped her, I smiled at Lindsay just to be met with her blue-steel glare. When Ryan said, "Ooh, Haleigh, we may need you to move in with us. You've got the magic touch," Lindsay walked out of the room and didn't come back for an hour.

Josh's parents, Wanda and Mike, were high on Ryan and Lindsay, endlessly bragging about their most recent accomplishments ("Lindsay was nominated as one of the best fitness instructors in Downers Grove"). Wanda hugged Ryan constantly. Mike and Lindsay struck up private conversations about nutrition. It was just the four of them in their close-knit habitat while Josh and I sat on the outside, observing it all. Different from how he was with just Ryan, Josh was stoic around the rest of his family, like he was watching a movie about a life that wasn't his. I understood how upsetting family dynamics could be though. Josh and I spent many nights talking about the things we would do differently than our parents if we had kids someday.

"Haleigh, so good to see you. Feels like it's been a long time." Ryan hugged me tightly.

I squinted as I recalled what today's date was, let alone the last time I saw everyone. The days all blended together when confined to the house chasing a little one 24/7. "Almost three months, right? Hunter's birthday party?"

"You're right. That's too long."

We say the same thing every time. It's always too long to go between visits with each other. We all group text or FaceTime so we can see the kids, but nothing beats seeing each other in person. Ryan had become one of my favorite people. We were very similar so we regularly lost ourselves in deep conversations about literature or were the last ones standing in long-running competitive card games. Sometimes my brain seemed wired in a way others didn't understand, having to explain my thoughts or repeat my statements to confused faces. But I never had to do that with Ryan. He got me.

"I married my brother," Josh once commented after drunkenly watching Ryan and I break into hysterical laughter over slapping each other's hands instead of the deck of cards in an intense game of War. I shrugged in response, "Just means you love a particular type of person. Nothing wrong with that." Josh was dozing off but repeated one more time for emphasis, "I married my brother."

"Hi, Haleigh." Lindsay popped around the corner. Her blonde hair was straight and perfectly edged her face. She wore athletic yoga pants and a loose white shirt that would make anyone else appear frumpy, but on her long-limbed frame, she looked like a model as usual. She put a hand on each one of my shoulders for my least favorite type of hug, but the one she preferred. It was the "I will hug you because I should, but I don't want to actually touch you" hug, which felt unnaturally cold.

Lindsay and I tolerated each other enough, but from the first day we met during a double-date in the city, we couldn't find common interests. If we were left alone, we would sit in silence, both on our phones ignoring the other, and we were fine with that. We wouldn't be best friends, that much was clear. At least it was an unspoken agreement.

"How are you, Lindsay?"

"Oh you know, working hard and balancing two kids. I've increased my class load, so it's been busy. All the gyms have child-care so the kids can come, too. It's easy to work and still be a mom these days, you know."

Most people would listen to Lindsay and think she was genuine in responding. But I've had enough faux female friend-ships in my life to know when someone was condescending. Ryan also let the truth slip once that Lindsay hated I didn't work because it was a slap in the face of feminism. She also thought her load was ten times heavier than mine just because they'd produced two children versus our one.

"That's great, Lindsay. What a wonderful bonus that you can combine work with your personal exercise time, and your kids can be in the same building with you. I'm sure a lot of women would love to be in your shoes." I flashed an exaggerated smile as I passed her and walked into the living room. I caught Ryan hiding a discreet grin behind his water bottle.

The birthday theme was warrior princesses, and Grace was Xena, which wasn't what I expected. I couldn't help but laugh once I saw her stud-covered leather costume with a shield. "How in the world does she know about Xena?"

"Who the hell is Xena?" Josh asked while texting on his phone.

Ryan's cheeks flushed. "Remember those giant cardboard cutouts I had? Xena was one of those. The warrior woman one."

I probed, "Um, you collected cardboard cutouts?" the same time Josh called out, "Oh yeah, she was the hot one! I might have used her for inspiration now and then." I shoved Josh in the arm once his comment registered. "That's gross!" Lindsay, however, found it to be the funniest thing she'd ever heard. I didn't even know she could giggle like that.

Ryan ignored Josh's comment and turned his back on both of them. "It started as a high school prank. My friends and I found a couple in an alley garbage can. But then it became an ongoing challenge to steal them from stores or events."

My mouth dropped open as I feigned dramatic shock. "Wait, you're supposed to be the big law-abider! School counselor with a rebellious past stealing life-sized cardboard cutouts of random characters? Say it isn't so!"

He grinned while handing me a bottle of water. "About twenty years ago. I've matured a little since then."

"What was the oddest one you found?"

Ryan thought for a moment before answering with, "A talking Austin Powers. Staples was having an event promoting the movie. We ran out of the store with it."

"And it talked?"

"Groovy, baby."

It was a terrible accent, but I was laughing as hard at him as Lindsay had at Josh.

"Do I make you—" Ryan started in the voice again to say one of the most famous catchphrases from the movie. Lindsay cut him off before he could say "horny."

"Ryan, stop! Kids are around." She rolled her eyes. "It's not even that funny, anyway." That last line was a jab at me for laughing and encouraging it.

I ignored her. "You have yet to explain how Grace knows about Xena."

"Ahh... I still have a few in storage in the basement. She plays with them. Austin Powers didn't survive, but Xena did."

"You've been carrying them around for twenty years?"

"I felt bad tossing them. They're like giant-sized people, you know? They have actual personalities now!"

"Lindsay, you let him keep those things?" Josh interjected without looking up from his phone.

Lindsay groaned and touched Josh's shoulder, which was the magical solution to make him finally tear his eyes away from his device. "Trust me, plenty of fights have ensued. I would have burned them from the beginning."

"I'm surprised you kept dating him after he introduced you to them."

She scoffed and lifted a hand as jingling bracelets slid down her wrist. "He kept them hidden until after we got married. I found them stuffed behind other boxes one day. Trust me, it would have been a deal breaker if I wasn't already caught in the marriage."

That was harsh to say considering there wasn't a light note in that entire statement. To bring the topic back to the birthday girl and avoid more marital spats, I asked, "Has Grace watched Xena?"

Ryan's eyes lit with excitement. He may be a bigger fan than he was letting on. "Oh yeah, you can find all those old episodes online. I'm convinced it will come back. All the older TV shows are getting reboots; Xena will be one. Especially with the girl-power themes these days."

"You have quite the passion for Xena, huh?"

"She's a badass! Just like my Gracey." Ryan's pride adorably beamed.

Wanda walked into the room, hugging and kissing us hello. She held on to Ryan, and I noted the flicker of ache on Josh's face before it disappeared. "Are you going to stand around chatting all day? We have a beautiful little princess excited and waiting!"

"*Warrior* princess, Nana!" Grace ran into the room to correct her and tugged on Lindsay's arm. "Mama, I'm ready, I'm ready!"

Ryan clapped. "Okay! Let's go celebrate you!" He tickled her sides, chasing her out of the room as we all followed.

Watching all the children play together increased my enthusiasm for the prospect of having a second child. Especially seeing the way Grace and Adam took care of each other, making sure they were both included in the games with the other children and that they had their drinks and snacks at all times. It was beyond precious.

There were six additional kids, all belonging to friends of Ryan and Lindsay. The split between who were Ryan's friends and who was closer to Lindsay was obvious. Ryan's group was welcoming and inviting, on the ground playing with the kids and exuding friendliness in every way; Lindsay's group was comprised of women in activewear standing linked together with immaculate makeup and skin. I'm not sure if any of them brought their husbands since they didn't talk to anyone else except each other.

Josh and I stuck by Ryan's group since he knew several of them since childhood. I assisted Ryan with getting the food out on the table and refilling drinks since Lindsay appeared too preoccupied with her friends to play hostess. Which shocked me since she was usually on top of all party-planning-related activities. I wondered if there was a problem between them because she was typically very affectionate toward Ryan, but I had scarcely seen her look at him, let alone touch him, since we arrived.

It was easier to point out what's wrong in other people's relationships instead of acknowledging the way it mirrors mine. Josh, usually more affectionate with me when his family was around, avoided touching me the entire time. It's what I had been looking forward to the most, that confirmation he still wanted me. Maybe it was because there were so many other people standing in the room, too. But as Josh loaded up on drinks and I watched one bottle disappear after another, I knew I was losing the potential of his closeness even more. My heart cracked.

Hunter suffering from it was the worst consequence. Josh wasn't just overlooking me, he was ignoring his son. I finally reached my breaking point when we sat down to eat. Josh and Ryan stood at the edge of the table, both with a drink in their hands. On the other side, Hunter created the biggest mess; threw food on the floor, spilled juice down his shirt, rubbed cottage cheese in his hair. He was fifteen months old and doing it quite well.

As Ryan and Josh talked, Ryan handed me napkins. Then a glass of water to dunk the napkins in. Then Hunter's milk cup that he had whipped across the table. Ryan did all these things without missing a beat. Acknowledging my struggle and helping while maintaining a discussion with Josh.

Josh never once looked at us during the fiasco. Sweat beaded my forehead while fighting Hunter on eating and keeping things as clean as possible. When Josh finally remembered we existed, Hunter had taken his last bite and I was cleaning the last of the mess. Josh rolled his eyes, "Oh geez, what happened now?"

I wanted to strangle him. I didn't answer, and he didn't care. He turned to one of Ryan's other friends and struck up a new conversation.

While I was throwing away all the napkins from the clean-up, Ryan joined me, his arm brushing mine as he threw in his own trash.

I blew the hair out of my face, eager to wash my sticky hands. "How do you do it with two kids?" My voice pleaded for answers. Everything about me felt frenzied.

"Like how do we do life with two kids?"

"Yes, exactly. I mean, holy crap, one is exhausting."

"It takes two parents in equal partnership to make it run smoothly," he cocked his head to the side, in part to sympathize with me and in part implying he saw what many others missed.

I whispered so no one else could hear me, "I have a newfound appreciation for single parents. Not for the faint of heart."

Ryan chuckled softly. "You're doing great, Haleigh. You are such an amazing mom. It may feel like a whirlwind inside, but you make the mom thing look easy. You're a natural."

I didn't realize how hurt I had been by an unspoken sentence until Ryan said exactly what I had been craving to hear. I recalled all the family moments. In the living room, as I played on the floor with Hunter while Josh sat on the couch. When I made Hunter giggle, the deep-belly ones only found in childhood. I'd look up at Josh, expecting him to be observing us with a smile on his face, treasuring the moment as much as I was; yet, he was engrossed in the TV instead.

"Did you see Hunter roll over? He did it mostly on his own!"

"Did you see him crawl?"

"Did you see him take his first steps?"

"Huh? What?" Josh wouldn't tear his eyes away from the TV. He wasn't watching us. He was *never* watching us.

Ryan spoke the words I wished so desperately to hear from Josh's mouth. I would tell Josh all the time what a great dad he was, but he never told me I was a great mom. Instead, it was "Did you put sunblock on him?" questioning if I did what, of course, I always did.

I looked at Ryan, my eyes filled with tears.

He met my expression with one of understanding. He knew how Josh could be. And Ryan also knew that I was indeed a great mom.

Chapter Fourteen
Him

Work is what I am the best at. I am motivated by knowing that all I have to do is work a little harder or learn a little more to move on to the next level. It is the one place I am consistently praised at. I hate to admit I need that reassurance, but I do.

It is also my safe zone. I know what to expect.

Everything outside of work is a gamble, and I'm not much of a risk taker. That was why meeting you was such a challenge. I met you through work, so I wanted to keep you in that section of my life, locked up where everything was predictable.

But we are meant for bigger things. You are the first risk I ever thought was worth it. And I'd bet everything on you.

CHAPTER FIFTEEN
HER

The summer Josh turned six and Ryan turned eight, Mike started a new tradition: taking the boys on camping trips for male bonding. They would aim to go four times a year but as life became busier, the trips tapered to annual occurrences. No matter what, they went, never missing a year. It was one reason Josh and Ryan were excited to have sons. They wanted to pass down the tradition by eventually including the boys on their trips as well.

Only weeks after our four-year wedding anniversary, the camping trip that year marked one that neither Josh nor Ryan would forget.

I heard from Ryan before I heard from Josh.

"Is he home yet?" he asked on the other end of the phone.

"No, should he be? Are you home already?" I panicked, wondering if something happened to Josh on the way home.

"I'm almost home, but wanted to call you first." Ryan sounded out of breath as he ran through his words. "We know Josh can easily spiral and withdraw. I saw the signs already. I need your help."

I had no clue what he was talking about. Usually, the camping trips resulted in a very laid-back, even if slightly hungover Josh returning home. After a hot shower and a warm, home-cooked meal, he was more refreshed than before. A trip like this was necessary for someone who worked as much as he did.

"Did something happen?"

The emphasized hum of air leaving Ryan's lips told me all I needed to know about how serious this was. "I don't think I should be the one telling you, even though I wish I could. But it's about our dad, and it's not good. Josh is pretty shaken up about it. We both are. I needed to forewarn you, Haleigh. I know how he can be and I want you prepared. Please let me know if he doesn't tell you, okay? I tried to coach him through his feelings before he left but he slammed the car door in my face."

I knew what Ryan was referring to all too well. When Josh got like that, it was like trying to rescue somebody who fell down a well and refused to be saved. They want to sit in the damp, cold darkness and just be. The dangling rope is next to them, and they refuse to grab on. It was hard to pull Josh out of those moods, and I prayed it wasn't that bad.

"Thanks for letting me know, Ryan. I'll keep you posted. And I'm sorry... for whatever it is... if you all are hurting, I'm so sorry to hear something is causing it."

"Thanks, Haleigh. We'll talk soon, I'm sure. I just pulled up to the house and should tell Lindsay."

I hated that she would find out first. Before I could fret over it much longer, Josh walked in the side door. He slung his boots off and threw his bag, caked with mud, against the wall as dried pieces scattered to the floor.

"Hey, welcome home," I acted as though I didn't receive a warning of bad news. Controlling my nerves, I tried to kiss Josh on the cheek, but his shoulders immediately rose, and just like that, his invisible wall was constructed.

"I need a shower."

I stopped moving. "Oh, okay." I dropped my hands to my side, unsure of what to do. "I made beef stew and yeast rolls. I'll have those ready for you."

"Okay." Josh hadn't moved. After several beats, he finally

mumbled, "My dad is dying. He has cancer. The clock is ticking on his life."

My heart shattered. My mind hadn't had time to conjure worst-case scenarios, but if it did, this would be one of the worst. "Oh, Josh, I'm sorry." I walked to him with my arms up, ready to embrace him, hold him, let him cry if need be.

He held up one hand as his gaze strayed to the floor, stopping me. "Don't. I need a shower. I stink."

I didn't care what he smelled like. I wanted him in my arms. But I knew how quickly he could crack. The wrong move could cause Josh to retreat further from me. "Okay." I twisted my hands together, fighting my urge to offer a shoulder to him, tempering my desire to know more and for him to confide how he was feeling.

Josh didn't say more. At least, not that night.

Over the course of a full week, Josh gradually filled me in on everything his dad had told him, what should have taken five minutes to relay. Mike was diagnosed with stage four prostate cancer. They planned to attack it with hormone therapy and possibly chemotherapy, too. There wasn't a cure; only hope to manage it as best as possible to prolong his life.

Every time Josh mentioned his dad's fate, his voice remained monotone, blocking any bit of emotion from sneaking through. He refused to talk about it with Hunter, even though I told him it would be important, a chance for Hunter to learn an essential life lesson about how to cope with death. Josh was unwavering in his argument, "He's a kid, he doesn't need to know that stuff. He needs to be protected from it."

Disagreeing as civilly as I could, I stated, "It's never too early to learn those concepts. We don't know what life will deal us. Children need to be emotionally equipped for it all."

Josh groaned loudly. "You sound like Ryan with all that psychology bullshit. I will not let my father's damn tragedy be your opportunity for a teaching lesson, Haleigh. Stop trying to use it as one. Hunter doesn't need to know anything. He just needs to enjoy his grandpa as he is today."

"There's nothing wrong with being honest with Hunter about what's going on around him." I had to stand my ground. Kids can sense when there's something wrong, and if we aren't the first to divulge the truth, more harm than good could result. We were both trying to protect Hunter, just in the method we both thought was best.

The slam of the door was Josh's response as he retreated to the basement.

I kept my mouth shut, attempting to respect Josh's wishes since it was his father. But finally, one night after we returned from dinner at Wanda's and Mike's house, I couldn't stay quiet any longer. Hunter was an old soul. He didn't leave to play the moment dinner was over like other kids; he sat at the table, making eye contact with everyone, listening to every word spoken. As the adults whispered about Mike's current state just to keep it from Hunter's ears, I was the only one who noticed his furrowed brow as he watched their mouths move, trying to process what it all meant. That night, I sat Hunter down on his bed and calmly explained Grandpa Mike was very sick and could leave this world soon.

"Oh no. He needs to get to the doctor's office."

I held Hunter's little legs, rubbing his kneecaps with my thumbs. "He's been, love."

"Doctors will save him." Hunter was confident. He believed it to be true since he received a doctor's kit the previous Christmas and had healed and saved all his stuffed animals. He saw the power of a plastic stethoscope and a few surgical tools. Surely Grandpa Mike could be saved just as easily.

"They will try, baby. But if they can't, we need to prepare for a day where Grandpa Mike may no longer be around."

"We can't go see him anymore?"

"We will visit him as much as possible while he's still here. That's why it's important for us to appreciate all the time we have with him. Soak him in, embed memories of him in our minds forever. There may eventually be a day where we can't see him again for a long, long time."

Hunter thought about this for a moment and said, "Okay. Is he the only one that's going?"

"For now, baby. He's the only one we know."

"Okay, Mommy." He hugged me when noting the tears in my eyes, further proof of his strong intuition and caring personality.

I pushed Hunter's long blond bangs aside and kissed his forehead as he continued to play with his Transformers.

I wasn't sure how much had soaked in for Hunter. But the next several visits to Grandpa Mike, Hunter was continually touching him, holding his hand, and staring at him as though trying to memorize everything about him. I'm not sure if Josh realized what Hunter was doing or if he ever pieced it together. He never asked me. But my Hunter was showing maturity beyond his years, and I was so proud of him. He managed to step up more than his dad did.

———

Lindsay called. She hadn't ever called me directly. Either something terrible happened, or it was a mistake. I debated whether to answer. I gave in on the last ring.

"Hello?"

"Haleigh? Lindsay." Short, concise, expected. "We are taking the kids to the water park tomorrow and wanted to know if you and Hunter would like to join."

The invitation surprised me, a first from her to do anything outside of the normal family celebrations. "Sure. I can see if Josh can take the day off, too."

"Okay, good. We figured in light of Mike's news, family is more important than ever and we all need to be closer."

I wondered if this may be a turning point for Lindsay and me.

Maybe there was hope for us yet. "Yes, I agree. We will meet you there tomorrow."

"Great. Would ten o'clock allow enough time for you to get here?"

Did she think I slept in just because I didn't work? I shook off the thought. "Absolutely."

Lindsay hung up without saying goodbye. I assumed it was painful for her to make the call, Ryan forcing her to do it. The thought brought a smile to my face.

When Josh came home later that night, I shared the invite and asked if he could join us.

Twirling fettuccini on his fork, he stopped mid-bite. "No, sorry, can't." It was nine o'clock, and Josh had missed dinner yet again. I had to warm it up once he came home. Hunter was already in bed, and I was preparing to follow suit.

"You seldom take days off. They won't care if you take one vacation day. That's why PTO exists."

"I can't, Haleigh. It's last minute, and I have meetings planned. It's not like I sit at the desk twiddling my thumbs. I swear sometimes you forget how the corporate world works."

I ignored his jab. "I don't see how it's any different from a sick day that suddenly arises."

"I'm not sick!"

"You know what I'm saying. It's family, Josh. It's important."

He took a sip of red wine before responding, "Yes, family is important. Going to the waterpark is not. The answer is no."

I didn't have the energy to argue, resigned to the fact that Josh's stubbornness was greater than my own. Instead, I swallowed my pride, kissed his cheek, and forced my obstinacy down to say, "Thank you for working so hard for our family. Goodnight."

I was asleep before Josh made it into bed.

———

I foolishly expected Josh to spend the night thinking about it and decide to devote the day to us. As I stood in the kitchen the next morning with a cup of coffee in hand and watched him grab toast and run out the door, I questioned why I was surprised he still went to work. Instead of becoming more calloused over time with dashed hopes, my heart still splintered when he chose other things over time with us. But I knew I had to take a step back and see it through his eyes.

Josh viewed work as taking care of his family; he just didn't consider spending time with us as the same thing, although that time with him was what I craved. Even when our relationship was strained, I felt the difference between when he was around and when he wasn't. I would take him being home every time. Even through the tension and pain... it was important. Especially with Hunter in our lives.

Hunter and I packed to go to the waterpark without him. Hunter's excitement swept me into his happiness. I was thankful Lindsay called us. We needed this. The sunshine always made things better.

We located their family of four at the surprisingly empty waterpark, set up and waiting. It clicked then that Lindsay must have taken the kids out of school considering it was still a week-day. Hunter had preschool only two days a week, so we didn't have the same school restrictions to be concerned about.

Lindsay stretched out on a chair, her scalloped black bikini defined her tan skin and toned body. With her oversized sunglasses and hair pulled into a topknot, she looked like a model. Men and women alike snuck glances at her.

"Perfect timing! We were about to get in the water," Ryan greeted us while helping Grace put on her floaties. "Are you excited to swim today, Hunter?"

"Yes!" he exclaimed loudly, uncharacteristic of such a composed and quiet child. Apparently, we needed to take more trips to the waterpark.

While applying sunscreen on Hunter's skin, I attempted to

put it on myself simultaneously knowing as soon as I was done, he'd be ready to jump in the pool. I stripped off my cover-up, feeling confident in a new olive one-piece with crochet inserts and an edgy deep v-neck that made it stand apart from the typical mom swimsuit.

As usual, Lindsay and I were total opposites.

She eyed me as I removed everything. Her first words outside of "hi" when we arrived earlier was, "One piece, huh? That's bold."

I didn't respond because it was an ignorant comment. Since when did a one-piece swimsuit become the bolder choice over a bikini?

Lindsay tanned poolside while Ryan and I took the kids to the water. We splashed around, challenging who could make the largest waves. Hunter kept jumping on Ryan's back for rides as though he was a water horse. Ryan didn't seem to tire from it, no matter how many times each kid wanted to take a turn. He was having as good of a time as they were. It made me ache, wishing Josh could be like that with Hunter, yet unsure if he'd be in the water playing or in the lounge chair like Lindsay, most likely with a drink in his hand.

I caught myself staring at Ryan, his body capturing my attention more than I would have expected. I had seen him without his shirt many times before, all while in various pools or beaches on family vacations, but it had been some time since our last outing. Mercifully, dark shades hid my eyes since I couldn't stop staring. Ryan wasn't necessarily ripped, but he was defined. More than he had been before. Muscular arms, incredible back lines, and curvature of the hip bones that gave a sexy peek-a-boo before disappearing into the waistband of his swim trunks.

My eyes traveled across this primitive sight, noting a few stray hairs poking out of his chest—a sign he may have chest hair too, but shaves, just like Josh. I watched Ryan's arms flex as he dipped Grace in and out of the water. The sun was shining down, but damn, it suddenly became hotter.

Ryan had been a distant best friend for seven years. We naturally connected like we read each other's minds. Maybe we would have been even closer, but it sometimes felt strange, like we weren't supposed to get along as well as we did. Once two families come together, you're pressured to like each other, but yet there's a line between familial camaraderie and getting along *too* well.

Being so attracted to Ryan might have been a sign that Josh and I were spending too much time apart. *Oh God, when was the last time we had sex? Two weeks ago? Three?* I excused myself from Ryan and the kids to sneak back to my bag and pull out my phone calendar. *Shit.* The Pet Angels fundraiser fifteen days ago. And that was bad sex. Like *really* bad sex.

I made Josh go with me even though he was slammed with work, so he got slammed with drinks as his not-so-subtle way of rebelling. I still felt guilty that I made him attend, so when he crawled on top of me later that night, I gave in. It was clear I wasn't into it, and after a few minutes, he rushed to finish. We didn't say a word after. Empty, dark silence until his snores broke through. Not good at all.

I texted Jessi as I sat on my chair.

> How often should married couples with a kid have sex?

Her instant reply,

> Ask Siri.

> I'm at the waterpark. I can't vocalize that. You're the lifestyle expert.

> I just checked. Siri isn't helpful. I say three times a week.

I suppose I shouldn't have asked someone who was in the middle of a dating hiatus, unmarried, and willingly childless. But I didn't even remember a time when Josh and I went at it three times a week outside of the first vacation we took together, which was seven long years ago. That bothered me the most.

Another ding on the phone.

> Is your silence telling me that's far from reality?

> Far from MY reality… but in line with my dreams.

Defeated, I leaned back on the lounge chair next to Lindsay, eyeing her husband while she napped.

Hunter fell asleep in the car on the way home from the waterpark. He was sun-streaked, damp, and handsome in every way. As I glanced at him through the rearview mirror, I couldn't help but wonder what type of woman would steal his heart someday. I would make sure he was the best man in this world. I was set on it. He already had a heart of gold and an old soul. I wouldn't let anything or anyone taint that.

The truth of it was, I could try to influence him as much as possible, but Josh would have a more significant impact. It was natural for a son to look up to his dad for guidance. There were parts of being a man I could help shape, but Josh had to be the one to demonstrate it. Josh needed to see the importance of his role and understand the long-term effects of how he treats Hunter and me. I just didn't know how to address it without leading to a fight.

When Josh came home that night, he never asked how our time was at the waterpark. We had to remind him we went. Sometimes, it was like he didn't think of us during the workday. I knew he had pictures of us—or at least of Hunter—on his desk and one on the background of his phone. That had to remind him of us throughout the day, no matter how brief those thoughts may be, *right*?

———

Ryan appeared in my dreams that night. We took a drive together. I don't know where we were going, and it didn't matter. The windows were down with cold air blowing in, yet the heat was on high. He had one hand on the steering wheel and the other casually resting on the armrest between us. He suddenly pulled over and turned to ask, "If you had a five-minute free pass with me, what would you do?"

I laughed him off with a wave of my hand, "You're too funny."

"I'm serious, Haleigh." He put his hand tenderly on my thigh and blonde hairs I didn't know existed there stood to attention. I shivered in the cold air as I willed his hand to go further up my thigh, to push the navy lace skirt out of the way and to dive behind my panty line.

Suddenly, I felt bold and flirtatious. "When would the five minutes start?"

"Whenever you'd like them to."

"Okay." *Challenge accepted*, I thought. "Lean your seat as far back as it'll go."

Ryan reached for the lever and obliged as the seat squeaked into place, and the headrest tapped the back seat. He leaned back into it and gave a playful submissive look with his eyebrows asking, "What's next?"

"And you're sure about this?" I prepared for someone to play a mean joke, to be revealed the moment I made such an audacious move.

"Five minutes. I'll even set the alarm. The only rules are we don't go all the way, and we never talk about it again." He reached for his cell phone to set the timer.

I exhaled and shivered again. This was so sexy I couldn't handle it, even before it started.

"Ready?" he teased with his hand on the button.

"Go." I made as graceful a dive as I could over the middle console, wrapping a leg on either side of him, pushing his legs together with my thighs so I could fit on the seat, too. Like a greedy wolf, I was eager to pounce and devour my prey. My fingers brushed through his hair before gripping the strands roughly as I kissed and nibbled his neck, making my way to his lips where I pushed through with my tongue and thoroughly pressed my body against every inch of him. I was grateful I was wearing a loose skirt so I could feel more of his skin on mine. The "tick, tick" of the seconds was screaming in my ears, and I wanted to make sure I spent each one getting the most out of him.

Ryan wasn't wasting time either. He caressed my breasts, nibbled my ears, and grabbed my ass as though he had waited his whole life for this one moment. I thought dry humping was only a thing teenagers did, but here we were, and it was more arousing than sex itself. The desire to do much more but being so limited was the strongest seductress. The outline of his bulge underneath me allowed my imagination to go crazy as I rubbed over it and hoped the thin lining of my thong would continue to push to the side so I could feel him more.

Tick, tick, tick.

My eyes opened and adjusted to the dark room. My heart thumped loudly against my chest. Tingles ransacked my body. I wasn't in the car; I was in my bedroom. I just had a sex dream about Ryan. *Oh, Lord. Take me back, please.* I wanted to go back. The time wasn't over yet. I needed to see what happened next.

I rolled over to see Josh sleeping next to me. He was on the far edge of the bed as usual, so I scooted the distance to him. Curving my body into his, I reached my hand across his smooth chest, down his torso and slid into his boxers. It didn't take long for him to wake up and roll on his back, pulling me on top of him. I redeemed the bad sex from last time; it may have been our best in history.

It was the first of many dreams about Ryan. My sex drive finally returned.

———

My one scheduled outing a month was margarita night with Lacey. A year ago, we started our Mamas' Monthly Margarita Night to get out of the house and reward ourselves for a job done decently well in the world of motherhood. I wasn't a fan of margaritas until I became a mom. Then it became the one drink that felt like I was partying, even though I was sitting in a booth stuffing Mexican food down my throat.

Lacey and I were honest sounding boards for each other and saved a month's worth of juicy details for that one night. We would sit in various Mexican restaurant booths for a good four hours, exchanging stories and asking for advice until we knew we could no longer hold our drinks and still make it home safely. I waited until we started the second margarita to ask her the question burning inside of me.

"Do you fantasize about other men when you're in bed with Max?" They had been married for fourteen years and had four children, so I considered her the queen of all marriage- and child-related advice. I admired her and took everything she said to heart.

"Oh, totally. I'd say it's about fifty-fifty. Fifty percent of the time I'm with him; fifty percent of the time with some actor or musician. It makes sex more adventurous."

I nodded as I evaluated my mental checklist. Step one: feel better about fantasizing about another guy when having sex with my husband. Check. Step two: find out if there's a difference between fantasizing about someone I don't know versus someone I do.

"Do you only fantasize about famous people? Or do you think about some other guy you know, too?"

Lacey scoffed, "I don't get out enough to know any other men. But it's all the same. Either way, it's a fantasy of something that'll never happen. The point is to spark the desire in new ways so it doesn't become mundane."

"But wouldn't you be upset if Max was fantasizing about some other woman while having sex with you?"

Lacey bit a chip and contemplated it before answering, "As long as he wasn't constantly thinking about her or fantasizing about her, then no. Of course, he still has to be present when having sex with me at least half the time."

"Does he know these rules?"

She pulled her brunette hair into a ponytail and fanned herself. Once the margaritas hit hard, red splotches appeared on her neck like she was suffering from hot flashes. "If you haven't learned yet, you'll eventually discover that some rules are better left unsaid."

"Okay, then." I smiled as I sipped my margarita, taking the salt in with it, reminiscing about my latest Ryan fantasy.

"So, who is it?"

"Who?"

"Who are you fantasizing about? Or wanting to fantasize about? I'm assuming something specific brought this up."

I didn't think I was ready to tell anyone about my sudden infatuation with Ryan. It felt too risqué. But I was two margaritas in and feeling good, and if anyone could tell me I was being a bad wife, it would be this friend who I admired and respected. "My brother-in-law."

Lacey surprised me by grinning. "Aren't you two pretty close?"

"Yeah, I'd consider us good friends even. Something snapped in me the other day though. I saw him in a different light. Ever since then, my body overheats at the mere thought of him."

"What do you think changed?"

"Well, I did see him without his shirt recently and was shocked by how incredibly defined he is these days." I briefly closed my eyes, ordering the picture to the front of my mind, as clear as it was the day I saw him. "But it's more than that. It's sinking in how much Ryan gets me and how little Josh does. It's not like I'm comparing them, because I knew they differed from the beginning. Josh is Josh. He's who I married." I felt defensive and vulnerable all at once and shifted uncomfortably in my seat. "It's so not good, Lacey. Tell me how terrible of a person I am."

Lacey stirred her margarita with a straw and shook her head. "You're not bad, Haleigh. Give yourself some grace. Most married couples feel how you do at one point or another. Like you're not jiving and not understanding each other. I get it. I can't tell you the number of times Max and I have been there." She paused and considered her next words carefully. "The only difference is I have no one else to compare him to. I'm not looking at another guy and thinking he gives me the feeling I wish Max would give me. I unassumingly wait it out until Max and I are on the same page again. Because it eventually comes around again."

Lacey's advice was clear: I needed to be cautious and guard my heart, making sure it stays open only for Josh.

The only thing I couldn't verbalize was the difficulty of keeping my heart open to someone who regularly closes off his own. The fantasies made me feel alive while reality sucked the life out of me.

"Do you think that other feelings are manifesting themselves in the form of this fantasy? Maybe it's something different than just attraction to another man?" she probed.

"Like what?"

"Motherhood can cause some weird thoughts. I find myself jealous about things that I wouldn't have been before and I have to check my emotions. Why does Suzy's baby sleep through the night and mine doesn't? Why does Mary look better and thinner post-baby while I somehow aged overnight and can't seem to lose the forty pounds I put on? Why can everyone else wear high-waisted jeans but it makes me look like an old lady? Why can

Sarah do those crazy trampoline exercise classes and I pee myself every type I jump? Stupid stuff that I never cared about before."

Maybe since I was thinking about Ryan still, my thoughts took me straight to Lindsay. *Was I actually jealous of her this whole time?*

Wow, yes. Yes, I was. But it wasn't because of Ryan.

"My whole life, I wanted to be a mom. Now that I'm a mom, I feel like I'm mourning an important part of me that had to die to be here. I don't create playlists anymore. I can't even listen to half the songs that once meant something to me because it physically aches to do so. It makes me sad when I think about them. Deep down, I know that if I didn't marry Josh, I'd be in California, actually finding out if I could make it in LA. I was close to going after it right before we got serious. Now I'll never know if I could have. I should have chased those dreams first, then become a mom." Lindsay was being a mom while still doing what she wanted to do in life. But to do what I wanted, I'd have to move half a country away.

"Well dang, how long have you been harboring those feelings?"

My cheeks flushed. "I have no idea. Between your good questions and these sleepy-time margaritas, it's like hypnotherapy. Didn't even realize that was bothering me."

"So, what are you going to do about it now? Do you think Josh would consider you all moving out there together?"

"Maybe," I said.

But in my heart, I already knew the answer.

Chapter Sixteen
Him

Fatherhood brought a whole new competition with Ryan.

Everyone says how great of a dad he is. How he drops everything to be with the kids.

I don't know how to be like that. I want to be like that. But I don't know how.

I can't compete.

I remember watching you at our first work event, the way you took care of everyone, the way you floated through the room to make sure we all had what we needed even though you were presenting just like the rest of us. I watched you in awe and thought to myself, "That woman will make an excellent mother someday." I noticed that before I noticed your looks. I've never had a thought like that about anyone before.

When I finally met you, you continued to make those words true. You're selfless, loving, and devote yourself entirely. You make me want to be exactly like that. You give me hope that maybe I can be. Someday. I'm trying. With you as my guide, I'll get there.

Chapter Seventeen
Her

"Hi, good to see you all!" Hunter and I made rounds with hugs as we arrived at Ryan and Lindsay's house. Once we got to Grace, I whispered, "Happy Birthday, sweet girl," and tickled her sides until she erupted into giggles.

Wanda peeked out the open door. "Where's Josh?"

I slid off Hunter's shoes so he could run through the house with the rest of the kids. "He didn't text you? He was supposed to let you know he had a last-minute business trip, so he's unable to make it."

"Oh." She shut the door in disappointment. "He probably sent Ryan a message."

Ryan walked into the foyer, handing me a bottle of water. I was never without water in my hands. "Where's Josh?"

Evidently, Josh let no one know he wasn't coming today.

"Another work trip."

"Sounds like a lot of those lately. That's a good sign, right?"

I shrugged as I scraped at the bottle label with my fingertip. "I think so. He seems happy there."

"It'll pay off for him, that's for sure," Wanda said, beaming, expressing how proud she was of Josh the one time he wasn't around to hear it.

I wanted to challenge her, ask her at what cost do you keep sacrificing time with family for forty-plus years to make working worth it all, but I knew I would appear rapacious. Wanda didn't support the fact I was unemployed since she worked her entire life. Lindsay was conducting fitness classes and earning a paycheck, so Wanda considered her part of the full-time work-force. However, since I only volunteered these days, I was looked down upon, despite the fact it was her son's suggestion to leave my full-time job. I knew she would attack me the moment I verbalized my opinion that he worked too much. "Someone has to pay the bills, honey," would be the response. It could have come from Wanda, Lindsay, or Josh, for that matter, since they all shared the same mind at times.

Ryan must have noticed the strained look on my face because he put a comforting hand on my shoulder and spoke before I could, "It makes me grateful for the school schedule. I'm glad I took the path I did. I don't think I could make it in the corporate world without the long holiday and summer breaks."

I turned to face him, noticing for the first time that he'd grown out his beard. It was quite fitting on him, giving him a Hugh Jackman appearance. Jessi would have been proud of my actor reference. "Give yourself some credit, though. The school system is challenging for different reasons."

"That is true. But at least there's no travel outside of a few conferences. I don't think I could be away from the kids so much."

"You're a great dad, Ryan." I didn't mean it as a slant against Josh; it was genuine. Every time I saw Ryan with his kids, the attentiveness he showed them blew me away, almost carrying more motherly instincts than some women. It's the way I thought Josh would have been based on the way he used to talk about his future kids.

Grace's fifth birthday party only had family in attendance since they already celebrated with Grace's school friends the previous day at the Discovery Museum. Without Josh there, it felt smaller. Lindsay disappeared, too, soon after we had arrived, citing sickness. Ryan said she had been under the weather for a few weeks, so I found myself once again picking up the roles that Lindsay should have done. Ryan and I worked well together, as we moved about the kitchen to prepare the food clean up. It was a flawless dance. We didn't have to ask who would do what; we easily fell into a routine.

The entire time, we didn't stop talking about life. Nana and Papa were watching the kids play outside while Lindsay's siblings were watching the game in the basement. My days of getting out with friends had significantly reduced with Josh's recent work-load, so having this time with Ryan and no kids around almost felt like *me* time for the first time in ages. I cried from laughing so hard, from things that weren't even that funny, but it felt so good to laugh, my heart bursting as I clenched onto that feeling, refusing to let it go, savoring it. Hearing another adult's genuine laughter reverberate from my own was addicting and fulfilling. I didn't want it to end.

Ryan had a natural sarcastic banter that played off my own. I had to reel in my sarcasm with Josh; he wasn't very receptive of it, and instead, it would launch him into a defensive mode, as did many things that came from me.

Ryan, however, got it. He understood my sarcasm, my take on life, my humor. He would tip his head back with a deep, hearty laugh when I would be the one to end (or otherwise win) our back-and-forth teasing. "Not many people leave me speechless, Haleigh, but you always manage to."

"I feel like I should get an award and have an acceptance speech ready for something that big."

"You don't even know the half of it," Ryan winked, and a warmness flowed through my body that made me lightheaded. I shook my head, wondering how two brothers who were as close as Josh and Ryan could differ so much in their personalities.

Sometimes I wanted to talk to Ryan about Josh, about the intricacies of our marriage, the good and the bad. No one else would understand them like Ryan would. But that's a delicate balance, a thin line to walk. Ryan and I had such a great friendship, but above all, Ryan was Josh's brother. I often wondered if Josh talked to Ryan about me at all. But anytime I'd tell Ryan a snippet of what was happening in our lives on our family level, he acted as though he was hearing it for the first time.

"How often do you and Josh talk these days?"

Ryan stopped washing the dishes and leaned against the sink. "I'm not sure. We text when there's a good game on, but it's more about the game than anything else. I can't say we've really hit on anything personal in a while. We usually save that stuff for when we're together, and obviously that hasn't happened recently between the kids and his work schedule."

I relied on Ryan to have a more positive influence on Josh, but that would require time spent together. Another priority buried under Josh's workload along with Hunter and me.

Ryan stepped closer and lowered his voice to make sure no one else could hear. "Is there anything I should know about? You'd tell me, right?"

Oh, there were so many things I was desperate to share with him. They had been building up for years. I also knew I couldn't lie to him. "There are always things for you to know. I struggle with whether it's my place to share them."

He nodded, comprehending what I meant. "I'll try harder to get together with him. Surely we can find a few free hours soon."

"That would be good."

Ryan touched my arm to comfort me. Instead, a shock wave rocked my body. I held his gaze, and he held mine, and everything around us stopped. All I could focus on was his five fingers resting on my arm, feeling his skin connect with my nerve endings. It seemed like he didn't want to move either.

Then the basement door opened and Lindsay's brother-in-law, Grant, stepped through it. "Hey man, you're running low on good beer downstairs. Can we restock with the garage supply?"

"Sure, sure. I'll help." Ryan didn't move his hand from my

arm until he said, "It'll be okay, Haleigh. I promise you. I will never break a promise to you. Ever."

When Ryan and Grant disappeared into the garage, the impact of his words sunk in. As did the emptiness I felt now that a part of him was no longer touching me. Ryan was the greatest man I knew, and I was grateful he was in my life. He provided the comfort I needed the most, even when he lacked knowledge of specific details. It didn't hit me until a few hours later what had actually clicked during that moment together.

The kids were all crashing from their sugar highs, and it was past Hunter's naptime, so we said our goodbyes. One-by-one, hugs down the line of family members to get out the door. Ryan was my last, and he was peering at me the same way I was at him.

It took seven years and eleven weeks from our first meeting. I spent many nights afterward falling asleep to that look. The beautiful reflection of me in his eyes, and the understanding of what was between us. The deep, dark secret we wouldn't be able to acknowledge, but we both knew. If we wrote it down in a letter, it'd have to be burned. No one else could find out.

I was in love with Ryan.

And he was in love with me, too.

I didn't believe the stories that described how the world stopped when you found true love with another. I was the last person to believe in anything romantic in nature. But that's exactly how it happened. Everything around us paused and became smoky, a distraction as the purest emotion known to man was lit on fire. Even when looking at everyone else for a final time, Ryan was my last look. The eyes I would repeatedly seek out for the rest of my days.

Shit. Shit. Shit. I hit the steering wheel three times, grateful Hunter passed out in his car seat so he couldn't witness my meltdown.

I fell in love with Ryan.

Shit. Shit. Shit.

Then I cried. Because what else could I do when I finally

found the greatest man in the world, but he was the brother of the man I married?

Six days later, Ryan and Lindsay announced they were pregnant with baby number three, which explained Lindsay's sickness. My first thought was how unfortunate it was. Then I had to scold myself for being selfish and inappropriate before forcing out a congratulatory text to them. Babies never failed to change relationship dynamics. With it being their third, I knew Ryan would slink further away because his life was about to get that much fuller.

Loneliness struck hard. My friendship with Ryan was fulfilling areas of my life that Josh should have been. At all of our Claystone family get-togethers, I only felt like I was a part of the family because of Ryan's inclusion of me, of his reassurance I wasn't outside the mold like I felt, that I could be understood and accepted. But now with one more little person to deservingly steal his attention soon, I prepared to feel like a wallflower once again.

———

Mike died eleven months after his cancer announcement. It seemed to be a steady, controlled decline, and then all of a sudden, he was gone. We all believed he stayed alive long enough to meet Ryan and Lindsay's newest addition, Brinley, who was born one month before his passing.

It was the first time I had seen Josh cry. I held him for hours the week following the news. For once, he let me. Josh took two weeks off work, which was unheard of, and spent every waking minute with Hunter and me, appreciating our time together as a family as we drove to various area beaches to play in the lakes. It felt like he was becoming the dad and husband he once promised he'd be.

I longed to text Ryan and ask him how he was. We had a brief hug at the funeral, but we were preoccupied with the kids, the list of things to do, and speaking to everyone that came to pay their respects. I wanted to comfort Ryan and be there for him, but that wasn't my role. I could only hope Lindsay was selflessly fulfilling it. Instead, I relied on updates from Josh anytime he would talk to him. Ryan appeared to be holding up okay, but I knew Josh looked fine on the outside, yet broken inside.

I also didn't dare reach out to Ryan because my feelings for him needed to recede. Josh and I were learning how to be happy again. His dad's death shook his core and forced him to view his loved ones in a new light. It was an unexpected blessing born of tragedy.

The thing about tragedy is that the initial stun eventually subsides. The pain lessens and isn't always at the forefront of your mind day in and day out. Life goes on, and we all get comfortable once again with the idea that tomorrow will be a brand new day. It becomes easier to push things off and later realize we never did what we meant to do because tomorrow came and went.

Josh and I were strong for nine months after Mike's death. We spent our evenings cuddling on the couch and watching movies after Hunter went to bed. There were sweet touches in the morning, sexy exchanges of texts during the day, and several times a week, we'd end the night wrapped around each other. It almost felt like the honeymoon stage again. Josh opened up, sharing regrets of things he wished he told his dad before he passed away, reminiscing about his favorite memories, dreaming about the traditions he planned to pass on to Hunter. I fell in love with Josh all over again. A different man replaced him. One who unfortunately had to break before he became comfortable in his own skin and in tune with his emotions and feelings.

Nine months of a healthy marriage left me smiling in bed as I counted my blessings. Hunter was happier, too. Thoughts of Ryan rarely crossed my mind. I felt complete. I had my boys: Josh and Hunter. Life was good.

Until suddenly I was realizing how annoyed I was becoming with everything Josh did. For once, it wasn't Josh pushing me away; it was me walking away every time he was near me. I could barely stand to be in the same room as him.

First, it was chewing his gum too loudly. Then, it was the smell of the gum. Then, it was the way he'd throw Hunter in the air like he was going to drop him or hit the fan and it gave me a damn panic attack every single time. Then it was the smell of him after a run or how damp his socks seemed to always be.

The worst was the maddening hocking sound Josh would make when trying to transfer phlegm from the back of his throat to the front to spit out. Josh would do it four times a day. Minimum. I wasn't even around him for twelve hours of the day typically; yet, I still heard it at least *four times a day*, morning and night.

That's all I could hear as I sat in the bathroom, waiting for the pregnancy test to give me an answer for my missed period. I wondered if it was why I had been so annoyed with Josh lately. Hormones. I couldn't remember when I had my last period.

Then the results appeared.

I walked out of the bathroom with the stick hiding in my robe pocket. Josh sat on the bed with the TV on, remote in his hand, and his laptop opened on his lap. I crawled into bed and sat on my knees looking at him. "Honey?"

"Yep?" His eyes didn't shift from the TV as he pressed the buttons on the remote.

"Can I have your attention for a few minutes?"

Josh sighed melodramatically. For a brief moment, I considered waiting until my stomach grew bigger, forcing him to ask, "Are you pregnant?" But I released the stubbornness. This should be a happy time.

"Yep." He begrudgingly closed his laptop and muted the TV. "What's up?"

Beaming, I pulled the stick from my robe and handed it to him. "I'm pregnant again. We get to make Hunter a big brother."

I expected the news to thrill Josh. This is what he and I both wanted from the beginning. Children. A family that we can mold to be what we want and not what we grew up with.

"You weren't on birth control?" was not the reaction I predicted.

"No... I told you it was making me feel crazy, remember?" I looked at him expectantly. Josh shook his head. "You said, 'fine, I want another anyway.'"

"I don't think so. I would have remembered that conversation. If I said something that absurd, it would have been when I was drinking. Why would I want to bring another kid into the world right now?"

I pinched the bridge of my nose to calm my nerves and to will the nausea back down into my stomach. "Since when did your desire for more kids change? We're getting exactly what we always wanted."

Josh sighed, flipped off the TV, and rolled off the bed as though me ruining his time with the tragic news was the worst part of this conversation. "What do you want out of me?"

"To be excited! To be happy! To celebrate that we get to be parents again!"

Josh didn't respond. He just stared at the wall and kept his back to me.

I slid off the bed and took a cautious step toward him. "Josh... what's wrong? What's changed?" It felt like the longest pause in the world. My heart raced as my mind replayed how crappy I had been treating him for the past month. "Honey, I'm sorry that I've been mean to you. I know I've been getting annoyed easily lately. Now I know why. Clearly a new round of hormones is kicking in. I'm more aware now and I'll control them better—"

Josh put up his hand to cut me off. "Just stop."

"Josh..." I put my hand on his shoulder and turned him around to face me. His eyes were wide as though he was hiding something and suddenly caught. "What is going on?"

"Aren't you tired of this rollercoaster, Haleigh?"

Us. He was tired of us. That's what he was saying by his question. His voice asking that beckoned a resounding "yes" from the cave deep inside me where I could feel it the most. The same place I stored all the things I didn't know how to fix. I had a baby inside of me and one outside of me, though. Josh was not allowed to give up on us. He already broke one promise of how he said he'd be as a dad. He wasn't allowed to break this, too.

"This is normal, Josh. It's a marriage. We're in this for the long-haul. It's not always going to be easy or smooth. There will be times that we both feel exhausted by it. But look at what we're creating." I put his hand on my belly so he could feel the bump. I expected a change in his eyes, but he immediately pulled his hand away like he touched fire. "This is what you always said you wanted."

"I also said I wanted to stay home with the kids and not work all the time, and that didn't happen," he muttered.

"Are you blaming me for that? It was *your* idea that I stay home with the kids. I'll go back to work, Josh. If that's what will make you happy, I will. I'll go back to the firm. Or what if we went to California? What if we could go there and start over?" I knew this was the wrong time to bring up the idea of chasing my old dreams, but I was searching for any suggestions that may spark a light in him again. His eyes looked lifeless. Gray. Like the light had fully flickered out.

A part of me didn't want to give up all the tiny moments with Hunter I loved, like getting to hold his hand every walk we took together throughout the days. But Josh suddenly felt like he wasn't just distracted by work, but fully slipping away. That couldn't happen. Our children need their dad. I know because I needed mine.

Josh's eyes narrowed in on me. "Let's not kid ourselves here, Haleigh. You can't make as much as me. What are we going to do? Live in a fucking box?"

I ignored his jab, desperate to keep him holding on. "Does that even matter if we finally get the family we once dreamt about?"

"You think this is the family we wanted back then? Me working all the time? You picking at every little damn thing I do? This the dream life, huh?"

I fought back the tears stinging my eyes but he was cutting deep. "Then find a different job, Josh. There are other options. One that allows more flexibility and less travel. Or at least let me try to find something. I haven't been out of the workforce for *that* long."

He stared at me, his eyes burning a hole in me like I said the worst thing I could say to him. I didn't understand why he suddenly turned so dark. "Are you really that fucking disconnected from the real world now that you think it's just that simple? Just snap my fingers and there we go. The right job just appears. Everything is fixed. It must be nice to live in your special little bubble where you don't have to worry about a damn thing."

I bit my inner cheek hard to keep from exploding as the taste of metal hit my tongue. I reminded myself that Hunter was next door. Although I didn't mind him knowing his parents fought, I didn't want him to hear something he shouldn't.

Instead, as was my general reaction when I would become upset, I cried. Which only provoked Josh more.

"I will not feel sorry for you if that's what you're trying to do. You're the one that got off the pill and didn't tell me. This is the weight you carry, not me."

"So I'm raising this kid on my own?" All the fears I harbored, stemming from my dad's abandonment, came rushing back and I thought for a moment I might pass out. I breathed in and out slowly.

"Of course I will still be here. I'm the *father*. Fuck, Haleigh. You didn't leave me much choice, though, did you?"

The tears fell freely now. I couldn't stop them. "I hope someday you look back at this conversation and deeply regret having said these words. What a great way to welcome your second child into this world."

With that, I shut the door to our room and curled up next to

Hunter in his bed. With one arm holding on to him and the other wrapped around my stomach, I wondered how Josh could be so heartless, and why I never felt deserving of better.

If Josh and I starred in a flipbook, a happy couple snuggling next to each other would grace the front. But by the end of the flipped pages, a giant cushion would wedge between them and erupt in flames while the couple sat opposite each other on the couch with folded arms. We eventually stopped spending time in the same room, and tension was once again a constant presence peering over our shoulders.

———

In, out. Hot, cold. Up, down. Pairs of words in the flashcard game I would play with Hunter as he learned antonyms. But also words that could describe Josh during the waiting period of our second child.

Josh was present in certain ways. He handled the housework, grocery shopping, and paying the bills, so I didn't have to do anything except relax and focus on my time with Hunter. The second pregnancy was hard on my body, and for Josh to step up without asking what I needed spoke volumes. *He's in this. He really is*, I would convince myself, attempting to forgive and forget the terrible night we had when we discovered our family was growing.

But during conversations, he was distant, unavailable, barely present. Even with Hunter. If I said something to Hunter, Josh would repeat my words, like wanting to own the words I was saying to earn lackluster participation points instead of contributing ones of his own, as though it was enough. How could I complain, though, when he was picking up more duties around the house? I would appear ungrateful.

Sex became clumsy and difficult. We had sex throughout the first pregnancy with Hunter frequently with no problems. This one was bare bones. It might have happened twice during the first two trimesters mixed with a few late night hand jobs when Josh said he needed a release. I wondered if Josh wasn't being considerate, knowing I was in constant pain. I also questioned how it was possible for him to be satisfied when I felt anything but.

"You would tell me if you need more, right?" I asked him one night, compelling him to talk, to share, to prepare for how our lives were about to change even more.

"Sure."

"Okay... because I want you to feel comfortable with being honest. It's my job as your wife to help you with what you need."

He patted my hand as he flipped on the TV. "You're doing fine."

"Josh, look at me for a moment, please." He turned his head, his eyes peering into mine, shocking me with a jolt. I studied his denim irises and long eyelashes like I was seeing him for the first time again. *How have I not noticed we don't look at each other anymore?* There's always something else to pay attention to, and we fell last on that list. "Are you happy? With us? With this life?"

Josh squeezed his eyes and scratched the back of his neck. I braced myself for the growing pit in my stomach, a warning sign of bad news to come. He took a few minutes before responding. Even though I wanted to press him more, I knew that would be counterproductive.

"Yeah, I think so. It's just a lot right now. With work being so busy and the pregnancy, and Hunter going through the toddler stage. It'll get better someday, and I know that."

I let out a breath, not realizing I was holding it in. "So, you don't hate me? You don't want to run away?"

Josh turned his body to face me. It had been so long since I was his sole focus. "I could never hate you, Haleigh. I'm happy we're having another child. I am. I know I wasn't at first. But look at Hunter. He's amazing. Even in his difficult periods, he's a hell of a great kid. I'm sure the second one will be great, too."

I threw my arms around Josh's neck, gripping like he was a

buoy in choppy waters at sea. "I'm so happy to hear that. I thought I was making you miserable."

Josh's chest heaved in and out under mine. I couldn't tell if he was emotional or if he was taking a deep breath. Intimacy between us had been broken, becoming difficult to discern what his physical responses were anymore. Eventually, he put his arms around me and squeezed tightly. I froze, hesitant to move. I didn't want it to change. I didn't want him to stop holding me this way.

The pacing of his breath increased, as did mine. Soon his hands were sliding down my arms, to my hips, where he held on, before rounding out my belly. Josh had shown little interest in this pregnancy, so when he stopped his hand to feel for a kick from the baby, I choked back tears.

We made love for the first time in months. At one point, tears slipped down my face, and I was convinced they were hormone-induced. But soon, Josh's tears joined, and I knew what we shared at that moment was more than anything physical; it was a desperate outreach to save a marriage.

———

Baby number two was a girl we named Hannah. I loved Josh's look when he first laid eyes on Hunter, but when he looked at Hannah, it was even more beautiful. A sight I wouldn't forget. She would be the apple of his eye. He would spoil her, fight off any guys that came calling, and be a pain in the ass to deal with when it came to prom, let alone her wedding day. I was relieved.

I knew in my heart no matter how difficult he and I had it at times, Josh would be diligent in showing Hannah what it meant to have a man adore her and treat her like a princess. He would be that kind of dad for her, which is all I wanted. Hannah would end up with a man who was worthy of her someday, thanks to the confidence Josh would help instill in her. He would give her what my dad never gave me.

All wrongdoings that happened before her arrival were erased.

Josh and I were starting fresh once again, and hopefully, for the very last time. I envisioned a stable future with our newly completed family. It was safe to assume there'd be no more kids.

As I snuggled Hannah and kissed her sweet bald head, watching Josh fall asleep on the couch in the hospital room and knowing Hunter was safe with my parents, I cried. I cried because this was what I knew we could be. This was what I knew I'd been fighting for all these years.

Josh matured in his parenting role with the addition of Hannah to our little family. He was a fantastic father. He was present when he could be, helping them, teaching them, and loving on them. When he was gone, he missed them terribly by the look on his face (and their faces) when he'd walk through the door after his work trips. What I neglected to see was how I wasn't a part of anything he was missing.

The kids were in bed by eight o'clock at the latest every night. That left two hours alone with Josh and me. We could look like the happiest family in the world for the first couple of hours leading up to that point in the night. But as soon as the kids were asleep, it crumbled. I didn't notice at first how much Josh's drinking increased. Mostly, he waited until after the kids were in their rooms before starting.

Now and then, if work had been particularly stressful, he would have one with dinner. Most of the time, he would retreat to the wet bar in the basement. My nightly routine involved picking up beer bottles surrounding his passed-out body on the couch, and it terrified me. My mom used to do the same thing with my dad, and I'd watch from the doorway with a blankie in my hand, wondering how Daddy could hold so much liquor without peeing.

I made the mistake of addressing the increase in drinking with Josh, believing that was the right thing to do. I had even taken a few weeks to determine the best approach so he wouldn't default to his defensive mode right away. My strategy didn't make a difference.

I sat down next to him on the couch, waited for a commercial break, and calmly asked, "Is everything going okay at work? And elsewhere in life?"

His guard shot up before I even opened my mouth.

Josh grunted and continued to stare straight ahead. "Why would you ask?"

"For the past couple of months, you've had several drinks a night. You rarely drink like that unless there's a problem. I don't mind the drinking; I only want to be available to you if there's something more you want to talk about."

"You think I'm a drunk now? I'm not my fucking dad, Haleigh."

The castle walls were being built higher with cannons placed on top, ready to fire. "No, I didn't say that. I was only concerned that there may be a reason."

"Now I can't have a drink in my own fucking house without calling attention to myself? Fine, I'll hit the bars after work instead. At least I can drink in peace there."

"You're not listening, Josh." I steadied my voice, but my emotions rolled, this argument reminiscent of the ones we had while we were dating. It was scary sliding back there again, back to a time I thought we had grown from and worked so hard to get past.

Then it got worse.

I jumped as glass shattered behind me. I didn't turn my head to confirm the mess. Instead, I continued to stare at him, my lips pressed together to control the quivering of my chin.

"What? I can't do that in my house either?" Josh threw another bottle over my head against the wall where it broke apart like the first. "I can do whatever the fuck I want to, Haleigh. I spend all day working my damn ass off for you and the kids. I can do whatever the fuck I want. Do you hear me?" Crimson painted his face, or maybe it filled my eyes; that was all I could see.

I closed my eyes, pushing the tears back, searching for something to change this, for the right words to say, for a way to glue our broken pieces together and make it all better. But I had nothing. I stood on the edge of a cliff, ready to fall, preparing for the sound of another broken bottle, my body geared for flight mode.

Josh grabbed another beer, and I grimaced, imagining the bottle coming straight at my face instead of over my head. But he flipped the top off with his teeth and continued glowering at the TV. That was my cue. I stood, walked up the stairs, and quietly closed the basement door. I paused for a second before sliding down to the floor, crying, stunned, shocked, my heart beating fast, my life threatened.

In my daze, I didn't remember making it up to my bedroom to fall asleep. I awoke at 4:03 a.m. to an empty bed. Josh never joined me. I tiptoed downstairs, opened the basement door to see the light from the TV on. I slipped down the stairs as silently as possible. Josh was nowhere to be found. I flipped on canned lights that highlighted four empty beer bottles on the couch as though they were trophies, when they were anything but recognition of winning.

Lines of stained liquid ran from the dents in the wall to the pile of broken glass on the floor. Retrieving cleaning supplies, I swept the bottles, vacuumed the carpet, and scrubbed the wall until it looked somewhat normal again, minus the dents that would forever be a reminder of that moment. Fortunately, someone had to look hard to know they were there. But I would always know they existed. I'd never forget how scared I felt.

It was the night I grasped the extent of our wrecked marriage.

I practiced deep breaths as I continued cleaning. At least our kids were happy. For now. I'd keep them as protected from this as possible.

———

Josh didn't apologize for that night; it wasn't brought up again. But he decreased his drinking. Maybe every other night or every third night he'd have a couple, but I would take it. Kristen's words haunted me; her question from years ago about whether Josh became physical frequently visited my mind. Those were words I once thought I could leave behind. But I saw a flash of it that night. Anger so severe that he wanted to do something more, even if that something more was punching a wall. Knowing physical violence lived just below the surface put me on edge.

After a few weeks, I stopped counting the beer bottles and Josh stopped drinking as much. An uneasy balance that worked for us and maintained a neutral level of tension in the house.

Josh also remained on the main floor after the kids went to bed. He wouldn't immediately retreat to the basement like before. I liked having him in the same room. After all these years and merciless moments and situations, I still adored spending time together, even if we were doing our own thing. I realized I was gripping on to whatever good I could; every little thing that wasn't bad carried more weight and meant a lot more than it would have in any other situation. "Decent" became the new status quo for intimacy.

One night, as we were getting ready for bed, I finally asked a question that was years overdue, "Should we try couples therapy?"

Josh sighed while plugging in his cell phone. "Listen, Haleigh, I'm trying. I know I don't always, but right now I'm trying. You see that, don't you?" Josh had his own way of doing things. It wasn't textbook, but I couldn't deny I saw some recent effort.

I nodded. "Yes, and I appreciate that."

"Let me try for a little longer, okay? Then we can discuss if we need to bring anyone else into this." He stepped closer to kiss my forehead before heading to the bathroom.

"Okay," I mumbled.

It did get a little better in time. We rose from misery, back to contentment. At least it gave me hope. Although I couldn't shake the fear that everything was cyclical with us.

Except for this time, Josh had a vasectomy. I didn't argue when he suggested he should. That meant the new baby stage of our cycle would break and we had a chance of continuing to move forward as new stages of life presented themselves, rather than ones we've trudged through with little success.

Hope for change was all I had left with Josh. I had to cling on to what little I could.

Chapter Eighteen
Him

For so long, there were only four people who knew the truth about my parents' marriage. My dad was an alcoholic for the first ten years.

Most weeknights, we listened to them yell endlessly at each other, waiting for the doors to slam to signify the end. Several weekend nights, we witnessed him hit her. Sometimes a push against the wall, sometimes a slap in the face, and once, a punch in the stomach.

The day Ryan punched him back, that's when it stopped. Dad disappeared for three months. When he came back around, he was a different man. He was submissive, catering to our needs, serving Mom and his family to no end, striving to put us above him. We could see him still struggle when things got hard. Like when he lost his job and had to find a new one at forty-five. But he persevered. He proved to us that he was stronger.

No one warned me alcoholism could run in the family. No one suggested that we should be aware of similar signs of addiction like my dad exhibited. We didn't receive that support.

I didn't realize it was a problem until it was too late. And there was already too much on the line by then.

If only I knew, if only I had coped better, things could have been so much different.

Chapter Nineteen
Her

Admittedly, I was losing my mind.

The first couple days of Josh's absence were always somewhat enjoyable. The kids and I would continue our days as usual with few changes. After Hunter and Hannah were in bed, my free time could begin. There was nothing else I was required to do, no one else I had to please. I loaded up on chick lit and rom-coms thanks to Jessi cultivating my addiction to a now-enjoyable genre. I realized how much of a needed escape it was. Popcorn was my dinner followed by endless glasses of red wine for dessert. My typical ten o'clock bedtime turned into midnight and beyond, as I soaked up as much "me time" as possible.

By day three, the kids were wild, sick of me, and veins popped out of my forehead. We FaceTimed Josh, but usually he would quickly check in before running off to another meeting or dinner or whatever they packed in the agenda for him.

"Hey, I wanted to say goodnight to the kids before bed." It was seven o'clock, the traditional last phone call of the night when he was away. Josh glanced at the screen but mostly watched something above his iPad.

"Hunter and Hannah! Come, say goodnight to your dad," I

called out. As I waited for the patter of their footsteps, I asked, "What in the world are you doing?"

Josh flipped the iPad camera to the TV in his hotel room, "Cardinals and Cubs."

I rolled my eyes. "Of course."

"Dad, Dad, Dad!" they chanted while crowding in front of the screen.

"Is it hot there, Dad?" Hunter had inquired about Texas earlier and since I had never been there, I said it was hot and that's about all I knew. I figured tomorrow we could dive in and do a study about Texas, a little internet research and a fun art project. Hunter had my nerd-like genes and enjoyed learning when an opportunity presented itself.

"Pretty warm. About forty degrees warmer than Illinois."

"Sprinkler time?" Hannah asked in her sweet little voice. She had started talking around sixteen months, and the words she'd say shocked us. She was a sponge, her little ears soaking up everything said around her.

"Oh, I wish, sweetie. That would be more fun!"

"Sprinkles, sprinkles!" Hannah clapped.

"Let's all go to the waterpark!" Hunter added. "You'll come, right, Dad?"

I knew where this was headed if I didn't curb it. The kids would form ideas and be relentless until I gave in. I wasn't ready to have a solo battle right before bed.

"Okay, babes, blow kisses to Daddy and head on upstairs!"

Hunter and Hannah blew many kisses, outdoing each other on the number, and Josh blew one back. Their interactions with each other would eternally make me melt. The kids snuck into the living room instead of up the stairs, stealing TV time while Daddy distracted Mommy.

"What are the plans for tonight?"

"Dinner with brokers and whatever they decide afterward, I suppose." Josh's eyes were back to the game.

"Hopefully you're going someplace with a TV?" I joked to grab his attention. I wasn't quite worthy of it the way the kids were, which made me insecure, as though he couldn't stand to look at me. At the beginning of the year, I challenged myself to go makeup-free for as many hours as I could stand each day. Hannah's curiosity about my beauty supply drawer recently increased. I wanted to teach her the importance of embracing her natural beauty and tried setting a good example for her. Nonetheless, I couldn't fight the voices in my head telling me that's why Josh stopped looking at me. I wished he would tell me I looked better without my makeup, that he was glad I didn't wear it. But he never acknowledged it.

Josh glanced at me and forced a tight-lipped smile, "It's about over with anyway." He paused and watched me for a moment, clearly recognizing he had nothing else to say. "I should head downstairs to meet everyone."

Eager to start my personal downtime, I didn't fight it. "Okay, I need to get the kids in bed, anyway. Have fun tonight. We'll talk sometime tomorrow, right?"

"Yeah, I'll try to call between meetings. It's pretty back-to-back though, so we'll see how it goes."

I knew the drill. That's how it always went. "Okay, love you."

"You, too." Josh was gone in a flash.

I shut the computer down with a sigh. Sometimes I wished I missed him more than I did. After a few days of indulging in romantic books and movies, I was left feeling empty. It's probably why I subconsciously avoided watching them for all those years before Jessi entered my life. I coached myself to be grateful for what may be just a decent partner in life, but a fantastic father to our children. "Other people have it worse," my mom's words echoed in my mind, as I realized how much I became a product of her over the years. And Josh never walked away from his family. That was more than I could say about my dad.

The laughter and smiles of two adorable children waiting for me was all the proof I needed that every decision I made had been worth it. Everything was meant to be and in due time, it would get better.

Twelve years since I met Josh, and I never once let go of that belief. It was bound to get better. Surely.

———

The next morning, sunlight poured through my bedroom window, awakening me from a bad dream. I couldn't remember the exact details, but red wine was known to produce weird nightmares for me. I rolled my shoulders to shake off the remaining oddness, contemplating making the switch to white wine instead. With the sun finally shining after multiple days of snowy bleakness, nothing would get me down.

Knowing that I woke up before the kids, for once, only added to the mix. I hurried into the bathroom to enjoy ten minutes of an utterly blissful, super-hot shower. Yes, it would be a good day indeed.

Three knocks. That's how long it took for me to get to the front door from the kitchen. I was in the middle of baking muffins to surprise the kids, determined to bribe them to get on the good day train, too. I would not lose my sanity today like I did yesterday. Maybe like Hunter had suggested last night, we could go to the indoor waterpark resort to break the winter blues.

However, the kids waking up by loud knocks on the front door early in the morning wasn't aiding my plans for a successful day.

Two police officers on my doorstep didn't help matters either. "Mrs. Claystone?"

My eyes surveyed the neighborhood behind them; my mind examined possibilities of something occurring in the safe cul-de-sac we lived in. My car might have been stolen, or I hit something while driving home yesterday in my frenzied, distracted state. "Yes..." I responded warily.

The officer who spoke had crystal blue eyes that reminded me of a waterhole Josh and I discovered once while hiking through Kauai. We found it after we detoured off the main trail and climbed down a rocky path that could have led to our deaths if we slipped. We didn't, and the risk was well worth the reward of that sight. I stood at the waterhole and stared for a good hour, watching the waves crash against the black rocks all around it. The rocks stood tall, protecting the waterhole, acknowledging it as a source of purity and guarding it against elements that could otherwise taint it. Josh had found his own spot feet away, sitting on one of the rocks connected to the cliff, watching the endless ocean with a faraway look in his eyes. For years afterward, we reflected on the serenity of that moment and how it was one we could never replicate.

As the officer's words tumbled out, I couldn't look away from his eyes and the way they carried me back to Kauai. Like an out-of-body experience, I could see myself walking back to Josh, wondering what he was thinking about as he stared at the water, his brown hair ruffled by the wind. When I reached him, I touched his knee, snapping him out of his trance. Josh gave me a smile that was almost identical to the one he gave me at Starter's Lounge after five months of dating; the one that told me maybe I finally had his heart; the one that was genuine yet rare for someone who smiled so little. Josh grabbed my hand and carefully led me to a small patch of rocks in the water. Despite the slippery surface, he slid down to one knee, displaying unbelievable balance and endurance, and asked me to marry him.

His mom, my mom, his brother, our friends. Our children. Where do I start? Who do I call first? How can I make the fewest calls possible? I hated to repeat myself.

"Mrs. Claystone? Did you hear me?" The officer gently reached for my left hand and put both of his own around it in a comforting embrace. He covered my wedding ring. My mind read the actions out loud like a narrator in a story.

I nodded and slowly sank to the doorstep. The officer

crouched down with me. I looked into his eyes and watched the waterhole of Hawaii sway in the breeze. Dizziness. When I closed my eyes, I repeated verbatim, "Josh was in an accident. Unfortunately, he wasn't able to be saved." I opened them again. This time, the water was replaced with an empathetic man staring back at me. I summarized in my terms, "My husband is dead."

The officer lowered his head. "Yes, ma'am..."

Josh was gone.

———

The following days were chaos. There were many people to call and infinite decisions to make. Josh and I said we would make a will but never got around to it. Someone asked almost every hour what Josh's funeral wishes were. The remorse was a heavy cloak as I stumbled through decisions about what he would want as his final sendoff. "I'm sorry, I'm sorry." I couldn't count the number of times I said those words, nor could I count how many times they were said in return. Those words that carried no meaning were the easiest to spit out when other emotions plummeted to pieces, impossible to grasp.

The only things in clear view were my children and their eyes as they sought to comprehend what their days would look like from here on out. Daddy would no longer be a physical part of those, only in memory, which we would be sure to honor. I encouraged them to cry and express their emotions, most of which was confusion, and I could fully relate. Someone who had been a pillar in their lives from their first day in this world was now gone. I spent more time in their beds than mine; not because they needed me, but because I needed them.

The day of the funeral, I stood in my bathroom, staring at drawers full of makeup and beauty products, suddenly incompetent. So many random pieces that held no real value. How much time did I once spend in the bathroom using them? And for what? Did Josh recall whether I used eyeliner? I emptied drawers of useless products, one by one, expelling them into the bathroom trashcan and replacing a new liner when it got too full, just to fill it up again. At least brushing my hair was instinctive and one I could easily command my hand to do. I gently placed the hairbrush on the bathroom sink while everything else would meet the garbage truck on Thursday. I needed to make sure I took out the trash. Josh would care that the garbage was taken out on time.

A black dress lay on the bed, imitating a body in a coffin. Maybe I put it out, maybe my mom did for me. I was uncomfortable once it was on. I didn't think it fit me well, but never cared enough to look in a mirror to find out. None of that mattered anymore.

Cars, procession line, flags, service, open casket. The visitation blended with the funeral. Everything I had prepared to see. Except for the coffin. "I'm sorry, I should have cremated him," I said that to someone. Wanda probably. She was nearby, I think. Regret shook my body. The kids shouldn't see their dad like that. Not for the final time. I didn't want them to remember him this way. But it was too late. They were letting us look first, before everyone else arrived.

I placed my hands on their shoulders as we walked closer. Josh looked so handsome. Asleep in a grey, three-piece suit. Why did I choose a suit? He's not the businessman; he's our Josh. He needs a tee and cargo shorts. His favorite Cubs hat. I wanted to undress him, to change his clothes. "I'm sorry..." I muttered.

"Daddy..." Hannah whimpered. Hunter put his arm around her shoulder. He was such a brave kid. No one would know how heartbroken he was except for a quiet sniffle that escaped him.

Hunter inspired me to find my strength long enough to bend down next to them and whisper, "This is our chance to say goodbye to Daddy. We don't remember Daddy like this though. We remember him as the man who would play baseball with you for hours, Hunter, and then go and have tea time with you,

Hannah. We have so many pictures and videos of Daddy as he was. We will remember Daddy for who he *truly* was." Hunter nodded bravely, but Hannah immediately turned into my arms and buried herself in my neck, her curly hair attaching to my lips. I was grateful for her maneuver and held on to her like a comfort blanket. I didn't want to let her go.

Once people arrived, I couldn't handle watching them view Josh. I stared at my hands, knotting them over and over again. Callouses that weren't there last week appeared. I couldn't stop playing with my ring. I had yet to think about my ring. *When do I take it off? When is the right time to no longer pretend I'm still married? Because I'm not married, right? But why didn't I get to have a say in it?* I didn't choose to stop being married. Yet here I was. And there he was. In a casket.

He wasn't supposed to leave me.

A dull ache hid behind my eyes, and it continued to grow in intensity. I wanted to cry but couldn't. The pain worsened, and the fog grew heavier. People wanted to have conversations. I didn't. I spoke because I had to. But I was tired of talking. I was tired of pretending that tomorrow would be a new day. Josh was no longer coming home.

Finally, everyone left. One by one. More handshakes. More hugs. More final words. More promises of visits that would never transpire. Most people would go home after the funeral and life would be the same for them the next day. They wouldn't think about how mine stopped.

Family lingered. Wanda was in as bad of shape as I was. She lost both a husband and child in such a short period. That's not something you expect to experience in life, and you pray every day you don't. Yet here she was. I hugged her the longest.

"Please let me know if you want to come by anytime."

She nodded. "I will. I know we have a lot to discuss yet. I just can't quite yet."

"We have time, Wanda." I didn't want to tell her I couldn't handle it either. The funeral arrangement discussions were hard enough. We clashed several times as she thought Josh should be cremated like Mike was. I had to tell her repeatedly that Josh and I had multiple discussions about death and what to do. I knew what his wishes were even though we didn't get around to writing them all down.

Then I realized how absurd it was that Josh and I rarely talked about our lives, about our futures, yet we talked about our deaths. Death didn't seem like a possibility. That's probably why it was so much easier. Our lives were too much of a hard reality to discuss.

I choked back a laugh. It was gurgling out of my throat. Instead of coming out, it resulted in a coughing attack where someone, I don't even know who, fetched me a bottle of water.

I stared at that bottle for a while, scratching off the label as tiny, cold pieces fell to the floor around my feet like snow. I didn't know what time it was, or where I was, until someone else stood in front of me.

Ryan.

I took one look at him and whatever was left of my composure seeped into thin air like a soul leaving a body. He put his arms around me, gathered me up, pulled me close to him. His chin rested on my head, as I sobbed heavily into his chest, knowing I was soaking his shirt, but I couldn't stop.

It was as though I was hugging Josh again, and I gripped Ryan's shirt even tighter. If I closed my eyes, Josh was hugging me back. Josh and Ryan were so similar physically, it didn't take a lot of imagination. *If I could embrace Josh again, if I could have said a better goodbye, if I could have made things better before he left us...* Why did he leave us when things were so rocky? Why couldn't we have made things right? Why couldn't he be standing here with me right now with his arms around me, and my arms around him, and both of us crying as we talked about life and not about death? *Why did we talk about death?* We brought it on ourselves. My knees wobbled, and I held on tighter.

"Hey," Ryan put both of his hands on my shoulders to steady me, tilting my chin up and leaning in until my eyes met his. I couldn't tell if his were watering or if mine were. Everything was a blurry mess. "You're going to be okay." His voice cracked as he added, "We will all be okay. I promise you, Haleigh. I will never break my promise to you." Just like he said before. But we never know if certain promises are out of our control.

CHAPTER TWENTY
HIM

But no more.

I'm done pretending. I'm done being scared. I'm done living a life other than the one I want.

I'm ready. It is time.

Chapter Twenty-One
Her

Life doesn't stop to recognize someone died. That's the hardest part of mourning. Three days of grace after the funeral to cry and figure out how to survive in this new world without my husband and the kids' dad before being forced to continue our hectic days, getting Hunter and Hannah to school and their activities, as though nothing changed.

My mom stayed with us and was my motivation when I could barely get out of bed. She gave me enough space to cry when needed, but never let me drown in my tears. She would whisper in the mornings, "Hannah is still learning how to grieve. You're setting the example. Show her the strength within you. You can do this." It was a necessary pep talk to get me out of pajamas and pull a brush through my hair.

After two weeks, Mom left. As she walked out the door, I wanted to grab her leg, beg that she move in with us. I was terrified. Absolutely, horrifically terrified. I didn't want her to get in a car or to leave us. I spent many nights alone while Josh was on his business trips, but it's different knowing someone is coming back. There was no one coming back this time.

My favorite pastime became calls with Jessi after the kids went to bed. She didn't ask me how I was doing. She rarely said things a person *should* say, only what she honestly thought and felt, which was exactly what I needed. Constant reality checks that were surprisingly comforting.

Two days after listening to stories about Chris, a guy who finally broke her dating boycott, the pieces connected. "Wait, Chris Umphrey?"

"Yeah, of course."

"When did you meet Chris Umphrey?" I had to repeat his name to make sure we were talking about the same guy.

"At Josh's funeral. Not the ideal place, sure, but kind of equal to meeting at a bar if you ask me."

"Chris Umphrey?"

Jessi groaned. "Yes, Haleigh. Chris something-or-another Umphrey. We haven't discussed middle names yet, so I don't know what it is. But I'm sure there wouldn't be two different Chris Umphreys at Josh's funeral."

Chris grew up next door to Josh and Ryan. They weren't close friends, though, until Ryan roomed with him in college. Suddenly Chris was everywhere, photobombing pictures and joining in on baseball trips. He was at most of the birthday parties for Ryan's kids, usually only popping in for an hour or so, and always flying solo. He was friendly, more of the studious type that gave the impression he'd be content at home with a good book rather than out at the club.

There was a contrast between him and Jessi, but I liked the balance. He was very good-looking too, standing a tad under six feet with the typical "Chris" appearance that pitted celebrities Chris Pine, Chris Evans, Chris Pratt, and Chris Hemsworth against each other in the most handsome Chris debate. I could see how he caught Jessi's eye amid tragedy.

"Why in the world is he single, though?" Jessi was already searching for excuses to dump him.

"Why are *you* single?"

"Touché."

"He's a good guy to go after. Ryan thinks highly of him."

Every time Chris showed up, Ryan would come out of his shell more. They had a childhood secret handshake. I couldn't help but grin each time they did it, while Lindsay would roll her eyes or make comments about how stupid it was.

"Hmm," Jessi coughs. "No offense, Hal, but didn't Ryan think highly of Josh?"

Ouch. "Josh was his little brother. There's blood there. Brotherly love. That's different." Jessi had such a harsh view of Josh, and I failed as his wife by painting that picture. Yes, things weren't perfect, but I shouldn't have let her hear as much negativity as I shared. Or at least I should have shared more of the good moments than I did. I used her as a sounding board too often. How could she view Josh as anything else when all she heard was the worst parts of our relationship?

"There were a lot of good things about Josh, you know." My voice was quiet as I choked back remorse.

Jessi's voice softened in response, "I know, Haleigh. I know you wouldn't have been with him otherwise. I'm protective of you."

"I just don't want to be the reason someone didn't see Josh's good qualities. My mom always said I was too hard on the guys I'd date, and I've been thinking about that a lot. I was too harsh with Josh, never giving him enough credit, never allowing him to be himself without criticism. I'm why he retreated further away from us." Tears liberally fell. "Now that I recognize it, I can't call him and apologize. He's gone. For good. I can't change anything now. I can't make any of it better." Sorrow rolled through my body like a monsoon, rocking my core, leaving ultimate destruction in the places that were already barely hanging on by a thread.

"Shh, shh..." Jessi soothed, although difficult over the phone. "Do you need me to come over? I can be there in fifteen minutes."

Once I cried, it was hard to stop. "No, that's okay." I sniffled, reeling back the sobs to finish our conversation. "Thanks, though. You're a great friend."

"I'm here when you need me. Even when you don't."

"I know. I appreciate that."

"And Haleigh? I think many people were aware of Josh's good characteristics. I mean, there were *a lot* of people who showed up for his visitation. I'm not sure you comprehended how many people paid their respects. He was a loved man."

I shook my head even though she couldn't see me. Both his visitation and funeral blended in my mind. I couldn't separate one from the other. "Everything was a blur. I went through the motions and spoke when required. The kids were all I could see. And my hands. I kept thinking about how damn old they look. I have sixty-year-old hands. I need to fix them."

Jessi laughed, and it made me smile. I haven't felt funny in so long, as though cracking jokes in this time of mourning would be an insult to Josh's death.

"Well, don't become a widow who gets addicted to QVC and spends the kids' entire inheritance on all the crazy good deals. Next time we go shopping, we'll make it our mission to track down cream so your hands won't look so old. You probably need retail therapy soon, anyway."

I looked down at what had become my normal attire. "As long as I can wear a baggy t-shirt and even baggier joggers, I'm in. Also," I used my thumbnail to scratch at a melted piece of chocolate on my shirt. "Stains must be accepted."

"Oh, dear," Jessi whistled under her breath, "You're in worse shape than I thought."

———

I needed to wear earrings. I had nowhere to go, but my ears had been bare for a while. Jewelry had gone out the window as much as makeup had. I wasn't sure how long it would take for the holes to fill in again, but I didn't want to risk it. My ears had been pierced since I was two years old. Maybe someday, I'd want to dress up again. Lately, barely presentable was good enough.

My pair of silver ear climbers were my go-to pieces and permanently sat on the top of my dresser, but I could only find one. Since I didn't wear a lot of jewelry, I rarely used my actual jewelry box that contained the random pieces I had been gifted or collected over the years. Opening it for the first time in so long, a layer of dust attached itself to my fingers, a robin egg blue velvet Tiffany's bag stood out. I knew what was in it.

A bracelet Josh gave me on our wedding day. I gasped when I dumped out the contents. A coating of tarnish covered the once-silver bracelet. An inscription I didn't even remember he engraved was impossible to read. The charm bracelet he gave me my first Mother's Day was also discolored. The only two pieces of jewelry from him in the box and both were spoiled. Nothing else was affected. Only the pieces that Josh gave me for special occasions, my most expensive jewelry.

Sobbing, I called my mom. "I neglected him."

"Honey, are you okay? Do you need me to come over?"

"I neglected him. He was covered in tarnish, and I didn't even notice."

"Tarnish? He was covered in tarnish? I'm so sorry, sweetie, I have no clue what you're talking about."

My sobs filled the phone speaker as I searched for better word choices but struggled to do so. *Why didn't she understand what I was saying? What was there to get? Why didn't Josh tell me how he felt?* The jewelry was more in sync with him than I was.

"I covered Josh in tarnish. All this time. I threw ugly words at him. I was never satisfied. He was ruined by me. I didn't take care of him enough. If I did, the jewelry he gave me wouldn't look like this. If I only took better care of us. If only I tried harder. We wouldn't look like this. The end of us wouldn't be so ugly."

My mom was silent before speaking again. "I'm not clear on what you're referring to, honey, but everyone knows you loved Josh. That you still love him. Josh knew it, too. And he loved you."

"But..." She didn't know the details. She didn't understand the struggles. She didn't realize what went on behind the scenes.

As though Mom read my mind, she continued, "Only the two people involved in a marriage truly know the ins and outs, what goes on, what's said, and what wasn't said but should have been. It's easy during the dark times to reflect on everything that went bad. And that's okay because it is part of the healing. You also have to look at everything that went right. Everything that kept you two together all this time. Everything you fought for, even if you simply showed up and committed to yet another day with each other. Focus on those times, all the laughs, all the happy things only you two know about."

Her words slipped through one of the many crevices in my heart, filling the brokenness with a different perspective. Mom was right. She spoke as though she had been in this same situation before, previous pep talks she gave herself when things were at the lowest point between her and Dad.

Mom confessed, "Your dad and I are naturally critical. I see it in you, and I'm sorry to say it's our fault. We failed to shield you from adopting one of our worst characteristics. My biggest fear as you repair your heart is letting this criticism take over. You cannot be too critical of yourself, and you can no longer be too critical of Josh. Things happened as they did, and you have to accept them for what they are. Otherwise, you'll drive yourself straight to the insane asylum for trying to grip onto things that are already gone."

It was the first time my mom mentioned being critical of me. After years of suffocating from it, a weight lifted from my chest a little, and I could breathe better with the simple acknowledgment.

"Thank you, Mom, for saying that. It helps."

"No more of this tarnish talk, okay?"

I turned the bracelets in my hand, still questioning how these could be the only tainted pieces in the entire box. The only two that were gifts from Josh. All I could do was put them back in the Tiffany's bag and get them professionally cleaned. Some of my memories could use a good scrubbing, too.

———

Josh promised to set us up financially, and that he did. Finding a job was not something I could manage right away after years of being out of the workforce. It would take a significant amount of energy I didn't have. The kids and I were still adjusting every day. Adding the stress of job hunting would have been disastrous for us all. Not to mention having to find someone to watch Hannah while I worked again. I was grateful Josh took care of us in that way, that he made it a priority. All the times I complained about him not being with us, he was out there working for us. I tried not to dwell on that and get stuck in a pity party once again. Crawling out of bed and facing the day was a big enough challenge.

Since Josh handled the financial details of our family, it took me weeks to browse through the paperwork in his office to get everything in order and find the right numbers to contact. Hours upon hours on the phone for passwords I couldn't locate, having to send death certificates and being passed from one customer account representative to another to prove that my husband passed, and I indeed needed access to our accounts. It was depressing proof of our subpar communication since I didn't know how many accounts we had or how to access half of them.

While I was on the phone with one of the three banks Josh used, I noticed the first email. It would have been buried deep in the trash folder, except I searched for "bank" in hopes to find information from Third Street Bank. Her last name was Banks. *Corinne Banks.*

Dearest Joshua- I can't wait to see you. I'll be in at 7:20 and will meet you by the baggage claim. See you soon. XOXO, Corinne.

A boulder crashed into my stomach. I checked the date. August twelfth. Six months ago. My hands trembled as I tapped open his calendar. He was in Denver then for one of his many work trips. Apparently, so was she.

Corinne Banks. Corinne Banks. Corinne Banks.

There were numerous emails from her. I clicked on the next email and the next, skipping over any actual bank emails and focusing on only hers. So many XOXOs, such excitement to see him on their many trips together, and a sickening over-usage of the word "darling."

I checked the "to" signature, to make sure it was supposed to go to *my* Joshua. I verified her email address wasn't spam. I confirmed the dates again, cross-checking with Josh's calendar. This couldn't be happening. This couldn't have happened.

Running to the bathroom, I made it to the toilet in time as I threw up the little breakfast I had eaten. Broken chunks of Cheerios floated in the water. When I was finished, I lay on the cold bathroom tile, pressing my cheek to the floor. The white toilet blurred in my vision as line upon line of emails filled the void in front of me.

I forced myself to admit the truth in what I read: Josh was having an affair.

But no, that couldn't be. There was no way he would do that to the kids. He *loved* Hunter and Hannah and wanted to set a good example for them. He wouldn't. He couldn't. The kids' pictures were all over his wallet and the first thing he saw when looking at his cell phone. What woman in her right mind would seduce a man who clearly cared about his family? Or at least cared about the kids? Wouldn't she know that she could break them? That if she broke that man's marriage, it was bound to break his kids? What kind of man would allow that to happen? Not Josh. No, there had to be something I was missing.

When I felt I could stand, I wobbled back to the office and sat down in front of the computer once again. I picked up my cell phone and saw the connection with the bank was now lost, so I placed it face down on the desk, as though someone was about to witness my next move. I typed eighty-eight words per minute on average, but I took six full minutes to find the power to type seven letters in the email search bar that would forever change me: Corinne.

Ninety-three results. They were all short and to the point—what most people would text another person instead of email. I suppose texting would be risky when the man had a wife and kids who could easily see his phone or iPad at any point. A shudder ran through me. The earliest exchange happened 364 days ago. Since it was clear in that message their interactions were already intimate, I could only assume the email box was cleared out a year ago, so none of the oldest ones showed up.

Josh had a mistress.

I couldn't read through all the messages. Each one was a knife slicing through my skin. The ones I skimmed proved all I needed to know: where he went, she went. All these business trips, he was never alone.

Before kids, I would go with Josh. He wouldn't even ask me; he'd book a ticket with my name. I once teased him for being so presumptuous about my desire to follow him. I'll never forget his response, "I want you there and will do whatever it takes to convince you. Buying the ticket is step one." I nudged him while we were in bed and asked him what step two was. Josh rolled on top of me and kissed my neck, "Step two is seducing you into saying yes." He once wanted me by him, and I didn't appreciate that as much as I should have.

The trips stopped once Hunter was born. We tried three within that first year, but they didn't work out. Hunter would get sick, or something else would happen to prevent my travel with Josh. After several fights ensued, it was soon dropped altogether. Josh left for his trips, and I stayed home. It became the norm.

The ache in my stomach turned into one of remorse. *Why did I let those trips stop?* If I kept going, if I prioritized him and let nothing stand in the way, none of this would be. I took the focus off of us. I stopped fighting for Josh. If I made those trips, we would have spent necessary time alone together. Our marriage would have been stronger. He wouldn't have needed her. He wouldn't have found her because I would have been by his side.

With shaking hands, I found the most recent email. She was meeting him in San Antonio. The last place he was. *After* the conference. After his meetings, after his scheduled dinners, after the conference agenda was completed. Everyone who was there would say goodbye and get in cars or planes to head back to their homes and families. But not Josh. He wasn't coming back home; he was going to her.

Anger and regret blocked my ability to cry. I failed Josh. I failed at my marriage. I drove him away. I drove him to death. Screw being critical, this was being truthful. If I were the wife I always thought I could and would be, the outcome would have been different. Josh could have been home. My kids would still have their dad. And I'd have a happy husband.

———

Sleep was a concept long gone. I didn't know what to do with this newfound information. I almost told Jessi. I almost told my mom. I needed someone to confirm it. Maybe I saw something else. Maybe I missed some obvious connection. Maybe other people knew, and I was the only one who didn't. *Was she at the funeral? How many people at the funeral knew about him and Corinne? Did she bring her family? Her friends? Did they know she was the other woman? Did they think that gave her more right to mourn?* All I could do was stare at the ceiling night after night and wonder.

I had to find out more about Corinne. I wanted to know if she saw Josh the day he died. Was he happy? Could I handle it if he was? Because she would have been the reason he was happy in those final moments. Not because of me.

Corinne Banks. She became my new drive, my new focus.

I needed time to dig. I needed space to think. I called Mom and asked if the kids could stay with her and Dad for a few days. The kids loved to stay with them since they rode four-wheelers and hung out with donkeys and got a little wild. It would be good therapy for them. All the while allowing me time to find answers.

I hugged on Hannah and Hunter extra hard before they left, a feeling deep inside that I may not be the same once they returned. The truth about our lives was about to change in ways they wouldn't know. I'd have to sweep it under the rug, just like Josh would have wanted. But kids are smart. They have a strong intuition. Especially Hunter. I wouldn't be surprised if he felt it. When he returned to this house, it may be different and it would be more than just the fact that his dad wasn't coming home.

"Thank you, Mom," I whispered and hugged her tight. Her eyebrows furrowed with concern. She questioned what I was going to do, concerned if I was planning to take good care of myself. I wasn't. I was about to open up old wounds and cut new ones. She didn't need to know that. Not yet anyway.

Four days since discovering the first email, I had an empty house and a plan written on a sheet of notebook paper I kept hidden in my closet, scared that someone may find it and stop me before I started. Sleep had become nonexistent since I couldn't think about anything else. There was a part of Josh's life I knew nothing about. A big part. A woman. A name he never mentioned. A face I didn't know.

I started with Josh's Facebook account. I logged in and was inundated with over one hundred notifications. People had tagged him in memories and messages. Overwhelmed, I immediately logged out, leaned into my hands, and closed my eyes. My head was pounding. This was a far cry from the financial battle I had initially set out to face by opening the first email on his computer. Now I was in a war with a woman I didn't know, salvaging whatever was left of my marriage with my dead husband.

Starting again, I typed in Corinne Banks in the Google search bar, hoping her name wasn't all that common and something would lead me to find her. Five LinkedIn profiles appeared on the first page. Each profile picture showed pretty girls I would typically not be envious of, but considering the circumstances, jealousy raged within as I carefully evaluated and judged each face. One Corinne Banks had straight blonde hair, a thin face with solid cheekbones, long nose, and bright blue eyes, similar to Lindsay. I knew it right away. That was her. She worked as a Financial Advisor for the JR Kriptzer Firm. Promising. It didn't take me long to figure out which password accessed Josh's LinkedIn profile and within minutes, I confirmed that this Corinne and my Josh were indeed connected.

I double-backed to his Facebook, ignoring his notifications as I searched his friend list. They weren't "friends" on Facebook, which was interesting. Either she didn't have an account, or it was all intentional.

Clicking back to LinkedIn, I studied every inch of Corinne's profile. With each pixel, I became more desperate to convince myself that I hated her. She was the enemy. I read her online résumé for clues to her personality. She went to Duke University for financial management and resided in Des Moines, Iowa. I *needed* to hate her. She had a fling with a man whose kids were on his phone, in his wallet, on his desk. I had to hate everything about her.

Before I realized what I was doing, I googled JR Kriptzer, Des Moines and located the phone number. As the phone rang, my heart swung a sledgehammer against my chest. The thought of hearing this woman's voice was enough to make me sick. The voice that Josh longed to hear. The one he wanted to listen to instead of mine nagging him. After two rings, I almost ended the call, until a woman answered, "Thank you for calling JR Kriptzer, this is Laura, how can I help you?"

"Corinne Banks." The words were a jumbled mess out of my mouth. I struggled to type her name; saying it aloud for the first time was a brand new challenge.

"I'm sorry, ma'am, can you please repeat it?"

I cleared my throat, "Corinne Banks, please."

Silence. Loud clicks on a keyboard. "I'm sorry, but Corinne is unavailable."

I ended the call before I could ask anything else I didn't need to leave a voicemail, and I certainly didn't need to grill an innocent receptionist. Or was she innocent? Had Josh visited Corinne at work? Did the receptionist know Josh?

If I were out of my mind even slightly more than what I was already, I would have called back to ask.

I shoved my chair from the desk and paced the room. I had to gather my thoughts about what I wanted to know before I spoke with her. What would I say? Would I ask her if she was at the funeral I arranged for my husband? Did she know he was married? Did she care he had kids who missed him every time he left the house?

Then a different line of thinking struck: Did she even know he died? Maybe they were supposed to meet, but he never showed. So she went home and cried because she was so upset, or went out drinking with friends, slamming Josh for ditching her. If no one knew they were spending time together, how would she have been informed? They weren't friends on Facebook, so she wouldn't have seen all the condolence messages. Would I have to be the one to break the news to her?

When sadness at the thought of Corinne's obliviousness overtook my other emotions, I realized even more what a screwed up situation this was. Why should I extend pity toward his mistress? Why the hell was the responsibility falling on me to tell her? And if she cried, was I supposed to hang up? Or was I to console her?

Suddenly, I no longer had the strength to care. It was easier to ignore the situation. It could be better for her to never know. Hell, I wish I never found out about her. Ignorance was bliss, after all.

I slammed the light switch down as I left the dark office and found comfort in the living room couch's embrace. After flipping through the TV channels, not comprehending what was on the screen, I poured a glass of red wine. I hoped the alcohol paired with the past several nights of restlessness would help me pass out.

I woke the next morning with drips of red wine on the couch. Some had spilled from my almost-empty glass, some had come out in the form of drool. The lack of sleep caught up with me. I lifted myself up on my elbows, staring at the stains. Josh would have been pissed if he saw I spilled red wine on the couch. He would have spent an hour scrubbing the stain then forbid me to sit on the couch for a good week afterward. Every time he'd walk in the room, he'd look at the couch for a long time with a dramatically-tilted head, analyze the faded marks, sigh loudly, make a show out of it to make me feel bad. I knew that's what he would have done. Because that's the way he handled everything. Yet he could throw beer bottles at a wall without blinking an eye. He could do things. But not me. He could cheat. But I couldn't.

The stains were staying on the couch. I wouldn't touch them. At least not yet.

Instead, I walked up the stairs to my bathroom, stalling my mind, delaying the inevitable. Sure, ignorance was bliss, but I always cared to know more than I should. I wouldn't stop searching for more information about Corinne. I managed to brush my teeth and shower, finding my way into another t-shirt and sweatpants outfit. I thought of Corinne in that picture with her straight hair and tailored suit, and I'm sure five-inch heels that highlighted her perfectly tanned legs. She wouldn't let herself look like I do. She was probably the image of perfection around Josh, everything that his wife was not. Obviously, he liked it.

I waited sixteen hours from the first call before I redialed the office. While it rang, I considered aborting my mission. But I had to talk to Corinne. She was the mistress, and I despised her role, but she may have been the last one to see Josh. I had to know what he was like that day. I needed this like I needed air.

"I'm sorry, but Corinne is unavailable."

Later that day. "I'm sorry, but Corinne is unavailable."

Even later that day. "I'm sorry, but Corinne is unavailable."

Seconds away from chucking the phone against the wall, I composed myself before calmly asking, "Do you know when she'll be in?"

There was a shuffling in the background. Visions entered my mind of them knowing it was Josh's wife calling. They had a plan in place to handle my call. I should have used a different number. Maybe Josh gave it to them as a precaution. Now my relentless calling was forcing them to deflect the crazy wife.

A hushed whisper from Laura, a voice I recognized from my incessant calling, "Are you the one who's called for Corinne the past couple of days?"

I mustered enough vigor to boldly reply, "I am."

"I'm so sorry. I'm not sure if you're a friend or an acquaintance, but you should know Corinne won't be coming back."

"Oh, is she working someplace else?" I grabbed for a notepad and pen so I could stalk the right office.

"No, ma'am," Laura's voice strained. "Corinne died in a car accident a few months ago."

CHAPTER TWENTY-TWO
HIM

I will fight for you. I will make this all better for us. It will be tough for a while. I know this. But I also know it'll all be worth it in the end.

Don't give up on me. I'll never give up on you. I promise you that.

I love you, Corinne.

Always,
Josh

PART TWO
AFTER

CHAPTER TWENTY-THREE
YEAR 1 – SPRING

I thought I hit rock bottom. Then I *actually* hit rock bottom and realized the old rock bottom was a Disney Cruise through the Bahamas, and I would do anything to get back there.

True rock bottom was an isolation cell on Alcatraz with no food, no bath, no light. No one knew I was there, and even if they did, they wouldn't be able to fathom the suffering I experienced.

The letter was the worst. When I found it stuffed in the lining of his briefcase, I thought Josh wrote it for me. While reading the beginning, I cried with guilt and regret that I didn't understand him more. I didn't comprehend what was in Josh's heart all these years.

Some people inherit the confidence in their lives to know who they are, to boldly be that person, to change the world and to follow their dreams.
Other people take a little more time in life to figure it out.
My revelation didn't happen until later.
When I met you.
Suddenly, everything became clearer.
I wish I could say it happened before. That I was the man I could have always been. But it didn't happen that way for me. It took

*extra time. I'm more shaped by my mistakes than my accomplish-
ments. I had to make a lot of mistakes to find what I needed the
most, to meet you, and to know what was right in this life.*

*Fuck, I made so many mistakes. But they're all worth it. Every
damn thing is worth it. Because it led me to you.*

*I didn't have passions in life. Until you. I didn't know what passion
was. Until you.*

*I thought life was full of decisions, all head, no heart. I didn't
know how to touch my heart at all. Sure, I had glimpses of it
before. Maybe a few close-calls. But you can't touch your heart
and then rebound back to cold and closed off. It doesn't work
that way.*

I wasn't in the right state of mind to meet you.

*Sometimes it takes being an asshole to realize I found someone
special. Anger was my default. I knew it, but I didn't know how to
change it, or if I wanted to change it, for that matter.*

Until you.

You make me a better man.

*My fears were unknown to you at first. Improperly directed anger
would become my reaction as I struggled to work through those fears.
Eventually, you caught on. Although I could see the pain cross your
face, knowing full well that I hurt you, you remained selfless. You
would suck down your own rage as a reaction, and instead, cup my
face and kiss me. You were proving to me you would stay, you would
try to understand the mess beneath the surface, and you would love
me no matter what.*

*That's when I knew I had found someone special. Someone I
couldn't let go of. No matter what.*

*Traveling brought out a different side of me. I was my best self. I
know it makes little sense to anyone else. "You have the perfect
family and the perfect life," people say. But that doesn't mean I
can't struggle. It doesn't mean I have to know who I am.*

*They always expected me to be someone else. Ryan was the perfect
child. My mom loved the most on him. My dad gave him the most
accolades. I was told I could be better. I spent my entire childhood*

keeping up with Ryan until finally, I surpassed him in every way I could.

I loved traveling. It's why I wanted that promotion so damn badly. I needed to travel. I needed to go where no one expected more than what they received from me.

You fell in love with me when I was traveling. That scared the shit out of me. I wasn't sure you'd love me when I wasn't on the road. I was still unsure of who I was.

You changed that though. You changed me. You helped me find the core of who I'll be from now on.

Few people know this, but I've fallen in love a lot. No one takes me for that type of man. I wanted the love that my parents had. So badly at times, I would force it when it wasn't there. I gave every good woman a chance. I didn't want to miss out on the right one. I got so damn tired of waiting. So exhausted with the self-consciousness that came from it all. I was never as confident as everyone assumed.

Ryan had found the perfect woman. He found someone that was exactly like my mom. My parents couldn't stop raving about Lindsay. Ryan started building a family when I wasn't even close.

I had to move. Fast. I couldn't let Ryan get too far ahead. I had to keep up.

The wrong reasons can replace the right reasons before you even know what's happening.

You were my wake-up call to everything I had done wrong in my life. You are my right. I know I need to fix it all to give you the lifetime of happiness you deserve.

Some people would say it's too late. I refuse to give up. I refuse to give you up.

I won't say I regret having a child. I just wish the timing was better. But Hunter stole my heart. He also scares me more than anything else in this world could. The moment I first held him, I sensed the weight of the responsibility I now carried. Providing for him, taking care of him, and influencing him the best I can.

My relationship with my dad is always in the front of my mind. I don't want Hunter to feel like he isn't good enough. I don't want him to carry resentment toward me.

That kid broke me. I didn't know what to do. So, I stopped doing anything that felt outside the norm of what I had already been doing for years. I stay focused on work. It is easier that way. It is the one thing I can do impeccably that will provide him with everything he needs.

I know he will appreciate that one part of me. I don't know how to do the rest. That's why I need you.

Work is what I am the best at. I am motivated by knowing that all I have to do is work a little harder or learn a little more to move on to the next level. It is the one place I am consistently praised at. I hate to admit I need that reassurance, but I do.

It is also my safe zone. I know what to expect.

Everything outside of work is a gamble, and I'm not much of a risk taker. That was why meeting you was such a challenge. I met you through work, so I wanted to keep you in that section of my life, locked up where everything was predictable.

But we are meant for bigger things. You are the first risk I ever thought was worth it. And I'd bet everything on you.

Fatherhood brought a whole new competition with Ryan. Everyone says how great of a dad he is. How he drops everything to be with the kids. I don't know how to be like that. I want to be like that. But I don't know how.

I can't compete.

I remember watching you at our first work event, the way you took care of everyone, the way you floated through the room to make sure we all had what we needed even though you were presenting just like the rest of us. I watched you in awe and thought to myself, "That woman will make an excellent mother someday." I noticed that before I noticed your looks. I've never had a thought like that about anyone before.

When I finally met you, you continued to make those words true. You're selfless, loving, and devote yourself entirely. You make me want to be exactly like that. You give me hope that maybe I can be. Someday. I'm trying. With you as my guide, I'll get there.

For so long, there were only four people who knew the truth about my parents' marriage. My dad was an alcoholic for the first ten years. Most weeknights, we listened to them yell endlessly at each other, waiting for the doors to slam to signify the end. Several weekend nights, we witnessed him hit her. Sometimes a push against the wall, sometimes a slap in the face, and once, a punch in the stomach. The day Ryan punched him back, that's when it stopped. Dad disappeared for three months. When he came back around, he was a different man. He was submissive, catering to our needs, serving Mom and his family to no end, striving to put us above him. We could see him still struggle when things got hard. Like when he lost his job and had to find a new one at forty-five. But he persevered. He proved to us that he was stronger.

No one warned me alcoholism could run in the family. No one suggested that we should be aware of similar signs of addiction like my dad exhibited. We didn't receive that support.

I didn't realize it was a problem until it was too late. And there was already too much on the line by then.

If only I knew, if only I had coped better, things could have been so much different.

But no more.

I'm done pretending. I'm done being scared. I'm done living a life other than the one I want.

I'm ready. It is time.

I will fight for you. I will make this all better for us. It will be tough for a while. I know this. But I also know it'll all be worth it in the end.

Don't give up on me. I'll never give up on you. I promise you that. I love you, Corinne.

Always,
Josh

When Corinne's name as the addressee was revealed, the letter flew from my fingers like it wanted to get as far away from me as Josh had.

Those secrets, the deepest parts of who he was; he didn't divulge any of that to me in the twelve years we were together, yet here he was, baring himself through words meant for only Corinne's eyes. All the details about how she made him feel... wasn't that the way a wife was supposed to make her husband feel? Wasn't that *my* role to elicit those feelings in Josh? I didn't truly know him. But she did. She knew everything.

After too much time on Facebook, I finally found the right Corinne Banks. I spent hours scrolling through endless posts from friends expressing their sorrow of her passing, remarking on how great of a heart she had, celebrating her grand accomplishments, and raving about her angelic soul. According to them, Corinne had plans to change the world. (Apparently, starting by butchering a marriage and coming between a family.) I couldn't stop analyzing her pictures as though she'd come alive and reveal the truths I should have known. There were none of her with Josh, no mention of him, so I wasn't sure if anyone in her life knew of him. No one may have known they died side-by-side while having an affair. I did, though. I knew.

One picture showed Corinne sitting on perfectly manicured green grass, with her arms wrapped around a beautiful merlot Australian Shepherd named Mixie. They both had bright blue eyes with hair blowing in the breeze, converting them into ad models. That one pissed me off the most. Did Josh take that picture of her? Did Josh mow that grass? Someone dared to comment underneath, "Her baby will never be the same without her." What about Josh's kids, huh? *Actual* children who lost a father. Do you think those babies will ever be the same without their dad?

Why the hell was he having an affair with someone who had a dog? The kids and I begged him to get a dog for years. Hunter was working on him from the time he was born with his first word being puppy. He gravitated to dogs, loving on them, conveying how great he would take care of one, dropping hints, helping me at Pet Angels to prove to his dad he was responsible. Josh was firm and unwavering. He told us we would never get a dog. But *she* could have a dog? Did he love that dog? Did he love her? Did he buy her the damn dog?

A hot shower rained on my body to wash away the deceit itching my skin. Dying to crawl out of myself, I begged to be someone else who didn't witness what I did. I cranked the water. Hotter. And hotter. I imagined my skin melting away by the scalding water. I didn't care.

What have we done? Why did we make these foolish choices? Why did we have to bring children into the mix? *Why did you have to die for these truths to be revealed?*

I screamed into the shower jet until my voice strained, unable to determine if the physical pain was worse than the emotional distress. It all just hurt. Somehow the worst moment of my life had become even worse.

———

I couldn't tell anyone what I discovered. As much as I wanted to expose Josh for what he had done, that wouldn't help anyone cope. It would crush his mom, break my mother's heart, and damage the memories the kids had of their dad. It wasn't worth it. Instead, I internalized my misery and split into two separate personalities. One side pointed fingers at each thing I did to drive Josh away, to make him choose her. As though I was the sole reason for his betrayal and death, as though I had that power.

The other part of me yelled out at him, demanding answers to questions that would never have closure. Why did he deceive our family? Why was he living two lives? Why couldn't he have the balls to tell me it was over instead of living this lie behind my back?

I had to suck down the anger like whiskey and prepare to

face Josh's entire family at once for the first time since the funeral. It was Easter, and they were having their annual celebration so the kids could hunt for eggs. Hunter and Hannah would forever be a part of the family. They had the bloodline. But I couldn't help but wonder when I would become the odd-man out. It was bound to happen. No longer married to anyone in the family, only the one who birthed the kids they wanted to keep around. I hoped we had a stronger bond than that, but does it indeed last with these kinds of changing circumstances?

I would soon find out.

We arrived at Wanda's house. From the start, the greeting was tender, different from the usual. Not as busy, not as rushed. Everyone in the room ached from Josh's absence on different levels. There was solidarity in that. No one felt the betrayal I did though. That was the most significant difference.

I didn't want the kids to feel the heaviness, so I attempted to elevate the mood. "Has the Easter bunny been here yet?" I rubbed my hands together to generate energy.

Grace beamed at me. "Not yet! We're supposed to be very good and not look. But we really want to see him!"

"Ooh, and have you been good?"

She pointed at Brinley. "*She* keeps trying to peek, so they sent us to the basement."

I laughed. "Well, he'll be here soon. I saw big, pink bunny prints as I was turning into the driveway. You better hurry back downstairs before he shows up."

Hunter grabbed Hannah's hand before they followed the rest of the kids to the basement. More affectionate since Josh's passing, Hunter had been quick to reach for Hannah's hand every time they were together, as though protecting her from any more surprises.

When I turned back around to scan the faces of Josh's family, all eyes were focused on Hunter and Hannah. I knew their concern mostly revolved around the kids. Mine did, too. I didn't know if I'd ever stop worrying about the impact Josh's death would have on them, especially as they grew up.

Wanda addressed the elephant in the room first, "How are they holding up?"

I rubbed my chin. "Hunter is trying to fill Josh's role in the house. He's constantly taking care of Hannah and me, and I have to remind him that his only job is to be a kid for now. But he's very attentive to our needs and in-tune emotionally if anything seems even a bit off-kilter. Hannah has been pretty quiet about it all, mostly following Hunter's lead. I'm not sure if she fully comprehends it yet. But I'm glad they have each other. Some nights they fall asleep in each other's rooms."

"Are you talking to them about it?"

I was extra sensitive but the question irked me, reminiscent of one Josh would imprudently ask. Did Wanda think I avoided the topic with them? I was a great mom. "Of course. I share when I'm feeling sad and regularly ask how they're feeling. Transparency is important both ways."

Ryan stepped in. "That's great, Haleigh. Most parents would skirt around their own emotions, but the kids need to hear them. They need to know it's okay to still grieve. I have no doubt you're doing everything right. They'll appreciate it even more someday." I valued his protection of me.

Lindsay and Wanda exchanged a look that revealed they had been talking about the kids and me. Whatever I said confirmed whatever they had been saying behind my back. Wanda drifted to Ryan and Lindsay's house more since they were all in the same town. Ryan told me the visits increased since Josh's death, like Wanda became even lonelier even though Josh was hardly around when he was alive.

As we walked into the living room, a spring of intense emotions bubbled inside of me. I couldn't discern what the cause was, Josh's death or his infidelity, which made it all that much more dangerous. There was new information that no one in Josh's family knew, shaping my feelings about Josh and being in the house he grew up in. If I didn't find out what I knew, I'd be begging to feel his presence. Instead, I was tenaciously dodging old pictures of Josh.

I couldn't handle any of them, especially those which resembled Hunter. How could I prevent Hunter from going down the same road? From making the same mistakes? From making decisions that damaged his family every single day? From lying? From living two lives? Especially when I wouldn't use his father as an example of what not to do. I loved the kids too much. Deep down, I loved Josh too much to let the final memories of him be seen through that broken lens. I'd be the only person who would know. The only person to carry this weight.

With the kids out of earshot, I asked, "Were all the eggs hidden yet? If not, I'd love to do it. It's a beautiful day and I could use the sunshine." *Please let me get out of this stuffy room before I suffocate.* That's what I was truly doing, begging from my knees for an excuse to get outside.

"We still have a few more to hide. Each kid has their own color to hunt for this year, so it's a mix of everyone's, not just Hannah's and Hunter's." Wanda handed me a basket of colored eggs.

"That's fine, I'll mix them up."

"Do you want any—" I shut the door before Ryan could finish his sentence. I needed a few moments by myself in the backyard. We only arrived minutes earlier, and I already couldn't breathe. I'm sure Lindsay would comment on how rude I was being. At least I knew Ryan would put a stop to it. I could hear him saying, "Everyone has their own way of grieving. Let her have hers. She lost her husband," in his soothing counselor voice that could talk a maniac off a bridge in a heartbeat.

I wasn't sure my grief would appear the same if it wasn't fueled by anger. That's what I hated. I would never know how much was sorrow and how much was pure rage. My heartbreak had been tainted.

My eyes blurred as I hid the eggs. Easter was my favorite holiday with the kids. I loved their anticipation as they searched high and low for eggs. I loved even more when the kids gave up, so I could help find them, too.

This year, I struggled to produce the excitement. Everything in me felt fake. I had to put on a mask while fighting for strength to set a good example for the kids, to help them, to be both their mom and dad. I prided myself on being genuine, but Josh stripped that away, his deceit forcing me to be fraudulent to preserve the false image of a good life together.

Lifting my head to the sky, I prayed for perseverance before sneaking my way back into the kitchen. The adults congregated in the living room while the kids remained downstairs.

Ryan was the first to see me. He quickly stood from his chair. "Are all the eggs hidden?"

"The Easter Bunny has officially left. All is set for the kiddos." I put on my best smile.

"Okay, then!" Wanda clapped. "Let's get started."

Lindsay called for the kids. Listening attentively for the announcement, they shot up the stairs like rockets. Wanda handed out empty baskets to each one, with a string around the top signifying which color of eggs each kid would collect. "There are fifteen of each, okay? Don't pick up someone else's color unless they ask for your help. Whoever gets all fifteen of theirs first gets an extra big egg with surprises inside."

"Ooh," the kids' collective delight sang.

Even the supreme bitterness that ransacked my body wouldn't let the delight of their faces escape me. I breathed in deep, as though their happiness was a potion I could inhale and bottle, a magical cure-all. Hannah and Hunter carried grins bigger than I had seen in much too long, a stark reminder of how life once used to be before elements like their natural joy faded. I was so grateful to see those smiles again.

"Is everyone ready?" Ryan asked in his best announcer voice.

"YES!" the kids all shouted at once.

"Okay! Ready... set... GO!" He opened the door as the children flooded out, somehow managing not to trip over each other and fall. Searching for the egg colors that were theirs, taunting when they would find ones belonging to others.

The adults poured out to the deck. Lindsay linked her arm with Ryan's and leaned her head against his shoulder. My heart ached. I wanted that, the comfort, being able to share this moment with someone I loved. I was jealous of them and jealous of her. I stepped past them onto the yard, putting them behind me and out of sight.

Hannah skipped from one egg to another, or her version of skipping which was more like a horse trot, but adorable none-theless. Hunter was a racing machine, similar to Dash in *The Incredibles*, bolting from one spot to another. They were both light on their feet.

"Hunter is fast," Ryan appeared next to me, out from beneath Lindsay's grip.

Cupping my hand over my eyes to block the sun's glare, I agreed, "I think so, too, but it's hard to know for sure. We're waiting for him to express interest in a specific sport and see if he doesn't take off. Or, *I'm* waiting anyhow," I corrected myself as I realized "we" no longer encompassed two people in the present tense. Not like it would have mattered. Of course it wouldn't, but it felt so bitter on my tongue. Maybe it was always just "I," but I used "we" as though Josh and I had collective thoughts and feelings on everything that included our family. Clearly, we had different goals altogether.

"Have you put him in any sports camps?"

"Only a variety sports camp. Each week they teach a new sport to the kids to give them a chance to experience them all. I thought he was leaning toward soccer, but lately he's been talking a lot about basketball."

"What about track?"

I shook my head. "They don't offer track until he gets a little older. I guess I could take him to a track and see if running timed laps gets a thrill out of him."

"I admire runners, but I'll never understand them."

"Someone would have to dangle a pizza down the track to get me to run."

"Not a carrot?"

"Am I a horse?"

Ryan chuckled as Lindsay stood next to him. "What's so funny?"

"Just talking about our hatred for running."

"Running is so good for your heart, body, and mind, though. You guys shouldn't be so quick to dismiss it." She patted Ryan's stomach. "Especially you as age sneaks up even more."

Well, that was a quick way to ruin a fun conversation. I stood and said, "I'm going to walk around and see if I spot any eggs."

"Don't point them out to the kids!" Wanda called from her chair as she sipped a glass of lemonade.

I didn't respond. I often wondered what type of person Wanda thought I was and how little she really knew me.

The kids finished in record time with Adam ultimately winning the big egg. Hannah couldn't find her last one so Hunter and I helped her. I felt terrible when I saw it was my fault for placing it above her eyesight, not considering her color of eggs would need to be much lower than all the rest. I told them I'd make sure they both got big eggs with special surprises once we returned home. They deserved it.

After the hunt, everyone picked their way through a small brunch assortment Wanda laid out, full of pastries and fruit to bump the kids' sugar high even more. The children wanted to play on the new swing set Wanda had installed. I told everyone to go on outside and enjoy the nice weather while I cleaned up. No one argued and took their drinks with them.

I was in the zone, entirely in my head as I washed the food trays when a voice startled me.

"Hey," a hand lightly brushed my back. A movement so quick I wasn't sure it occurred except for the tingling that remained. "How are you?"

I didn't turn to face Ryan but saw his body lean against the counter in my peripheral vision. The heat of his hands only inches from mine on the counter made the hair on my arms stand to attention. I continued staring out the window, watching the kids as they took turns down the slide. "I'm fine."

"Haleigh, it's me."

Yes, it *was* Ryan, someone I was vulnerable with and knew would be the hardest to keep my newest discovery hidden from. Ryan, someone I had fallen in love with. *Josh's brother* who I fell in love with. I was pissed about Josh running off with some gorgeous blonde, and yet my heart was split between brothers for how long? What a hypocrite. I'm *such* a hypocrite.

Shaking my head while wringing the soapy dish rag, I asked, "Life always goes on, doesn't it?"

Ryan drummed his fingers on the counter. "Life is pretty big, and the forces that be keep it in motion."

I leaned my hip against the sink, carefully choosing words that could relieve the emotions plaguing me without giving away everything. "But isn't it crazy how little impact we have? It doesn't matter who we are or where we are or what we do, we aren't a wedge that stops the spokes from spinning. Nothing stops just because we're gone."

"Isn't it a relief that one person can't put a complete stop to all of life, though?"

I knew I was too vague. I wished I could tell Ryan what I really meant, how little impact we have even in our closest circles, like family. Like how I couldn't be the wedge that stopped Josh's affair from occurring. That I couldn't prevent him from ruining our family for good. That I couldn't stop him from leaving. That I couldn't stop him from dying. That I couldn't stop from being the only damn person that would know the truth in all of this. Josh's death was more than a tragedy. He was in the middle of an affair at the exact moment his life ended. That Josh died with Corinne was as though they had sealed their fate as a couple. Like *Romeo and Juliet,* they were eternalized together, all in the name of love. I was made the mistress.

Ryan's eyes peered into mine, deciphering, and I looked into his, silently confessing. I never had to make sense when talking to him. He pretended he understood me, even if he didn't. He tried to, and that alone meant more than he could know.

I cleared my throat and broke eye contact as I composed myself before bringing my eyes back to his, "Enough about me. How are you?" I had been so caught up with Josh's affair that other people's well-being had fallen off my radar. I finally examined Ryan and immediately regretted failing to soak up every ounce of this moment. Getting a few minutes of Ryan alone was a rare event, as the shouting of the kids in the backyard reminded me how small that window of opportunity was.

Ryan shrugged as he repositioned his body against the counter to face me. "Heartbroken. As I get older, I stumble across new fears. Losing my brother wasn't one that crossed my mind. Not like that's one you can prepare yourself for anyway." He wiped his hands on his jeans. "But I'm getting through it. The days are busy, so that helps. If I have a beer, it's a silent salute to him. Josh wouldn't want us dwelling on it."

"What do you think he was doing in those final moments?"

Ryan glanced at the ceiling and grinned. "I imagine listening to a killer soundtrack, windows down with blue skies, thinking about how great his life has been."

I turned to look out the window again so Ryan couldn't read my face. "Yeah, that's a good thought." Except add in some blonde girl who was holding his hand, listening to the same music and looking at the same blue skies as they headed to their hotel room together.

"You're grimacing."

I shook my head, waking up from my ruthless thoughts. "I think we're getting a dog."

"Oh yeah? What kind?"

"I don't know. Maybe an Australian shepherd." The picture of Corinne hugging hers flashed through my mind, aiding my pain. "Josh wouldn't let us get one."

Ryan nodded. "You should definitely get a dog. Hunter would be awesome at taking care of it."

My heart clenched at Ryan's words. The dog debate had been such a sensitive topic with Josh that it felt strange to talk about it freely, as though it was an actual possibility. It was almost like Ryan approved our dog wishes on behalf of Josh, in replacement of his absence. Ryan at least understood how responsible Hunter would be with one. "Yeah," I managed, "we probably will."

Ryan nudged me with his arm. "Just make sure you choose a good name. That can make or break the cool factor for a kid with a dog."

"Dad! Grace won't leave me alone. She keeps following me," Adam whined as he walked through the door.

Ryan quickly stepped away from me as though we were caught in something. "Well, she wants to be like you. Take it as a compliment."

"Dad, tell her to stop, please! I need my space. She's invading my bubble."

I let out a giggle. Where do kids get these things? Ryan grinned at me and lifted his shoulders in the air as if to respond to my silent question with, "I have no idea."

"Ok, I'll ask her to give you bubble space. But you need to let her play with you if that's what she wants to do."

"But Dad, she's annoying." Adam crossed his arms against his chest.

"She's fun. Try looking at her through a new lens. Now go on, I'll be right behind you."

Adam stomped out of the kitchen.

"Do emotional intelligence speeches always work on your kids?"

"Always. They're my little protégés."

"Or experimental hamsters for your therapy techniques?"

"Or that." Ryan flashed a smile that went from cheek to cheek like he found me flatteringly amusing. That smile made me blush.

He quickly turned the conversation serious again. "You do know you can call me if you need to talk, right?"

I forced a smile. *No, I couldn't.* We both knew that. I couldn't call without being put on speakerphone so Lindsay could hear the conversation, too. As much I would love to talk to Ryan, it wasn't only him and me. It would never be just him and me.

Instead, I responded with, "Thanks, Ryan."

He rounded the corner with one glance back in my direction, a flash of light breaking through the cracks of my isolation cell. At that moment, I wanted to crawl to him and cry and beg for the release of all these secrets, as though he could be the one to save me. Instead, I sank to the floor, leaned my head against the cabinet and hugged my knees to my chest.

No one knew. No one could know. No one would understand the agony Josh caused. No one except me.

Chapter Twenty-Four
Year 1 - Spring

We made it through Josh's birthday.

The kids and I celebrated it as though he was still alive. In the morning, we cooked a buffet-worthy breakfast of pancakes, waffles, bacon, eggs, and fruit. We ate with music cranked in the background like Josh would have done, an old soundtrack we created as a family for *It's a Wonderful Life,* the one Christmas movie we watched as a tradition each year. Afterward, we visited Josh's grave at the cemetery.

Typically, I would have knelt by his headstone to feel closer to him. Each trip we had before I found out about Corinne, I had fallen to my knees without thinking twice. The winter cold had prevented us from getting out of the car for a few months when we visited. Now that the ground was clear, infidelity was to blame for keeping me a safe distance back.

The observant eyes of the kids eventually pushed me closer. We had a routine. Each one of us would take turns talking one-on-one with him. I would let them down if I didn't do it, especially on Josh's birthday.

I stood closer and put one hand on his gravestone to appease Hunter and Hannah, as they played on the grounds. I searched for words that wouldn't uncover the wrath inside. Finally, I found some.

"I cut my hair." Josh had a thing for long hair, which was why I continued to let it grow, despite my standard ponytail since I hated styling it. I had spent years pining over Pinterest images of one particular haircut, saving the pins for a day I felt brave enough. One week ago, I finally did it. Hair that once rested at the middle of my back now framed my chin. Josh would have hated it, which only made me love it that much more. Corinne's hair was long. I pictured him running his fingers through the silky strands as they traveled in the car that day.

The birds chirping and the wind blowing through the leaves in the tree above filled my silence. This was such a gorgeous cemetery, sitting on the edge of Schaumburg, lined with evergreen trees on a hillside, bordering fields in the country. Josh didn't state where he wanted to be buried so I chose a place I wanted.

As I looked at the empty spaces around him, irritation suddenly broke loose. I kicked the ground next to his mound with the toe of my shoe. "I'm going to be buried right here, right next to you. When I die, our kids will put me *right here*. Why? Because we were married. Married people are buried together. We were married, dammit. Everyone else recognizes that. You were the only one who didn't respect it." Tears threatened my eyes.

I gulped air to hold them back. Josh didn't deserve my tears on his grave. "You didn't want me next to you while alive so how do I tell our kids you wouldn't want me next to you when we're dead? You would want *her*. And she's someplace in Iowa, far away from you," I sneered, my words a jumbled mess, reflecting the state of my heart and mind.

I clutched his gravestone until my knuckles turned white. "You should have been man enough to end our marriage. No one knows it was over. I didn't even know it was over. But you got to escape, and I'm left with a lie and forced to pretend we had a happy life. That's not fair, Josh. You got to love and be free. Now

I'm still stuck to the chain you've always had around me. And I hate you. I hate you so much for it."

Sobbing and shaking, I wanted to throw something; I wanted to punch something. All I could do was twist my hands together until they were raw, seeking out pain that felt stronger than the pain that gripped my heart. Especially when on top of it was a thin layer of guilt. *Guilt.* Guilt for hating him while he lay in his grave. Guilt for being the one to hold him back from the love he actually wanted. Guilt that I couldn't be enough to keep him at home, to keep him happy, to keep his priorities on our family. Guilt that I stopped traveling with him, that I stopped putting him first. Guilt that I didn't love him as the man he was because I didn't truly know that man.

Focusing on the gleefully singing birds, I swallowed, calming myself with nature. The birds were still happy. They were still singing. I'd find my voice again someday, too. I had to grip onto anything I could for inspiration, for strength, because my poise was fading fast.

A hand landed on my shoulder. Hunter. My rock. For being so young, he was so strong. He put his arm around my neck and leaned his head against mine. "I miss him, too, Mommy. But he's happier now, right? He can laugh like he used to."

I wiped tears from my eyes. "What do you mean, baby?"

"Daddy stopped laughing a while ago. Now he can laugh again, right?"

I recalled how Josh had been in recent times when he was home. He would still laugh with the kids; I could hear it. It was the one redemptive quality that made me forgive him more than anything else—the reminder of how good of a dad he was when he was spending time with Hunter and Hannah.

"Daddy didn't stop laughing when he was here."

Hunter shook his head. "No, Daddy's *real* laugh. Daddy hasn't laughed his real laugh in a long time, Mama. I waited for it to come back."

When I thought my heart couldn't shatter more, shards splintered into tinier pieces, and I wondered if there would ever be any recovery. I never noticed a difference in Josh's laughs, but of course the kids would. They sensed the teeniest changes. I succumbed to Hunter's belief, "You're right, sweetie. I'm sure he's laughing again like he used to."

Hunter smiled and patted Josh's gravestone. "That's good. Lots of people would like to hear that." Hannah gripped Hunter's other hand, and we stood there for a moment, the three of us joined in silence, looking at the remaining earthly existence of Josh. He was a gravestone now. With my recent discovery of his alternate life, the cold hardness of it was fitting.

"Can we go to Nana's now?" Hannah asked.

————

The greeting this time at Wanda's house was much warmer and more relaxed than Easter. The tension in my shoulders eased. I didn't want to be discarded as a family member just because Josh was gone. The Claystone clan would be the ones to understand the hole Josh left more than anyone else. There was a bond there, no matter how sad the reason may be. Especially on Josh's birthday when we were the people who loved him most.

"I love your hair, Haleigh! I've thought about chopping mine, but there's so much more you can do with long hair. I wouldn't know how to handle my options being so limited like that. But it's cute on you!" That was Lindsay's way of saying she didn't like my short hair. In the past, those comments would have bothered me, but I didn't care what she had to say anymore. She was just Lindsay and always would be.

Ryan dipped in for a hug as I wrapped my arms around his back. "You look beautiful, Haleigh," he whispered. The only other time he had said that to me was when I was standing in my wedding dress as he and Josh descended the stairs for pictures. Ryan said it before Josh could, leaving Josh with, "Yeah, you really do."

I beamed at Ryan while I touched the strands, still getting used to the length. "Thanks. It feels more like me."

"It looks more like you. Free."

Free. Not yet. But that's where I wanted to be.

The kids were happy to be together again. I was tempted to move closer so the cousins could grow up in the same town. But I wasn't sure I could handle Wanda coming over more, knowing full well she was comparing me to Lindsay, and Lindsay constantly won.

We celebrated Josh. Wanda made his favorite cupcakes: red velvet with cream cheese frosting. She lit a single blue candle in one and let Hannah and Hunter blow it out together. Before they did, I shut my eyes and silently wished *please let me forgive him.*

The children downed their cupcakes and milk while the adults made small talk. Once the kids ran outside to play, the memories of Josh slowly unfolded as we reminisced previous birthdays and the things he enjoyed. I tried to tap into those good memories, the ones spent laughing and smiling and genuinely joyful because we were wrapped in the present. There was no rough past, no foreseeable unforgiving future—we were happy at that moment. But I couldn't do it. The animosity was too great. Instead, I followed the lead of the others and laughed when cued, but stayed relatively quiet otherwise.

A crying child broke my trance. Apparently, the play outside was getting rough. Brinley had scraped her knee and Adam had a cut on his hand, so Lindsay and Ryan took them to the upstairs bathroom for bandaging. It left Wanda and me alone together for the first time since Josh's death. I spoke first.

"How are you holding up, Wanda? Especially today." We had gone too long avoiding our true feelings for each other. She wasn't one to wear her heart on her sleeve, so I was unsure how to relate with her. Transparency wasn't exactly her strong suit. Today was a different day though. No parent expects to outlive their children, and here we were commemorating what should have been a momentous occasion for Josh, her youngest baby, turning forty. Yet death had come too soon.

Wanda turned her gray eyes away. She didn't want me to see the tears she blinked back. "Every day is a new challenge. But I am grateful for what I still have." She turned with a thin smile on her face, hiding her brokenness physically, but it could be felt in the air. "Hunter is the spitting image of Josh, is he not? Maybe he'll grow up to be like Daddy. He already has Josh's athletic abilities."

I smiled back, pursing my lips. I didn't want Hunter to be like Josh. How do I keep my little man from breaking apart his family to pursue some fling? How do I keep him an honorable man, righteous and honest? Even though Hunter looked like Josh, he already proved to have a sensitive heart full of empathy with keen intuition. Perhaps Josh did early in life, too.

Wanda sighed, and I was surprised when she continued without prompting. "What makes me hurt the most is that Joshy died alone. I wouldn't have wanted you all to be in that accident with him, that's not what I mean. But if he was alive for a few moments after... If he knew he was dying and yet he was all alone..." She placed her hand over her heart. "As a mother, you want to comfort your child in those moments. I wasn't able to."

The venomous words slipped out of my mouth, "He wasn't alone."

"Oh, I know." She dabbed at her eyes with a tissue, the first sign of weakness she had ever shown me. "That poor colleague died with him," Wanda waved her hand, dismissing my comment as though that coworker—who wasn't actually a coworker—wasn't anything of importance. Except she clearly was important to Josh. He sacrificed his family's happiness to be with her. "But that's different from having your family when you need them the most."

I paused as the news she revealed clicked. "Wait, you knew someone else was in the car with him?"

"Yes, of course. It was in the articles."

The newspaper articles. I didn't read them. I refused to. Now

I wish I did. Although it still wouldn't have braced me for the emails I discovered. But at least I would have known that someone else died with him.

"Did they say the name?"

Wanda shook her head. "Not our paper, at least. Said the passenger was with a client company from Iowa. They only focused on Joshy."

I studied Wanda's face, searching for a hint that she recognized her son was unfaithful. She sipped her lemonade with despair imprinted within her wrinkles. No matter how critical she was when Josh was alive, she would look at him with nothing but rose-colored glasses now that he had passed. He could no longer do any wrong in her eyes so she wouldn't have picked up on the clues to piece it together.

To Wanda, Josh was innocently with a colleague that night. The betrayed part of my heart was tempted to reveal the truth, to shatter this perfect image, and in part, to share what was killing me inside. But as a mom, I knew it didn't matter. Wanda deserved all the good memories she had of her son and to continue thinking the best about him. No good would come out of assassinating that. I wouldn't want to know if I was in her position. And he deserved for his mom to speak of him fondly, for she didn't often when he was alive.

So my mouth stayed shut, and the truth burrowed further into my heart. I never had such a severe bout of heartburn before in my life.

———

A few weeks later, Brinley had the flu. Lindsay stayed home to care for her while Ryan took Adam and Grace to Brookfield Zoo in a strategic play to keep the other kids from getting sick. He asked if Hunter and Hannah would want to join.

The kids burst with elation as we hurried to stuff a bag with snacks and drinks and loaded the car for the thirty-minute drive. We were almost at the zoo when Ryan called.

"Oh no, what happened?" I assumed the worst these days.

"Hey! Nothing happened. Only wondering how far out you guys are." His sultry voice echoed over the car as my heart raced. There was something about the wiring of the speakers that made everything sound sexier.

"We are about three minutes away, but have yet to find a parking spot."

"That's why I'm calling. I've got one reserved right next to us. I think I've been honked at and flipped off once or twice, but we're determined to save it for you."

"Well, I'm flattered. Tell me where you're at."

Ryan gave me directions to the spot they found. As we navigated the large parking lot, we finally located them.

"Mom, is that Uncle Ryan?" Hunter asked, appalled.

I laughed so hard I snorted. Ryan was stretched out on a blanket in the middle of the parking spot, reading a book high in the air above him. Grace sat in a foldable chair texting on her phone.

Honking, I called out, "Hey you, out of the spot!"

Ryan shielded his eyes from the sun with his hand and then jumped up, grabbing the blanket from the ground. "All yours!"

Grace folded up her chair and stepped aside, never taking her eyes off the phone. She was accustomed to Ryan's crazy antics.

I parked the car, and we all filed out, embracing everyone. It was a perfect day for the zoo, sitting at a beautiful seventy-five degrees with the sun shining brightly. It resembled a fresh start. I inhaled this new life. Followed by coughing.

"Yeah, it's not exactly a fresh ocean breeze here."

"I was expecting the scent of Spring. Flowers, pretty stuff," I motioned to the vibrant plants surrounding the edge of the entrance. "But all I got was animal dung."

Ryan chuckled. "Zoos are potent. Part of the draw, don't you think?"

"Clearly, the kids are unfazed." The whole lot of them were skipping, jogging, and trying to stay somewhat close to us as we had demanded they do, but running ahead through the entrance in excitement. We discovered it was easier when they were all together. The older kids led the pack, the younger ones followed, and all kept each other entertained.

Ryan cleared his throat as we stopped by the first exhibit. "Can we get one question out of the way since no one else is around for once?"

My body tensed, wondering if he would seize this moment to talk about us and the look we exchanged years prior. The day Ryan unknowingly claimed my heart as his, the lock in his eyes I bring to mind anytime I need a reminder that my corpse of a heart was once alive. At the time, everything seemed overwhelmingly complicated, yet nowhere near as complicated as it was today. Life was funny that way; certain moments feel as bad as they can get until it proves things can always get worse.

"Sure," I whispered for no other reason than it was as loud as I could speak, preparing for the confrontation.

"Are you doing okay? It'll be the last time I ask outright. I don't want to bug you. I just want you to know I'm here for you. I'm here if something comes up. Even twenty years from now."

I smiled at the nervous energy radiating from him. The elements between us were always more layered than the words we spoke. "I'm as good as I can be today, but I have a lot of healing to do. Many things I have yet to figure out."

We sat on a bench as the kids ran from cage-to-cage, fascinated by the animals. "I think about you all the time." Ryan stared straight ahead as his knee bounced up and down. "You know, wondering if you're okay." He took a deep breath and turned to face me.

I held his gaze, unable to remember the last time we were free to be this close and directly study each other. The past several months aged him twice as fast. Strands of gray were woven through his brown wavy hair, new lines etched in his face, barely visible under patches of scruff. But I noticed. Because I knew every inch of that face. "How are you?"

"I'm acknowledging his and our dad's death as a part of me that will forever feel lost. There's no other way to put it." Ryan's chest heaved. "It's been a rough few years. Difficult to not feel beaten down, worried about what else could go wrong. Praying it will be the last funeral these kids have to attend for a while."

Watching our children playing and laughing ignited hope for the future ahead. I knew the loss Hunter and Hannah felt from their dad's death wouldn't stop. It would be ongoing, and they'd feel it stronger at varying peaks in life. But they shelved the heartbreak to enjoy the trip. The happier times would add up and eventually weigh more than the sadder ones, as long as they continued to make the deliberate choice to live like that.

"They've experienced more death than they should have in their young years," I agreed. "I wasn't sure if Hunter fully comprehended Grandpa Mike's death, but now I see it helped him be courageous and quicker to accept Josh's." I sucked in my breath the moment his name was out of my mouth. Saying it out loud made Josh sit right between us, in the few inches that separated Ryan's skin from mine. "I wish Hunter didn't have to prove he was this strong, but I've been blown away by his maturity."

"We're more resilient as kids than we are as adults."

"It sure seems that way sometimes, huh?"

"Listen," Ryan angled his body to me, his arm rested on the back of the bench, strands of my hair lifted from the wind and danced along his fingers. I had every urge to lean my head into his hand, knowing the level of comfort that would come from it. The same amount of comfort that instantly came from all his touches. "I was thinking about continuing the camping tradition. Josh and I had talked about it before he... passed. Now that he's gone, too, it seems even more vital to maintain the legacy of the trips. Obviously, I am taking Adam, but I wondered if I could take Hunter, too."

I bit my bottom lip as my chin quivered. My fear of not being able to provide the father-figure Hunter and Hannah had come to expect surfaced. I was scared I wouldn't be enough to fulfill that side of him because my mom was never enough to replace my dad either. Ryan offering something as simple as the camping trip was an answer to a cry for help my lips never released. And brave of him for filling in for both his dad and his brother. I couldn't imagine the strength to still go knowing he was the only one still alive.

"Yes, definitely. That would be incredible, Ry." I would call him that in my head, but a nickname felt too intimate, even if it was just the shortening of his name. I held my breath as I watched his reaction to me saying it out loud for the first time.

Ryan tilted his head closer, his fingers twitched as if enticed to touch me. His eyes traveled around my face. Then he clenched his hand, removed his arm from the bench, and leaned back with a smile on his face, commenting, "It's gorgeous out today."

I lifted my head to the cyan-colored sky, a magnificent gift after the cold and bitter winter. The energetic atmosphere promised good things to come. The kids' laughter as they ran with each other toward the harbor seals enclosure only made it that much better.

While walking, Ryan's hand brushed mine and lingered, our knuckles grazing. I gasped, appreciating the electricity that shot through me, but cognizant enough to keep the emotions at bay. There was no sense in letting my feelings spring from this moment. Ryan would have to remain one of my closest friends in secret, but the brother of my dead husband to everyone who knew otherwise.

Hannah bounded into my arms, forcing the connection between Ryan and me to break. I turned to him and smiled, hoping to convey my gratefulness for him always making me feel alive, even when I felt otherwise. I couldn't read the look he returned, but I also didn't dissect it. Instead, I put my nose in Hannah's hair and breathed her in. I valued these little moments more than ever before.

After we parted ways with Ryan and the cousins, we went back home with bellies full of zoo sweets and fried food, and a little sunburnt, but joy reflected off our faces.

I couldn't remember the last time I had said, "It's been a great day." But as I was turning out the light that night before crawling into bed, I discovered a smile. I gently touched my face where it resided, encouraging it to visit more often. From beginning to end, it was a great day.

I wanted more of them.

CHAPTER TWENTY-FIVE
YEAR 1 — SUMMER

Cutting my hair short propelled me into a spiral, craving anything that made me feel equally free. Ryan had used that word, and it became like a drug. One I kept thinking about, dreaming about, wanting to inhale. I was ready to break through the chains holding me down—Josh chains, guilt chains, lie chains...

Rollerblading was my favorite activity as a teenager. While everyone else rode bikes, I skated everywhere, so I thought it'd be a breeze to pick up again. Rollerblading proved to be more challenging in my thirties as I convinced myself popping out two kids somehow knocked off my equilibrium. Within a few days, I exchanged the blades for outdoor roller skates instead. I was much better on four wheels evenly spaced out rather than five in a line. But I loved the wind through my hair, the speed, and the reckless threat of the danger, but the ability to mostly control it. Anytime I felt angry or frustrated, I would strap on the skates and go for miles at a time.

Because of a suggestion on Jessi's blog, which referenced a class her author friend Autumn took, I also attended my first Mixed Martial Arts class, which then turned into regular attendance. After one session, the instructor commented, "There must be a lot more to you behind that smile."

I blew sweaty hair out of my face while unstrapping the strike gloves and said, "You have no idea." Josh and his lies and the life he had before he left and the life he left behind consumed my thoughts in the first few classes. But soon, martial arts became the only time Josh didn't enter my mind. I focused on the art itself and learned how to protect and defend myself. It's so common for the protector role to fall on the male in the household. Well, now I was the one responsible for it all. Everything in my life, in the life of my kids, in the present and what was to come, now fell into my hands. I was stronger than ever before.

While putting on facial moisturizer one morning, I touched my nose, picturing what a stud would look like in it. I had brought up the idea to Josh years earlier and asked his opinion on nose piercings.

"Kinky is the first word that comes to mind."

"Kinky is a good thing, right? I mean, a kinky wife? Jackpot."

He peered at me over his financial magazine, unamused. "Kinky reminds me of an immature teenager. It wasn't a compliment."

And that was the end of that.

I dropped the lotion and picked up my phone to text Jessi.

Free tonight?

Busy tonight. Free tomorrow.

Want to come with me to get my nose pierced?

Yessss! Drinks?

Perfect.

My next text was to my parents asking if the kids could stay with them. Luckily, they were available. I was in dire need of a night out, and I think they knew that.

I spent too much time in this short life searching for acceptance from other people, relying on them to validate who I was. Not any longer. The only person guaranteed to be alive for my entire lifetime was me. I needed to learn how to love myself. I might take risks and fail, but it was long overdue.

———

"It's a quarter-life crisis." Sitting in the chair at Exquisite Tattoos and Piercings, I suddenly doubted my reasons for being here as I stared, entirely out of place, at the walls covered with Harry Potter and anime posters and bumper stickers of bands I had never heard.

"Except you're not twenty-five."

"Well, it's sure as hell not a mid-life crisis. And third-life crisis sounds just as depressing."

"Your husband died. It's allowed."

"SHIT!" Instinctively, my hand blocked my nose as the needle touched it. The silently judging, tattooed piercer sat back in her chair and waited for my freak-out to subside. "Okay, maybe that didn't hurt. Should it have hurt?"

Expressionless and monotone, she replied, "I didn't even do it yet," as she leaned in again and continued.

Jessi stifled her laughter. "Her husband died," she justified to the piercer.

"How many times a day will you be saying that?"

"Countless. It needs to sink in."

Admittedly, her words stung, but the real stinging of my nose as the needle penetrated the skin was worse. My eyes watered, and it was the closest to any crying I had done outside of Josh-related issues. I blinked back the blurriness as the piercer inserted the stud and wiped the blood from the edges.

"Done. Go look."

"Aww, yeah," Jessi hooted. "You're gonna love it!"

I looked in the mirror, analyzing the diamond stud that now

dotted the right side of my nose. I never wanted this when I was younger, but over the past several years, I thought about it a lot. It was a curiosity that had yet to go away. Now that I had it, I loved it.

"I feel like me. Is it weird for a nose ring to cause that?"

Jessi stood on her tiptoes, resting her chin on my shoulder so her face was in the mirror next to mine. "Not at all. It looks beautiful. I kind of want one now."

"Apparently you have to wait until your husband dies to get one."

"Screw that. You have time?" she asked the piercer who was in the process of throwing everything away and sterilizing the instruments.

"Let me clean up. Go pick out a ring, sign the waiver, and sit down."

"Are you really doing this?" I touched the side of my nose away from the piercing, noting how strange it felt there was something else in there, too.

"Hell yeah. If I don't like it, I can take it out, right?"

The piercer snorted and grumbled, "And they say our generation is impulsive."

"Hey, lady, we're bonding here. Don't ruin it." Jessi smirked at the tattoo-covered woman, who rolled her eyes as she continued setting up. I realized how similar she was to Kristen, an ache reminding me of a great friendship that no longer existed. I wondered if Kristen had heard about Josh's passing. I was angry at her for how long it took to confess her relationship with Josh, but ultimately, it was all on him. I see that now. His time with her obviously wasn't the last time he cheated on me.

"Shit!" Jessi's cry interrupted my thoughts.

"Hurts, right?"

"Yeah, man. I thought you were being a baby about it."

"All done." The piercer pulled off her gloves, tossing them in the trash before leaving the room, clearly tired of the antics of these old ladies.

Jessi joined me in the mirror again, except this time a tiny gold ring hooked on the edge of her right nostril. "Well, that's not how I expected tonight to start. But we look damn good." Jessi swept her hair to the side so that nothing touched her ring. "I mean, this is exactly what I needed. I didn't even know it. But I look good."

I grinned at her self-admiration. "I love having a crazy, spontaneous friend."

"Let's get out and celebrate! Now that I have this in my nose, I feel like Pink. I need everyone to see it."

Shaking my head, I acknowledged our changing plans. "You want to go to Kimber's, huh?"

"You know it! I've got to d-a-a-a-n-n-c-e!"

We paid for our piercings and grabbed a bite to eat before heading over to Kimber's. Only local bands played there, and the best acts typically don't go on stage until later.

While we ate, Jessi asked if she could invite Chris to join us. "If you want a girls' night, I'll tell him to find something else."

"But you want me to hang out with him." It wasn't a question. With how independent Jessi was, I knew a night out with me would have been her first pick. For her to consider Chris joining us, there was a reason. They were getting serious.

Jessi chewed her burger instead of saying anything and avoided eye contact.

"You like him."

As she swallowed and slurped her shake, she admitted, "Yeah. It's weird because he's the opposite of me in a lot of ways, but he brings me down a notch. I don't mind staying in with him. He's like you. You're the peace to my crazy, and I need you for that reason."

"I'd like to get to know him more, but..." Wiping my mouth with a napkin that I then rolled into a ball, I prepared to speak the name I feared would ruin my quest for freedom, "He won't bring up memories of Josh or anything, will he? For at least one night, I'd like to pretend I don't have a heart-wrenhing past."

Jessi vehemently shook her head. "No, I'll kick him in the balls if he does."

I knew that's exactly what she would do. "Give him the green light then."

We finished our food with bloated stomachs; between the double cheeseburger, chocolate shake, and cheeseballs, it was like we had devoured a whole cow. I recognized how little I had eaten since Josh's death. For the first time, food tasted good again. We abandoned our car to walk the five extra blocks to Kimber's to burn off some of the fatty and fried deliciousness.

The summer sun was bold, even at eight o'clock, so it took a while for our eyes to adjust when we entered Kimber's. All black with colorful strobe rays twirling from the main stage, where live music reverberated every day, except for the two nights a month when the environment faded into a more intimate setting for slam poetry. We found Chris sitting at a table by himself. I leaned in for a hug before Jessi could bowl him over. "Hey, good to see you again," he said above the music.

"Shh," Jessi threw herself in his arms. "Tonight, this is my new friend, Haleigh. She doesn't have a past or a future. Just a present. Only tonight."

"Nice to meet you, Chris," I added with a wink.

"Nice to meet you, New Haleigh." He turned to Jessi and kissed the tip of her nose. "Looks even better in person."

She wiggled her nose and tilted it in the air with pride. "I knew you'd like it." Jessi grabbed my arm and lifted me from the chair. "We're getting drinks! Be right back."

"Don't worry about the beers," Chris nodded toward a figure walking to the table with a tray.

"Ryan," I gasped, his presence freezing me in place like a statue. "What are you doing here?"

A slow smile spread on his lips. "You got your nose pierced." I loved how quickly he noticed little changes about me.

Blushing, I looked down to the ground, suddenly self-conscious, hoping dried blood wasn't caked around it. "I've wanted it for a while so I figured, why not tonight?"

"It looks good on you. Not surprising." Ryan squeezed my shoulder before turning back to the table with the drinks.

I hurried to the bar with Jessi and grabbed her arm. "You didn't mention Ryan would be here."

She shrugged as she handed me a shot. "Chris must have invited him. Does it matter? You know he won't bring up Josh."

Yes. I wanted a night of pure freedom, no chains, no reflection of who I had been before tonight. Ryan signified too much of my past, and more of my present than I could admit. Resentment arose in my throat, a force compelling me to stay in the lines outlined by Josh, his version of who I should be and who we were around his family. I had to remind myself that Ryan knew me. That's who was here, the one who had always known me best.

Instead of sharing my hesitations with Jessi, I mumbled, "No." We clinked glasses, the Jameson watering my suddenly parched throat. Before I could request another, she grabbed my hand and led me back to the table where Chris and Ryan held out beers for us.

"You actually saved one for me?" I asked, surprised, as I slid onto the stool next to Ryan.

"Why wouldn't I?"

Because Josh would have drunk both to punish me for taking a shot without him, that's why. Smartly, I bit my tongue. That was precisely why Ryan being here tonight wouldn't be a good thing. I had too many default expectations; the holes of quicksand I had to navigate around and jump over to avoid sinking when drinking was involved. Ryan wasn't Josh, but he was a reminder.

I changed gears with my thoughts. "Well, cheers to a surprise night out with you." I turned to Jessi and Chris, "And with you guys." Then as customary, we all held up our glasses to the gigantic 3-D red-haired woman popping her head through the wall with a smile largely disproportionate to her tiny nose and small eyes. Her name was Kimber. She was a creepy part of

Kimber's Bar, and also part of the charm. No two people saw her the same.

I thought she was a dead ringer for Ellie Kemper, but couldn't get anyone else to agree. It was the Kimber Bar mystery, and also a good gauge for how many drinks were consumed throughout the night. Kimber always changed after each drink. One night, a man jumped off the stage screaming, convinced Kimber was trying to eat him with her suddenly enlarged teeth. That may have been a sign he'd been overserved.

"Hey, isn't that the band you introduced me to the other night?" Chris asked while playing with Jessi's hair. For once, she sat unmoving, a peaceful smile on her face and eyes closed like receiving a massage.

Jessi popped an eye open to look at the band that was setting up on stage. "That's the one." She turned to me and Ryan and explained, "I did an article on those guys. They're the ones actively trying to bring back the 2000s emo scene."

"Ooh! Talk about good timing!" Nothing like being greeted with nostalgia on a night out. This was exactly what I needed.

Jessi's eyes widened and she whispered something excitedly in Chris's ear, popping off his lap, and running up to the stage.

I watched her talking to the band and immediately felt heart palpitations. "Chris... she's not going to try to set me up with someone up there, is she?"

Chris shook his head with a laugh. "No, I'm pretty sure they're all married. She wouldn't do that."

Jessi ran back to the table with a half-hop and clapping her hands excitedly. "Haleigh, come with me! We're getting the best seat in the house tonight!"

I looked around. Our table was about as close as it got to the band without the floor being crowded with standing room. "This looks pretty solid to me."

"Haleigh..." Jess prepared me by enunciating each of the following words carefully. "You. Are. Going. To. Sing. With. The. Band. Tonight!"

"What? When was this decided?"

"Since the New Haleigh said she wanted to go out tonight and a band that I knew took stage!"

Confusion crossed Ryan's face. "Did I miss something? New Haleigh?"

My cheeks flushed. I didn't want to explain to Ryan what it was all about. I didn't want to clarify I was running from my past, desperate for one night where tragedy didn't exist. I didn't want to offend him by sounding like I was already blocking Josh out of my life. If only he knew the truth. If only he knew Josh abandoned me a long time ago. Then he'd understand why I needed this.

The Old Haleigh wouldn't have gotten on the stage. Josh would have been embarrassed and disapproving. I was so worried about his opinion of me, continually sidestepping eggshells around him. It's the same reason I never cut my hair or rollerbladed or got my nose pierced. He would have hated it. Josh had me pegged as a particular woman from the beginning, and he did everything within his control to make sure I stayed within those lines. In hindsight, I could now admit I was the one that let it happen. I lost myself because I wanted whatever ounce of love I could get from Josh. I became what I feared, retelling exactly how my mom was with my dad in those early years. I'm done with that now.

Instead of answering Ryan, I left my chair and followed Jessi to be introduced to the five men who formed Kicks Tuesday. They were all wearing dark skinny jeans cuffed at the ankle with tees and various haircuts but most with longer strands on top and thin side-swept bags covering their foreheads. It's like emo guys never went bald. It brought me back to my high school days, drooling over every live show I watched, imagining I'd marry a drummer someday.

As soon as my eyes landed on their set list, I knew the perfect song. "Let's do this one," I informed him. "A Praise Chorus" by Jimmy Eat World, taking me right back to my emo-loving, song-writing-dreamer, ready-to-conquer-the-world-with-words-that-made-people-bleed-emotions roots. I missed that spontaneous and uninhibited side of me and was ready to connect with her again.

I didn't return to the table with Jessi while waiting for them to finish setting up. I didn't want to think about Jessi or Chris or Ryan or anything else that could make me, even for an instant, think about Josh. This moment was about me. This was about finding myself again.

As soon as I stood on stage, the lead singer, Brandon, introduced me as a guest singer. Then the floor began shaking as the bass kicked in, music flooding my senses, becoming all I could hear, breathe, taste, feel, and see. It made me *alive*. Dancing, whipping my hair, belting out each note, the words penetrating my heart. Free. *I was free.* The lights were so blinding I couldn't see anyone else. I could only hear voices rise with mine and feel the energy collide.

The song was four minutes long, and the last note was a ringing disappointment of the end.

Hoots and hollers sprayed from the crowd as per usual. It didn't matter if someone was great, terrible, fun, or boring—the audience reacted the same, which made it the perfect place for first-time bands. It was an unspoken rule of the establishment; if anyone dared to boo, they'd be kicked out in a heartbeat and likely banned from returning. I replaced the mic on the stand, high-fived the lead singer, and stepped off the stage in euphoria, letting the band go right into their next song. For a moment, I forgot I was with anyone else until my eyes located our table once again.

Ryan stood and applauded, whistling with his fingers in his mouth. My nerves from the very beginning returned and embarrassment replaced my high, quickly humbled as reality set in around me again.

Someone slapped my butt. I hastily turned around, relieved to see Jessi was the culprit. "Great job! Now it's our turn!" Gripping Chris's hand, she pulled him to the floor space reserved for dancing as he balanced his beer so drops wouldn't splash over the side.

I glanced back at Ryan. My breath caught in my chest as I picked one foot up and then the other to return to my seat next to him.

"That was awesome, Haleigh! I've never heard you sing. You have an incredible voice."

Fairly certain he was exaggerating, I chuckled, "Always sounds better in the shower."

"Everything is always better in the shower," he replied with a smirk. How can such an innocent statement carry such heat? My heartbeat kicked up a notch and warmth filled my body as our eyes locked.

Our intimate moment was interrupted when we erupted into laughter at the same time. Chris was standing stiff as a board in the middle of the dance floor, lifting his beer to and from his mouth with one hand like a robot, while Jessi danced all alongside him and on him, oblivious that Chris wasn't dancing at all.

While we watched their theatrics, the air around us changed, as it usually did when I felt wholly in tune with Ryan. Like a plug into an outlet sparking a fire, a hazy aura drifted in my sight, clouding my mind like a drug. Most people wouldn't have noticed the small movement as his knees angled more toward me than the stage, now barely brushing mine, perceptible only by breathing and feeling them separate with every inhale and touch with every exhale. As though intense electricity zapped my chair, I melted, nothing left but helpless remains.

Strangely, falling in love with Ryan seemed even more a betrayal now that Josh was gone. The pain and confusion of losing Josh had put any feelings for Ryan on the back burner. But now, sitting next to him in an environment where anything felt possible, Ryan was intertwined with every breath I had.

Once Chris and Jessi finished their show, we applauded and whistled like everyone else. Chris bowed, apparently loosening up during the charade. Jessi took advantage of the spotlight to fiercely kiss him, tangling her fingers in his hair and gripping tight. The audience loved it, rambunctious shouts fueling Jessi even more. She lived for this type of attention.

They made it back to our table with sweaty hair matting their foreheads. Jessi worked up a sweat dancing, and Chris was worked up from her.

"We're grabbing more drinks. Another round for everyone?" Chris stuffed his hand in Jessi's back pocket, squeezing tightly. Jessi's face silently conveyed their plans for a detour. Drinks would be delayed.

"Yes for me, please." My response was swift, but I desperately needed more alcohol to relax my nerves. The heat from Ryan's leg was intense. My entire body was on fire. I refused to move, hoping Jessi would return with a straitjacket to help me keep my hands off him.

"Ryan?"

He looked at his watch, the black Apple band reflecting 10:55 p.m. "I probably shouldn't." A wave of disappointment in his words hit both of us. He didn't have to say it; he needed to go back home. To his life. This wasn't our reality. Just a much-needed escape.

"C'mon, man. A shot before you go?"

Ryan glanced at his watch again, hesitated, and looked at me as though I asked the question. "Okay, sure."

He didn't break eye contact with me even after Chris and Jessi left. I wished our gaze could feel awkward. It never did. We were having a normal conversation, only without words. Those deep brown eyes were so beautiful and soulful. They showed everything he was thinking and feeling. I felt safe with him. I trusted him. I knew him. All things that weren't true with Josh.

I finally cleared my throat, predicting my words would ruin our shared moment, but I had to keep a hold on our real situation, despite wanting to disregard it all. "Do you need to make a phone call or anything?"

Ryan continued looking at me for a moment before finally

pulling out his phone. "Let me send a quick text. Before I left, I said I needed a night out. It's overdue."

Pulling my eyes away to give him privacy, I surveyed the room, trying to focus on anyone else other than picturing the face of who he was texting. New Haleigh doesn't know Lindsay. *Do not picture her.* Ryan was a big boy. If there was anyone else who needed a night of freedom, too, it was him.

Fortunately, Chris returned in time, slamming the tray of shots down a little too hard. He was panting, and Jessi's face was red like Chris's facial scruff had been all over it. I shot Jessi an amused look, and she beamed back.

Ryan wasn't oblivious either. "Tell me you at least ordered these after, and not before?"

Jessi passed around two shots for each of us. "Ryan, your boy has skills. Don't you worry about the timing part. He's a pro."

Ryan slapped Chris on the back, who had a smile as big as Jessi's. They were adorable together. It was strange to see Jessi date since she had been swearing off guys for years. Yet it was fun to watch her in a new element with Chris, the winning man who stole her heart.

We played a game, challenging who could drink their shots the fastest when someone on stage sang a word that rhymed with Kimber. Almost every weekend night, someone would sing Pitbull's "Timber" as a tribute to Kimber. The timing couldn't have been more right, or wrong in hindsight, as the next duo took that one on, leaving eight empty shot glasses at our table within minutes.

It all felt good for a short period. We were laughing and singing as loudly as we could and playing weird games that made no sense with the shot glasses. My throat burned from all the yelling and my cheeks hurt from all the smiling.

I soon realized I couldn't hold my whiskey like I once could. Age and having two babies made a difference in my body's capacity. The shots kicked in, and the high took a turn to a lowest-low, as I slurred a few words, slid off the chair, and stumbled to the ladies' restroom. Everything was blurry. After a few steps, Ryan had my arm in his, guiding me like he was helping an elderly lady cross the street.

I barely made it out of the bathroom, unable to remember if I even went in the first place. As soon as we returned to the table through drunken stumbles, Ryan said, "Chris, you take Jessi home. I've got Haleigh."

Hugging Jessi goodbye, she whispered something in my ear. I'm sure it was inappropriate, but I don't remember what it was. I only recalled her warm breath and giggles and knew it had to do with Ryan.

As soon as we made it back to my house, I ran straight to the bathroom and vomited, like I was back in college. I didn't even try to get off the floor. That wasn't exactly what New Haleigh had in mind for the night, but at least I had fun for a few hours. Picking at the threads on the soft bathroom rug, I curled up with an aching belly and fell asleep.

———

I woke up dizzy, nauseous, wondering if I would lose whatever was left inside my stomach. Light danced on the ceiling, which didn't help the spinning. Closing my eyes, I rolled over on the couch and opened them again, surprised to see a fire burning. The dawn light peered through the open curtains. A figure sat in the chair next to the window. I popped up, defensive, ready to put my Martial Arts skills to good use. Either I was fighting an intruder or running away from a ghost.

My gasp got his attention. "Haleigh, I didn't mean to scare you." It was Ryan. He rose from the chair, grabbed a glass and a small plate from the side table, and crossed the room. "Here, try this."

The glass was full of ice water, the coolness welcomed by my raw throat. My body was inflamed, and I couldn't determine if it was from the whiskey, fire, or Ryan. All three were synonyms in my mind, equal culprits. I sipped water while wearily eyeing the crackers. "Small bites," he encouraged as he sat on the floor, leaning against the couch, turning his attention to the fire.

I nibbled at the crackers, waiting to verify the nausea subsided before I opened my mouth. "What are you doing here? Shouldn't you be back home?"

Ryan didn't remove his eyes from the fire. "I just said we had too much to drink and I was staying with Chris." We intentionally left her name out of our conversations, easier to ignore the fact that there's a stake in the ground he's tied to with Lindsay's scent all over it. "Besides, Jessi was in as bad as shape as you were, so there was no one to make sure you got home, and there was no way I was sending you that drunk alone in a random Lyft."

Silence. Comfort. Peace.

"Thank you," I finally muttered while chewing another cracker. My stomach gradually felt more solid, and it felt good to be cared about with such consideration.

I examined the back of Ryan's neck, enjoying the moment to study him. Long hairs dotted the base of his neck, telling of his need for a haircut. But I also liked his unkempt, shaggy ways. There were three moles, all various sizes, peeking out from underneath his collar. I had the urge to drag my fingers along them. They were ugly moles, but on him they became alluring; seductresses that pulled my eyes to his skin, longing to see more, desiring to feel everything under his clothes. The fire, the whiskey, the dawn light, all my biggest fans screaming from the bleachers to bring my lips to his neck, to force him to moan and fall into me.

Bringing my palms to my face, I shook my head, coaching myself to calm down. I pulled my hands through my hair and patted it down, attempting to look somewhat presentable, even though Ryan was a witness to my chucking-in-the-toilet episode not long ago. I grabbed a strand and smelled, praying the vomit didn't catch. Thankfully, it still had a tinge of vanilla from the shampoo, overpowering the odd smoke smell that even nonsmoking bars carried with them. Relieved, I asked, "Did you have fun tonight?"

Ryan chuckled, angling his body to place his arm on the couch merely inches away from my leg. "Did *you* have fun tonight? You were the best thing about that place. I never took you for a band girl."

Heat rose in my cheeks as I extended my hand in the air to confess, "First-timer here."

He raised his eyebrows in surprise. "You seemed so natural."

"Well, that's what whiskey can do to you." I raised my water glass in salute. My stomach twisted at the word "whiskey." No more alcohol, ever.

"I'm not sure the hardest liquor could convince me to get up on stage and sing. But for a moment, while watching you, I thought about how fun it could be. That's the closest I've been to considering it."

I sipped more water. "Well, it may be my last time since I am never drinking again."

"You've had quite the adventurous night, huh? Nose piercing, your musical debut, drunkenness. Anything else I missed out on?"

Joining him in soft laughter, I added, "The perfect trifecta for letting go."

Ryan rotated his body to face me completely, the fire illuminating him with an angelic glow. Concern washed over his face as his brown eyes narrowed in on me. "Do you need to talk about anything? I'm here if you do. You know that, Haleigh."

The softness in his voice pierced me and, combined with the exhaustion of the night, sadness overtook me like a tidal wave. That's the third time he asked me that question and it seemed to be the key to unlock everything I had held back. My control slipped rapidly, my grasp failing as I watched my composure slide over the cliff. Secrets I've been holding in burst through the dam I built around them, threatening to flood us. Ryan was one of the last people I should share any of it with, but the first one I desired to confess to. The only one that could feel my pain and anger as significantly as I was. I was sobbing before I realized it.

Ryan scooted directly in front of me on the floor and put his hands on my wrists, the safe zone. "Haleigh, talk to me. Don't hold this stuff in." I would bet all that I owned on his ability to see through my eyes and read everything behind them.

I sniffled in an effort to stop the tears. Ryan continued to hold my wrists, a move I would later appreciate even more. He wasn't handing me tissues to urge me to stop; he was encouraging the outpour of emotions, despite how messy it was turning.

My voice shook, and I doubted he could understand me, "Did you know Josh didn't die alone?"

Ryan was silent for a moment and then slowly nodded. "Right. A client was with him."

I stared at the couch, a blurred vision in front of me as I picked at the fabric. "Something like that." The emails, the words, the secret messages all swirled through my mind. "She wasn't even supposed to be at that conference. She went to meet him there."

As Ryan digested my words, a jumbled billboard of emotions crossed his face, with anger shining the brightest. It was as though the thought had crossed his mind before, but only now was he given the permission to confirm it. "Corinne." It was said simply, very matter of fact. Not a question, a statement as obvious as saying the grass is green.

Appalled, I couldn't repress my voice from rising in a fragmented shout, "You *knew*?"

Ryan removed his hands from my wrists and joined me on the couch, the cushions sinking in as he sat down, bringing me closer to him. For the first time in thirteen years, I wanted to push away from him in fury, to distance myself from this accomplice to such a terrible, cruel secret.

He shook his head, "No. I promise, I didn't know anything, Haleigh. But I caught Josh texting her once while we were at a ballgame and next thing I knew, we were meeting her at a bar. It was a brief encounter, but I warned him to be careful because she was flirtatious. Josh didn't seem concerned, so I didn't put much weight on it." Ryan rubbed his temple, looking pained. "I now realize how easy it is to recall her name. She was frequently brought up in other conversations."

My shoulders sunk, shipwrecked. It was one thing sleuthing and pulling together evidence and theories, but something entirely different when someone else certified it. This wasn't just a story I was caught up in because I was reading about it. This was *my* story, *my* truth, *my life*.

"Do you remember saying the same thing when you first met me? You said, 'your name has been brought up enough over the past few months.'" I didn't forget any of Ryan's words.

Ryan looked down at his clenched hands. "I did, didn't I? I'm so sorry, Haleigh. I should have known. I guess we knew Josh was a bit of a playboy, but we thought you changed him. All of us believed that. Mom, Dad, even Lindsay. I thought he got it out of his system. I told him from the first day I met you that you were the best thing for him. I never thought he'd do... that... not to you, not to the kids. I can't believe he did that to you."

Even in the dim light, Ryan's color loss was evident. I shouldn't have told him. I didn't want him to be burdened by this, too.

"It's so maddening. Sometimes I want to blast it everywhere, to tell everyone what he was doing right before he died—and for what, even a couple of years before I found out?" I glanced at Ryan to confirm the timeline of Josh's scandal, but reverted my eyes to the couch before he could. I didn't need to know that; I couldn't handle it. The heartbreak grew stronger, rolling out of my mouth in crashing waves, desperate to unleash the intensity rising within. "Some days this urge to throw plates at his gravesite and call him terrible names devours me." My knuckles whitened around my water glass, and I considered for a moment if I had the strength to actually crush it, picturing the broken pieces cutting into my skin.

"But what can I do? What would change this? Nothing. It

happened as it did, and I can't do a damn thing about it." I softened my release and leaned my head against the couch in defeat. We were both guilty. All these years, we both hid secrets and refused to be honest with each other. We thought we were being martyrs for each other but for what? Did we really know what we were fighting for? "I keep imagining the scene of the crash..."

"That's terrible. You can't do that to yourself," Ryan interjected.

Hugging my knees to my chest, I agreed, "I know. But I wonder as Josh realized he was going to die... Was he happy to be dying with her? Was that what he wanted? He spent so much time and energy keeping her a secret, but in the end, was he happy to have her as his last look, the very last thing in this world he would see?"

"No, Haleigh. You can't do that. You know he loved you and the kids."

"I know. But..." I rubbed my stinging eyes. "It sounds stupid but it's like we loved each other and respected each person's roles, but we were business partners. We didn't have an in-love passion for one another." I squeezed my eyes shut, forcing the hardest part of the confession to roll out before I could stop it. "Tonight wasn't about mourning; it was about finding freedom. It's been the first time in twelve years I felt free to be myself. If Corinne made Josh feel that way, then I'm glad he found her. I'm grateful he could discover that in himself before his life ended. Clearly, I wasn't doing it for him. He didn't make me feel it, either." My words pricked, like granting approval for Josh to cheat on me. I knew this truth had been eating at me; to release it was daunting, humiliating, and painful. But also freeing. That's what New Haleigh was all about—finding freedom.

Ryan shifted in the cushion next to me. I had mentally disconnected our unspoken link in the middle of my revelation. I didn't have the energy to read him; I directed every remaining ounce toward surfacing the pain I had hidden deep inside, finally letting it pour out.

"I found a note he wrote to Corinne. He was ready to end it with me, to break apart our family, to be with her." The image of Josh and Corinne in the car together, holding hands, invincible and on top of the world flashed before me. I took a breath before continuing. "Josh told her things in that letter about his life that he never told me. Over a decade together and he couldn't open up to me the way he could with her. I don't get it."

Ryan cleared his throat. "Sometimes it's not that we don't want to, but we overthink the timing of it and then the moment is gone before we know it."

I looked at him incredulously. He put his hands up in defense. "I'm not saying what Josh did was right. I'm just saying I understand that part of him. I can be like that, too."

Ryan's honesty allowed me to admit another truth I had yet to acknowledge, "That's part of what I regret the most. We didn't make each other better. We got along because our worst parts were so compatible and it made us feel justified in our weaknesses. Does that make sense?"

"More than you know," Ryan muttered.

I continued like a freight train, unable to be stopped now, "Sometimes my anger toward Josh feels forced. Like I'm *supposed* to be angry at him for cheating on me. I am in the sense of disrespecting our family and me—I hate knowing the kids could find out and forever view their father as a cheater, an identity he won't be able to reconcile." I sighed, knowing I wouldn't have told Ryan if it wasn't for feeling so weak. "I just wish he was honest with me. It's unfair. He spent his last few years chasing his heart while I've had to keep mine locked up."

Ryan grabbed my hand, squeezing it once before letting go. His warm hand lingered on the couch inches away from mine, where energy pulsated from it as though our skin still touched. I wished he didn't let go. I needed his embrace. We watched the fire die as the morning sun flooded the silent room. My head throbbed, this time more from the tears than the alcohol. Drowsiness soon took over, coercing me into a heavy sleep. When I woke hours later, Ryan was gone, with no sign of goodbye.

Holding secrets in can make a person feel alone; but shedding those secrets and stripping down bare naked without a warm body for comfort, that was the loneliest I felt. I buried my head into the couch where he once sat, the cushion still shaped by his body's imprint, and cried some more.

CHAPTER TWENTY-SIX
YEAR 1 - SUMMER

Six days passed before I heard from Ryan again. As soon as I saw his name on my phone, my heart skipped a beat. It was a simple text,

> How are you?

I didn't delay in replying,

> I'm doing okay. How are you?

The typing dots oscillated, then stopped. Then started. Then quit. Exactly seven minutes passed when his earth-shattering reply finally came through,

> I'm okay.

I sat on a park bench watching Hunter and Hannah chase each other on the playground equipment. It was chilly once again after a week full of thunderstorms, but the warmth of the sun was finally heating the air, allowing layers of clothing to be shed throughout the morning and into the afternoon. We had been waiting for a day like this as much I had been waiting to hear from Ryan. Unfortunately, the latter wasn't as fulfilling as I had hoped.

Staring at the phone, I silently pleaded for him to type more. Anything else. *Just talk to me.* Nothing more came. I slid the phone and the book I was attempting to read in my backpack with a mixture of overwhelming sentiments. Frustration threatened to smother me the most.

I hastily arose from the bench, determined not to let this much-needed sunny day be ruined, and slung my backpack over my shoulder. It connected with something as someone gasped, "Oomph."

"Oh my gosh, I'm so sorry," I apologized profusely.

A man with dark brown hair and bright green eyes stood in front of me, rubbing his shoulder. He smiled, dimples filling his cheeks. "In a hurry?"

"Yes, and apparently, no one will stand in my way," I jokingly replied, as I turned to leave.

"Books?"

"What?"

"You must have books in that bag."

I slid the backpack off my shoulder and let it hang in my hand. "Oh, yeah, I do. A few."

"Any good ones? I'm always on the hunt, and it's a gorgeous day to read. I grabbed this," he said, holding up a newspaper, "thinking maybe I'd want to read it. But why read something filled with depressing news when the sun is shining this bright?"

"Oh, so you're putting stipulations on the reading material," I teased. "What if I have nothing but dismal books in my bag?"

The man grinned. "Do you?"

I reached inside my backpack and pulled out four books for his choosing.

"You were going to read all of these today?"

"I never know what I will gravitate toward so I come prepared."

He reached for the books, scanning the jackets on each one for details. "I haven't read any of these yet."

"I'll admit, I'm not very original. My time is limited with two kids so I need guaranteed good books. These were all on the *New York Times* list in the past month."

"You're smart. I read every single back cover in the bookstore before deciding on one. At least I have a fairly good track record with my picks." His intriguing green eyes were sparkling, like books were his favorite topic to discuss.

"What do you—" I stopped mid-sentence when I realized I was glancing at his finger to see if he wore a wedding band. It was bare and tan, so it's not like he had taken it off to pick up a woman. Jessi wrote an article on warning signs when you meet a new man for the first time, which had been stuck in the front of my mind. To keep my mind off Ryan in the past week, I digested all of her articles tagged with "dating" or "relationships." Occasionally I was excited to date again, but mostly incredibly fearful of how much the playing field had changed in the past decade.

What was happening with this handsome man in the park on a gorgeous day was all playing into a plot for a juicy story. My blue-eyed husband died, my brown-eyed true love dismissed me, and now I've met a gorgeous green-eyed, dimpled man who could teach me how to love again.

I snorted out loud.

"Is something funny?" he asked, a modest smile teased his lips as he realized he might be the center of the joke.

Shaking my head, I answered, "I need to go. Here, keep this one. Read it, and then pass it on to someone else someday." It was the book he kept returning to when reading the blurbs, so I knew it'd be the right one for him. I waved before turning on my heel. "Enjoy your day."

"Goodbye... and thank you!" He called out behind me, dazed by my rapid departure and gifted book.

Hannah and Hunter were challenging each other on the

monkey bars, so I called out in a sing-song voice, "Who wants ice cream?"

"Me!" They raced to see who could touch Mama first. Another kid came, too, and I had to apologize for such a broad offer. Once I explained I could only take my children, and he wasn't one of them, the little guy broke into tears and ran to find his mom. I was just now opening myself to the dating world again and already breaking hearts.

"Mom, are you going to date that guy?" Hunter pointed to the man on the bench, proving their protective eyes were always watching me. I knew Hunter had been paying more attention than he let on when Jessi discussed her love life with Chris. He understood more than we gave him credit for, but comprehending his mom's dating life would soon be new territory.

I glanced behind me. The man was still sitting on the bench, already a few pages into the book. It was encouraging to see he was a real book lover and not just using a pickup line. I had to collect all the evidence I could that there were still decent men in the world.

"No, honey. We were talking about books."

"Will you date someone someday?" Hunter twirled a strand of grass in his fingers.

Shrugging, I responded truthfully, "I don't know. Someday, maybe."

Grabbing my hand, he squeezed, "I hope you do."

"Me, too, Mama." I'm not sure if Hannah knew what Hunter was encouraging me to do, but she gripped my other hand as though offering her consent.

That was the one topic Jessi had yet to cover in her Lifestyle Blog, and I was desperate for answers. When was the right time to date once becoming a widow? And does that timeline get bumped up if the widow finds out her husband planned on leaving her years before he died?

I played with the ring that still sat on my left finger. It was time to slide it off.

CHAPTER TWENTY-SEVEN
YEAR 1 — FALL

Nine months. It had been nine months since Josh died. That was long enough. I needed to breathe again. His items scattered all over the house just sucked the excess air and turned it stale.

Every day still carried chaotic emotions. Sometimes, I was remorseful and wanted to reach out to apologize to Josh, accepting what transpired between us was half my fault. Other days, I was livid he had chosen to be deceitful instead of honest. Most of the time, I missed his presence and wished I could sit down with him again to ask all the "whys" that plagued my mind.

On the days I felt so numb that the pain and anger couldn't take hold, I packed away a few of his items at a time. Each piece I touched felt like it belonged to a stranger, and I wondered how well I knew him.

The letter, stuffed in the pocket of his moto jacket, sloppily handwritten as though he wrote it on the car steering wheel, was his words rising from the grave, despite being formed years before his death. Answers that I frantically wanted were revealed, and they weren't as fulfilling as I had hoped they would be:

Haleigh,

I met someone.

I've spent too long avoiding it. I need you to know now. It wasn't intentional. I was trying to make things work with us. I promise you, I was. But it happened so fast.

As soon as I saw her, I knew.

Even when I knew I was doing something wrong, it felt right. I have nothing else to go on, no other explanation. I know it's pitiful. I know you'll be angry. I can only hope that you, Haleigh, being who you are, can understand some part of this. You know this feeling, too. I know you do. Because you look at someone else who isn't me. To write these words feels like the relief that I needed for so long. To finally confess what I know you already know if you stopped long enough to look at me. You don't look at me like you should. Maybe at times I see it. Times when we trick ourselves into thinking we can make it work. But I see your eyes when you look at him. The jealousy almost ate me alive. Because believe it or not, I did love you. Very much. I know I didn't always show it like I should. I guess I felt like you settled with me. No man wants to feel like he's second place, especially one as competitive as me.

I had a lot of shit I needed to work through. And for whatever reason, I couldn't do that with you, Haleigh. I tried. But I could never be where I needed to be. Maybe that makes me weak. Maybe some people could do these things on their own and don't need someone else to rely on. But I needed help. I found that help once I met Corinne.

She looks at me the way you look at him. I am looking at her the way I once looked at you. The way I should have been looking at you all this time, but we weren't looking at each other that way.

You were one of two women I introduced to Ryan. Yet you chose him over me. Like everyone chooses him over me.

Corinne, though, chooses me. She barely acknowledged Ryan when he was in the room. I am all she can see. So she became all I could see.

I hate myself for having to leave this in a letter. But I couldn't find the words when I'm around you. Nothing works with us like it should. I tried. Trust me, I did try. You would say something, and I would get angry. Then it'd be off track from the way I envisioned. After a while, I stopped having the energy to get it back on track. Hopefully, in due time, you'll forgive me and we can co-parent Hunter together peacefully. I love him and am so glad we had him. I want to make sure he doesn't end up like me. I promise you, that's what I'll do. I'll make sure my son learns from my mistakes. Don't shield him from me. Don't be worried. I'll make sure he's a better man than I was.

I hope you find your happiness. I sincerely do. Because I know it's not with me and I want to give you the space to find it with someone else. Please call me when you've had time to think about this.

-Josh

The ink was illegible in some places, my stunned tears washing it away. I read it several times more than I should have, the agony thickening with each interval. Josh planned on leaving me before Hannah was born. I recalled his harsh reaction when I told him about my pregnancy with her. It's why he was so distraught. He had been prepared to leave us, to run off with Corinne, and I ruined that.

Josh's affair had been going on for far longer. They must have stopped it at one point though, right? Because we had happy moments, even after Hannah was born. Surely, he stopped to focus on our family, to give it another try. But what kind of woman holds on to a married man for that long? I stared at his words until they blurred, nausea striking as all the similarities between Josh and me, Corinne and me, Josh and Corinne, and Ryan and me became clear.

Just as the days were becoming easier, this letter arrived, bringing a new emotion that had yet to arise since Josh passed: shame. Josh knew I had feelings for Ryan. After reading Josh's letter, Ryan proved to be a sensitive topic. I'd assumed Josh's intense reactions throughout the years were because of how much Ryan meant to him, when really they were propelled by jealousy.

If Corinne and I were friends, we could have gotten a drink together and mulled over how we couldn't move on past a married guy no matter how hard we tried. Hers might have been Josh, but mine was Ryan, and no matter the differing physical affair details, the offenses of our hearts were the same.

If I stripped away the expectations of how I should feel while swimming in these truths of being the widow of a man living two lives, I was resentful. Josh went after what made him happy. He was willing to take the risk. I had committed myself to a life of contentment. I foolishly believed I could ignore the unhappiness in my marriage and somehow manage to get by with the happiness produced by our kids. That wasn't fair to Josh. That wasn't fair to me. And that wasn't fair to set up Hunter and Hannah to view marriage in that light. They didn't need to grow up in a household where everyone walked on eggshells.

All my life, I didn't want to end up like my parents. The very thing I was running from all these years is the same thing I ended up running toward. I clung so desperately to the idea of Josh being the best father for our kids that I didn't realize I was losing myself to hold onto him, and he was slipping because of his own neglected demons. We both let our pasts catch up with us instead of overcoming them.

If I had forgiven my parents, especially my dad, I wouldn't have been so laser-focused on finding a man with the one trait that could prove he was different than my dad. That one trait carried all the weight, and it blinded me to all the similarities that subconsciously drew me to Josh as the *result* of my dad.

Maybe I don't need to be New Haleigh. Maybe Haleigh by herself is enough. A Haleigh who actually forgives the wrongs done by other people, and those done by her. Like Ryan once said, "only through forgiveness can you move on."

Josh might have been selfish and misguided in the ways he chose to chase his happiness, but ultimately I was grateful he experienced true love before he died. Every person needs and deserves that. Maybe, someday, I'll find it, too.

———

"Hey, are you and Chris free today? I'm finally ready to clear the house."

At 6:52 a.m., I was tugging an army green hat over my hair. I expected to leave a voicemail so Jessi surprised me when she answered the phone. Although, she didn't exactly answer, it was a muffled "Mmm?"

"Could you come over later and help me move boxes to the garage? Maybe sometime in the afternoon?"

"Mmm..."

"Ok, see you later." I knew Jessi would stop by even if she thought my call was a dream.

Surveying the basement, I eyed all the boxes I created since waking up from a bad Josh-related dream at midnight and giving up on falling back asleep. The empty cartons were soon evenly distributed through the house, waiting to be filled.

The kids were staying with my parents for the weekend so I could seek closure in peace. I had prepared Hannah and Hunter to return to a house without their dad's belongings. Hunter walked around, analyzing everything that reminded him of Josh, grabbing the items he wanted to save and placing them carefully on a shelf in his bedroom. Hannah followed in his footsteps and took a pen from Josh's office, and that was it. That broke me the most. I wondered if that pen was last touched by Josh's fingers when he wrote the words telling me he was leaving. All before Hannah. Maybe Hannah was the glue that kept him in our lives longer. Even if he didn't plan to stay, at least the kids wouldn't know that. All they knew was a complete household before death broke it apart.

Sure enough, later that afternoon, Jessi showed up with Chris by her side.

"Chris said he would only help if you guaranteed him a playlist."

"A playlist? For what?"

"I heard you make the best ones, and everyone gets their own. I want to be part of the club," he explained while carrying one of the heaviest boxes to the garage door.

I blushed and touched my cheeks. "Oh, it's been a while since I've made one." *Any that weren't sad, that is.* I stuffed that side of me down for years but Josh's affair brought it back up. I also hoped no one would find the recent ones since they were labeled with derogatory terms. Making soundtracks for difficult situations was a form of free therapy for me. I seldom wrote in journals; I expressed myself through songs.

"Well, I'd say it's about time then, right? Who better to get you out of your funk than this cute tush for inspiration?" Jessi smacked Chris's butt. They were always going after each other's butts.

"You want me thinking about your boyfriend's ass for inspiration?"

Jessi pretended to snap pictures of it as Chris slowly bent over to lift a box from the ground. "This thing could stop wars."

They had arrived only ten minutes before and already had me laughing. That's why I needed them. Not to help me pack; only to keep the mood light and my sanity in check.

"What are you doing with all of this?"

I pulled the cap off of a black Sharpie with my teeth. "Well, a few boxes will be saved for the kids, one box I'm giving to his mom, and I don't know... I guess Goodwill. I don't think I could handle having a garage sale. There's something easier about giving it away for free than having to negotiate with penny pinchers on items that carry memories."

Chris spoke up, "What about letting Ryan go through some of it? I'm sure there'd be things he'd want to hold on to."

I stifled a groan as I sat on the ground next to a full box to draw a triangle on it, signifying its trip to the donation facility. I fully planned to ask Ryan to go through everything first. But with how awkward it had been since my drunken confession night, I had yet to work up the nerve to ask him.

"Sure, do you want to ask him if he wants anything?"

Chris began to protest, but then Jessi shot him a look that made him stop. Begrudgingly, he texted Ryan. Within minutes, his phone beeped. I tried to act indifferent.

"Umm... here." Chris held up his phone, so I could see Ryan's reply.

Whatever Haleigh thinks I'd want. She knows me.

I refrained from reacting on the outside, but inside I was dying. I nodded at Chris to recognize I read it so he could put his phone down, and I didn't have to see Ryan's name anymore. "Ok, I'll put a box together for him." I glanced at the one furthest to the left with a red circle. It was the one I already filled with the items I knew Ryan would want. Josh's baseball caps, some pictures of them together, and all the Cubs memorabilia he owned.

Chris's phone beeped again. "Ryan wants to know how you're doing."

I squeezed my eyes together. "Fine. Clearly, I'm fine."

Chris glanced at Jessi to confirm whether I was indeed fine. She shrugged. "Ok, fine it is," he relented and typed a quick message in return to Ryan.

Jessi gently tapped me with her elbow. "Is this hard on you?"

I rested my head on my hand and leaned against a box. "It's strange, that's all..." Removing Josh's items was officially declaring the end. Sometimes it felt like he was away on a business trip again. I missed his company and his relationship with Hunter and Hannah. That ached more than just about anything else. My favorite sounds in the house were his laughter mixed with their giggles as he chased them around each room. He could have been the greatest father if he believed in himself more and didn't assume he was a reflection of Mike's demons. Also, if he wasn't running away from me, he would have been there more for

Hunter and Hannah. When I thought about missing Josh, it was mostly in desperation for the kids to still have their dad around and to have given him whatever he needed to be the dad he had been set on being.

Discarding his items established I am alone and a widow, like I should have gray hair and be dependent on a walker and not in my thirties. It didn't really sting until Ryan texted Chris. Even in my most calloused moments over the years when Josh and I were mentally and emotionally as far apart as two married people could be, I never felt alone. I was so in love with Ryan that each memory of him floated me through the hardest days. Night after night when Josh turned away from me, sleeping far on the other side of the bed, I fantasized about Ryan holding me. I had conversations with him in my head, telling him about my day, him listening intently in support and then filling me in on his own. I made Ryan exist here; he lived in this house, too.

Now both were gone.

I didn't know how to tell Jessi I was more bothered by Ryan than Josh. Mostly, it seemed quite heartless, like laughing at a joke in the middle of a funeral.

Jessi put her arm around me, "You're doing good. You're strong."

She misinterpreted the tears welling in my eyes. No one knew the true source.

Soon after Jessi and Chris left and while throwing away taco wrappers and beer bottles, I picked up my phone to see if the kids had FaceTimed yet. A message from Ryan stared back at me. My phone was on silent so I didn't see his text until five hours after he had sent it.

> Can I swing by sometime to pick up Josh's
> things?

I held my breath and considered not responding. I could send the box with Chris the next time he traveled that way. My hands trembled as I set the phone down and finished wiping the counters. I missed Ryan and hated that truth with every cell in my body.

Reaching for the phone, I sent a text before I lost my nerve.

When?

Ryan must have been waiting because the reply came back within seconds.

I don't know. Soon. I hope.

That was the last I heard from him for several weeks.

———

Headlights flashed from the driveway. Nearly ten o'clock on a weekday night, I peeked out the window to see who in the world would pull up to the house at this hour.

"Ryan, hi!" I opened the door with wide eyes, while tugging at the bottom of my tank to cover my leggings, wondering why I couldn't be a woman who walked around in sexy lingerie.

"Haleigh," he was breathless, as though he ran the entire way to my house. "I was coming back from a conference in Indianapolis and thought I'd swing by for that box you set aside." He nervously glanced behind him.

"Is someone in the car?" I peered around his shoulder at his running vehicle.

"What? No. Just me."

"Oh," I gave a perplexed look that went unnoticed by him. "Well, come on in."

Ryan stepped in the doorway, shutting the door softly behind him. "The kids are in bed, I assume?"

I pointed upstairs, suddenly jittery that Ryan stood in my foyer with no one else around. It was such a surprise to see him that the distant intimacy took a few moments to sink in. We hadn't spoken for weeks. "Yep. Sleeping soundly. Or reading books under the covers."

He shoved his hands in his pockets, as though shrinking away right in front of my eyes. "How are you?"

I crossed my arms, debating if I should invite him to sit on the couch and talk, but the headlights of his truck were still on. Obviously he intended to quickly pick up Josh's items and go. "As good as I can be, I suppose. How are you?"

A scowl crossed Ryan's face, his eyebrows narrowed in as though I said something wrong. He opened his mouth only to close it again. Ryan did that anytime emotions were stronger than his words. I had only witnessed it twice before and both times made my heart quicken. The air thickened.

For the first time in all our interactions, awkwardness filled the silence between us. I hated it. This wasn't like us. "So…" I didn't know why I thought saying something stupid was better than not saying anything at all.

"The box," he finished my sentence.

"Yep." I opened the foyer closet to pull it out, sliding it across the floor as quietly as possible to not wake the kids. "Well, here it is. Do you want to see what's in it?"

Ryan shook his head. "No, that's okay. I'd rather go through it alone."

"I understand." I wrapped my cardigan tighter around my torso. Is this the way we would have been if we never got so close?

He picked up the box and opened the door. I couldn't believe he was leaving. After not talking for weeks, this is how we were going to be. What if we didn't know how to exist without Josh, without the boundaries put between us, forcing us away? Like a dream that looked real, felt real, seemed real, but couldn't breathe in the realms of reality.

As I came to terms with him leaving, Ryan suddenly dropped the box to the floor and pushed the door shut. He kept one hand pressed against it as he closed his eyes, steadying himself.

"Are you alright?" I touched his back. He flung around like my touch stung him. I stepped back in surprise, knocking into the plant on the entry table, where it wobbled and threatened to fall. I reached out and grabbed the vase before it could, stabilizing it again.

Ryan breathed heavily, and I noticed how red his eyes were, like he had been crying. "No. I'm not okay. Ever since I was here last, I haven't been able to eat or sleep." Linking his hands behind his head as he rocked on his heels, Ryan's navy t-shirt raised, revealing a thinner stomach. Scared to look at him too much when he first arrived, my eyes now drifted to the rest of his body. He had lost weight since the last time I saw him, concerning me even more. "Did you know Lindsay and I separated?"

"What? When? I'm so sorry, Ryan." Wanda had said nothing about it when she came over earlier in the week to drop off gifts for the kids. I couldn't believe she didn't mention it.

He waved his hand to cut me off. "No, don't—it was a long time coming. I wasn't sure who all knew. She told her family, and I've told Mom, but that's it so far. I wasn't sure if Mom said anything to you. We're keeping it under wraps until we can figure out living arrangements. For now, I'm in the basement."

Despite the gloomy news, his eyes sparked fury.

"Did something happen?" I searched his blazing eyes for an answer.

Ryan shook his head as he rubbed his face with his hands.

"It wasn't what I shared with you about Josh, was it?" Guilt surged in me. That was precisely why I shouldn't have told anyone, as I had originally intended. No one else should hold the anger toward Josh that I did. It wasn't worth it.

"Dammit, Haleigh..." Ryan exhaled, a man who never cursed now clawed at whatever words came first. "I miss you all the damn time, to the point where I feel like I'm bleeding out and barely have enough to get me through the days." He grabbed my hipbone as chills ran through my astonished body, his thumb pressing into my tank like he intended to leave his fingerprint. "I mean, you feel it, don't you? Sometimes I swear I'm having a conversation with you in my head although you're nowhere in sight. Am I delusional? I might be losing my mind."

Seconds that felt like minutes passed with us entwined in a heated stare. He was desperate for answers. I hadn't seen him like that before. I closed my eyes to kill the image, to grasp self-control, to remind myself to breathe when I realized I wasn't. Ryan finally said the unspeakable. Here was my chance to confess what I had been carrying around for so long, and yet all I could find to say was, "Are you sure you're not missing him instead?" Immediate regret followed. Now was not a time to feign defensiveness to replace my loss of words.

Ryan let go of me, covering his face with his hand and turned away, a mixture of irritation, disbelief, and hurt exploding from him. He shook, flexing his hands open and close to gain equanimity. "This existed long before he died."

I shuddered, an attempt to control the convulsing my body would have otherwise done with this reveal. How many nights have I spent dreaming about this man? How many days have I longed to be next to him, to freely admit all the ways he made my heart inflate and my body tremble just by being in the same room? Why was it easier to give in to these fantasies when Josh was alive than now, standing here, confessed into reality?

"I am in love with you. I have been for so long." It was a whimper, the last of Ryan's willpower wearing off. He leaned his back against the wall and slid down to the floor. "I—I can't help it. There's been far too much happening to keep a shield up any longer. He would have been so hurt. But I can't hide it anymore. I don't want to."

Ryan's vulnerability cracked through me as much as it did him. I slipped to my knees, joining him on the floor, desiring to comfort him, to protect him, to convince him it would all be okay... to be his strength when he couldn't find it, like he was mine when I needed it the most. Instead, all I could focus on was his lips. I placed my hands on his cheeks and lifted his head.

Countless nights I had dreamt about what his kiss would feel like, the brush of his beard against my mouth. Instead, we watched one another, testing restraint, questioning what our next move should be and discerning whether it was right or wrong.

My hands fell from his face into my lap, twisting together.

"I always thought you were too good for him. I loved my brother—I still do. But you deserved so much more, Haleigh. When you told me about his affair, I was furious. There were times I hated him for not treating you like I would have. He was given such a gift with you, and he threw it away." Ryan leaned his head against the wall, tears lining the edges of his eyes. "Maybe I'm a hypocrite with my own marriage. Maybe it's the same thing Josh did. But from the first day we met, I felt like you were more mine than his. And every day since, every time we are together, I know you should have been mine."

My head swirled with words I couldn't compose. Ryan poured out his heart, and I sat silent, unable to expose anything inside my hectic mind. He was still married. That's what it all kept coming back to. I couldn't do or say anything because he was still married.

"What happened with you and Lindsay?" The words tumbled out more nonchalantly than I meant. They should have been laced with concern, but I couldn't muster the energy to fake what I wasn't upset about.

Ryan pulled out his phone from his pocket and glanced at it before responding. "We've been struggling for years, as in about ninety percent of our marriage. We tried counseling, it didn't work. Each time we talked about separating, she would end up pregnant." He gave a shake of his head. "I'm not saying she did it intentionally. You know I love my kids, and I'm grateful for them. The timing was just off. I don't want to be the dickhead guy who leaves his pregnant wife or soon after a child is born. And we wanted it to work for the sake of the kids."

I thought back to all the family events we were at together and the way I'd enviously watch Lindsay touch Ryan or reach for his hand. I had to fight the tinge of jealousy that would strike. "She loved you, Ryan. That was clear."

"Yeah, she did. She does," he agreed easily, his mind working to explain the rest. "It's like what you said last time I was here. We're business partners. That resonated with me. We don't make each other better in this life. If anything, I feel more shallow. She likes the parties and the faux friendships and all the material possessions I couldn't care less about. I'm constantly trying to keep up with her and this image she wants to present. She gets bored with me. We make each other feel terrible about being who we naturally are. Both of us are guilty in that."

I understood very intimately what that was like. "Almost sounds like she and Josh were the same."

Ryan laughed a bit harder than I expected, startling himself even. He quickly covered his mouth and glanced upstairs to make sure the kids didn't hear him. After confirming the silence, he reached out and grabbed my hand, rubbing his thumb along my knuckles. Goosebumps immediately covered my skin, and I let a low breath escape.

"Did Josh ever tell you what our dad spoke to us about when we had our final camping trip with him?"

"Nope," I replied distractedly, watching his thumb graze my fingers, shocked from this sudden intentional affection.

"We were sitting around the fire. Dad was in his chair, smoking a cigar and watching the constellations above us. He declared something like, 'Funny how this world works, huh? How things come together. Even if they're not pieced perfectly, they still come together.' It was such a whimsical, profound statement."

I smiled, imagining the scene. "Typical of your dad."

Ryan sat up straighter and returned my smile, the memory of his dad warming the moment. "Yes, typical dad-ism. Anyway, he continued his thought as he reached out and tapped both of us on the knees, 'You both have great wives. You are lucky men, and we're lucky to have them in the family. But you got it wrong, and it makes me laugh and hurt every time I see you all together.'"

I raised my eyebrow as Ryan pulled my hand into his lap, holding it still with both of his. "Josh said that Dad was losing his mind quicker than we realized. But Dad's words stuck with me. We had Easter a few days later, and I observed my dad as he sat back and watched all of us. Every time Josh or Lindsay were talking, or you and I were next to each other, he smiled in a way that only puppeteers do when they've successfully finagled all the strings to get their puppets to perform as they want. He caught me watching him and said, 'You get it now, don't you? Look at the pictures, and it'll be even clearer.'

"It took me a week to finally do it. I was scared to discover what he already found. Dad had a certain insight that none of us could match. It's what made him such a great photographer."

Goosebumps reappeared down my arms in a mix of anticipation for what Ryan would reveal and his skin touching mine. He moved his finger up my arms, grazing the bumps, the magnetic force luring each hair to stand to attention.

"Did you know most of his candid pictures have you and me together? Not the ones we purposely pose for, but the ones where we're all just hanging out. You and I are always together in them. We were always captured together."

My face reddened, and a rash-like warmth flowed through my neck. I felt like I had been caught breaking the law, or in this case, busted flirting with my brother-in-law. It was never intended to be like that; it was a force that pulled me to Ryan every time I saw those brown eyes, to hear his voice and the words he had to say, to be closer because everything felt a little better when I was. I didn't hide it because there was nothing to hide; but now knowing it was so transparent, especially after finding Josh's letter to me, made me flush with embarrassment.

"My dad saw it before any of us. Josh was a better fit for Lindsay than I could ever be. And I..." Ryan trailed off as he gently kissed my hand. "I want to take you out on a date."

CHAPTER TWENTY-EIGHT
YEAR 1 - FALL

Two weeks passed before we set our first date plans.

Ryan was busy finding a new place to live. Moving out of his family's house was the most difficult part for him, officially having to explain the divorce to their kids and automatically sentenced to seeing less of them by no longer being in the house. All three of the kids took the news with mixed emotions based on their age and limited understanding of how much their lives would change. That was the part that made me the sickest; they were still my nieces and nephew, and I loved them and wanted to protect them. I had to remind myself this wasn't about me, and that it would have happened regardless. Fortunately, Ryan had plenty of experience in his job counseling children through divorces. Combined with his fatherly instincts, he was the best person to help them through the transition period.

Despite not seeing each other for weeks, Ryan and I spent hours on the phone every night after the kids went to bed. We struggled with feelings of selfishness at times, doubting the decisions we were making, until we reminded each other that we were allowed to be happy, too.

I struggled to keep everything from Jessi. Conveniently, how serious things had become with Chris was a constant distraction.

They were on a two-month-long holiday to meet all their family and friends, with an agenda that included Colorado (where most of Chris's family was from), Wisconsin (where Jessi was from), and visiting friends in New York, South Carolina, and overseas to Italy. Jessi said it was a perfect two-in-one deal because the trips would help her expand her lifestyle blog, too. Chris was a free-lance travel writer, so they both benefitted. I prepared for her to be engaged by the end of the trip. Short romance, but they were a perfect match.

Ryan and I wanted to explore what was between us before revealing our relationship to anyone else, especially our families. It made sense to mitigate additional complexities during an already tender period until we were sure our relationship would develop into a long-term future together. For the time being, it was our own little secret, and for once, we were free to test the waters.

Preparing to go on my first date in over a decade, nerves kicked in the hours leading up to it. I changed outfits ten times. I was desperate to call Jessi for help. This was a man who had already seen me in my best on my wedding day and my worst, sick with toilet paper stuffed up my nose, yet I still felt pressured to impress him by my external appearance. As casual as this date was, a lot was riding on it as well. Our dating would determine the truth in every underlying thought and feeling about each other from the past thirteen years.

Ryan arrived on my doorstep with a book and a bottle of red wine.

"Oh, are we staying in tonight?"

"Nope, I know you don't like flowers. I figured these may last a little longer. The book at least. I'm sure the wine won't."

It was the perfect way to woo me.

I reached for the book. "*Hotel du Lac*. I've been wanting to read this! Did you stalk my Amazon wish list?"

Pride colored his face. "Nope. I remember you talking about it after reading the article that quoted the book. When I looked up the details, it sounded like you. I was hoping you hadn't read it yet."

Floored by how well he had listened to me over the years, I kissed Ryan's cheek. "You are the best." Placing the gifts on the hallway table, I locked the door behind me.

Ryan held out his arm so I could hold it. "You are beautiful."

I giggled before I could stop. "I changed a ridiculous number of times. I am so nervous." No point in acting unruffled with Ryan. I shared everything with him, and I wouldn't stop now. His comment made me stand a little taller in my booties, skinny jeans, oatmeal lace sweater, and blanket scarf. I was almost back to the weight I was before Josh died, finally filling out my pants again and looking less like a skeleton. I felt more confident when I had meat on my hips, especially when recalling how Ryan had grabbed on to them, as though he couldn't fathom ever letting go, the night his confession changed everything.

Ryan laced his fingers with mine. "Me, too. This is the third sweater I tried on."

"You look handsome." I meant every word. The burnt orange speckled sweater brought out the gold flecks in his brown eyes. His eyes danced like warm embers when he was excited.

He opened the passenger door of his Tacoma as only a gentleman would do.

"Thank you," I smiled shyly at him as I scooted by, my arm rubbing his torso, electric currents rippling through me. I slid into the seat and glanced around, partly nervous to see any remaining sign that Lindsay once sat in this seat, too. I was relieved to find it professionally detailed. It made me feel like I was in my twenties and dating again, outside of the two car seats in the extended cab, a glaring reminder of changing times.

Ryan turned the keys in the ignition but before removing his hand, a grin spread on his face. It was a look so full of joy that it made me squirm.

"What?" I asked with a nervous laugh.

"You... here next to me... in my truck..." He shook his head and turned the keys as the engine roared to life. "It makes me happy." He backed out of my driveway and onto the road before continuing, "Can I admit a truth?"

Ryan may have taken his eyes off me to watch the road, but I couldn't stop looking at him. I knew what he meant, the disbelief he and I were in a car, driving somewhere that would also be just him and me. Alone. Together. "Nothing but truths, please."

He glanced at me and said with such conviction, "Always, I promise." As he turned onto Miller Road, he revealed one of many truths to come, "Remember the family vacation to Michigan?"

"Yeah, we rented cabins, right?"

"Right. Well, each night I would drop a hint that I was making a coffee run for everyone the next morning. And every morning I would wake up, go to the main living area, and hope to see you there."

I laughed, amazed by his admission. "You wanted me to get coffee with you?"

"I wanted to know what it would feel like to be alone with you, even if only for thirty minutes. I would think about this center console," he waved his hand over the driver's shaft where his hand rested, "and think about our elbows here, barely touching."

Like in my dream. My heart fluttered. "You wanted that?"

"Oh God, I wanted it so badly." Ryan chuckled. "I realize how lame it sounds, but I couldn't get it out of my head. I kept imagining it."

I moved my elbow closer to his. "Like this?" I winked at him, surprising myself with my flirty maneuver.

He exhaled as though it was the greatest thing in the world. "Yes. Exactly like that. It sounds so minuscule but I just wanted to know, even on the smallest scale, what being with you could be like."

I scoffed at the circumstances we were continually surrounded by, "Even hugging felt too scandalous sometimes. I get it. I doubt we could have left together without raising eyebrows."

"For sure." Ryan glanced at me bashfully. "That was part of my odd coffee fantasy, too. I kept thinking that maybe if you came with me to get coffee, we would stand in line waiting for it, and I'd be sure to hug you. I mean like *really* hug you. None of this five-second touch and let go stuff."

I wanted to melt into a puddle and laugh all at the same time. Instead, I wrapped my hand around his and brought it to my mouth. "It's weird, isn't it? How restricted we were that even the most innocent thing like hugging became something of desire." I squeezed his hand. "I wish I had gone to get coffee with you."

"Tomorrow."

"What?"

"Tomorrow. Let's get coffee together tomorrow. You can make it up to me." Ryan pulled into a parking spot down the street from The Bistro. As soon as he shut off the car, he unstrapped his seatbelt and turned to face me.

"We haven't even started our first date yet!" I feigned a look of surprise, but the colossal smile on my face undoubtedly gave me away.

"This may be our first date, but it's not our last. I'm not letting any more moments pass that I don't seize. I want to get coffee with you, and as we're standing in line, I will hug you and hold you, and I don't care who sees." The resolve in his voice made my heart skip, and a swarm of butterflies fluttered in my stomach. "I'm ready to explore the world with you by my side."

The food we ate and the environment of the restaurant were insignificant next to how I felt, Ryan's reactions to the things I had to say, and all the things he shared. I had never smiled and laughed so much. I had never been a part of "that" couple that the waiter stands over, dropping hints it was time to go.

I couldn't tear my eyes away from Ryan. My hand rested on his thigh, his hand on mine. He brushed my hair away from my face. Our hands entwined on the table, our knees touching beneath. We couldn't stop touching. The electricity ran rampant through us as it always had, except this time, with liberation.

There was so much we knew about each other yet so much we had to discover. I couldn't get enough of what he had to say, and we both didn't know how to stop.

Eventually, the restaurant shut down for the night, and we were all but kicked out.

The only time we stopped talking was when we walked out the doors of The Bistro. The temperature significantly dropped, so Ryan immediately wrapped his arm around my back and pulled me close, my head cradled by the crook of his neck. Our steps synced, and we watched our legs partner in a beautiful waltz as we dodged rain puddles on the sidewalk back to the car.

Ryan opened my door for me once again. Instead of sliding in, I turned around to face him, confident he could hear my heart thumping against my chest. His brown eyes were curious, inviting. I looped my finger on his belt. As my knuckle tapped his skin in the bottom gap of his button-down shirt, I pulled him closer.

"Truth," I whispered, Ryan's face lingering inches from mine. "I want to take it slow. Bottom line is, you're still married, and we should be cautious of those lines until the divorce is settled."

He closed his eyes and nodded in painful agreement.

"But," I continued as his eyes opened once again. "I have years of pent-up wants, desires, needs, fantasies, and now a reality that centers around you. I don't want to waste another second of you not kissing me and—" I couldn't finish my declaration before Ryan's lips were on mine, his hands wrapping tighter around my waist, his tongue exploring the taste of me. One hand traveled up my spine, neck, and finally through my hair to the back of my head. If he didn't have that grip on me, I would have fallen to the ground. My whole body became limp, with its singular focus to become one with him.

We might have been that way for hours. When we finally forced ourselves to pull away, both of our faces were red and scuffed from his scruff. I couldn't feel my legs, but we quivered as though the temperature was forty degrees less than what it was, contradicting how on fire I felt. Ryan placed his hands on the roof of his truck to break contact so we could breathe. His breath tingled my ear, so I turned my head into him more, my forehead touching his left wrist with his pulse tapping my skin. I never felt more alive.

The next morning, he arrived at my door to pick me up for coffee as promised. We stood in line and hugged like newlyweds on a honeymoon. Twice we were stopped and told how cute we were together. Those compliments continued to inflate the balloons that lifted us higher off the ground. For a brief moment in time, we believed we were invincible. But that rarely lasts.

———

There are many kinds of love. But there's only one kind of romantic love that feels pure, nonjudgmental, non-sacrificial... for the first time in my life, I experienced that. I wondered if Ryan was as great of a guy as I imagined him to be, pondering his deepest thoughts, secrets, if he had the same dark sides Josh had. The idea of a person isn't the same as the reality of a person. Despite feeling as though I knew Ryan, there was a mandatory barrier that prevented us from exploring the depths. Nothing would stop that now, so the ocean's secrets were being uncovered one-by-one.

Ryan was indeed the most wonderful person I knew. I hadn't been great at setting reasonable expectations in the past, but Ryan surpassed all of mine. The reality of him, even down to his sweaty feet, wasn't disappointing. His private struggles and fears and strange quirks all became more reasons to love him. Ryan was passionate, kind-hearted, generous, selfless, calming, a great listener, an amazing father, and did his best to be present in each moment he was in.

We dated for five weeks before I finally gave in and went to his place. At my house, there was an unspoken barrier. It was as though Josh was still around, monitoring our every move. We didn't necessarily feel guilty, but we were cautious, especially when keeping this early period of our relationship so protected.

But after five weeks, we direly needed unrestrained space to be free. Physically, I couldn't take it anymore. Five weeks was a long time for any new adult relationship, let alone one that had been in a secret game of foreplay for thirteen long years.

Ryan prepared to drive me home after our date at a local sushi dive.

I covered his hands on the steering wheel with mine and placed strategic kisses down his neck. "Your place," I whispered.

One kiss. That was all it took to feel his neck throbbing, which was an instant link to another part of his body mirroring that same motion.

"Are you sure?" He wasn't dim; he knew what it meant. Fewer restrictions to keep us apart. His divorce would be settled in another month. We planned to wait before elevating our relationship to the next level. But Lindsay was being difficult on a few of the financial terms to draw it out, so the date had been pushed back two different times. I reached my limit. We had been so well-behaved. But I couldn't wait another day.

Ryan maneuvered the car in the opposite direction to drive the twenty minutes to his place.

Arriving at his new bachelor pad, it was the first time I could see Ryan personified. His house with Lindsay always felt cold, and I could never put my finger on why. As soon as I saw his chosen living quarters, I realized it was because there was very little of Ryan in the house he shared with her. But this place was all him.

Ryan's apartment was an incredible loft in an old warehouse converted into several living units. Giant wooden beams ran across the eighteen-foot-high ceiling with a darker finish of wood used for the flooring. The bathroom was the only separate room with a door. Everything else was one enormous space—the bedroom, kitchen, living area—only divided by standalone short-ened walls to provide a contrast with the surrounding brick walls.

It was very artsy, cozy and magnificent, despite its vastness. I felt at home instantly.

"Ryan, this view!" I gasped as I looked out the floor-to-ceiling windows. Gorgeous full trees lined a river with an incredible walking trail that followed its length. Autumn was displaying itself in the leaves with bits of red, green, and yellow highlighted by the streetlights. It was like watching a starry night filled with fireballs.

"It's pretty spectacular. I only wish this place had a balcony, then it'd be perfect." He wrapped his arms around my waist. "Tomorrow morning, we should make coffee and take a walk on that trail. You'll love it because it winds through different nature preserves."

I turned my body into his and ran my fingers through his hair. "You're being awfully presumptuous with the idea that I'm staying the night."

"You must have forgotten already that I lost the car keys." Ryan dug into his pocket and flung them in the air behind him. They clattered loudly on the floor as he winced. "Let's pretend they landed in that river outside, and there's no way to get them back, so you're stuck here forever."

"And also pretend we live in a world without Ubers or hitchhiking?"

"Precisely." He kissed my nose as I melted further into his touch. "C'mon." Ryan uncorked a bottle of wine, poured two glasses, grabbed my hand, and led me to the large sectional couch.

"Is this where you light a fire and seduce me?"

He glanced at the open hearth. "I wish. There was a reason this was the last unit available. It's one of two with real wood-burning fireplaces. I need to figure out where to get firewood and relearn how to start a fire."

"Ooh, like a modern woodsman. That's sexy."

Ryan flexed his muscles and in a gruff voice said, "Wait until you watch me chop wood, little lady. I'll win you over yet."

I fanned myself with my hand and pretended to faint as I fell back against the armrest. When I popped an eye open to look at him, he was watching me, suddenly serious. Heavy thickness replaced the lightheartedness in a blink.

I brought myself to a sitting position and put my hand on his arm. "What's wrong? Did I do something?"

"Damn," he took a sip of wine and rubbed his forehead. "I swear I don't get this emotional on dates." Ryan tried to maintain the joking atmosphere despite whatever washed over him.

"No, don't do that." I grabbed his wineglass and put it on the side table, then reached for his hands. "Talk to me. There will never be anything typical about us."

He circled my hands with his thumbs. "I didn't realize how much this was eating away at me over the years. My heart was burning, and I didn't know what to do or how to handle it. There are so, so, so many pressures every day. So many people to be concerned about and protect. It was always about what everyone else wanted. My heart was on fire, and I couldn't save it. Until now. You being here with me is better than I imagined. Being able to touch you and kiss you is great. But just being alone with you without interruptions from anyone is the best."

I smiled with my lips pressed together as I held back my own sentiments. "When did you know?"

"Which part?"

"When did you know you loved me?"

"Oh," Ryan ran his fingers through his hair. "That's kind of embarrassing."

I nudged him. "C'mon. Truth."

"Ok, truth. Six years ago. You were at our house with the kids and getting ready to leave—"

"Grace's fifth birthday party," I interjected.

He nodded, eyebrows raised in surprise, hesitant to continue. "Yeah, that's the one. I stood there with everyone else saying bye to you, and I felt like there was this huge invisible wall standing between us. Everything in me wanted to bust through it and sweep you off the ground, put you in a car and run away. Maybe that'd be considered kidnapping, but man... it hurt. You left, and I spent the rest of the day in a fog. I couldn't stop thinking about you and attempting to come up with excuses for us to all get together so I could see you more. It felt like I was suffocating after that. Then I'd see you again, and it was like being able to breathe for the first time. Then you'd leave, and the cycle would continue."

My reaction wasn't ideal, but I couldn't control it. I laughed. I laughed so hard I couldn't catch my breath and snorted instead, which just made me laugh harder. Ryan poured out his heart, and I couldn't stop snorting. It was definitely not the textbook move that romance stories or movies suggest after a heartfelt reveal.

When I could finally get a handle on it, I took reasonable action as I should have from the beginning. I crawled on top of Ryan, one leg on each side of him, laced my arms around his neck, and leaned my forehead into his. Relief replaced confusion on his face.

"Thirteen years. It's been thirteen years of constant thoughts about you, wondering, wishing, wanting... Since the first day I met you, Ry, I was hooked on you. I thought I had this wire connected to you and could feel your thoughts and emotions filtering into me. They mirrored my own so much that eventually, I resigned to the idea that I was daydreaming.

"Six years ago, I was leaving your house after Grace's party and said goodbye to you. I swear there was a light shining down on your face, and I realized how much I was utterly in love with you. That look hasn't left me. For a brief period, I thought maybe you fell in love with me, too, before I chalked it up to yet another fantasy. What you just confirmed, is that it's true... we've always been connected. You and me, we're wired together."

A tear slid out of the corner of his eye and down his cheek. "Haleigh..."

But I was done talking. Done waiting. Done doing everything else except what I really wanted. So I kissed Ryan, hard, erupting like an active fire doused with more gasoline when it didn't need the assistance.

Ryan's hands traveled up my shirt, grasping, rubbing, clutching every inch of my torso, front and back. I did the same to him, only barely resisting the urge to rip his clothes apart to get to his body. Each touch elicited a moan from him and me. We had wanted this for so long that every part of our bodies ached for it; when finally getting it, the pleasure proved to be indescribable, even in something as tiny as a simple touch.

Ryan stood with my legs wrapped around him and turned to place me on the couch where he once sat. As his tongue explored my mouth, he grabbed a throw pillow and stuffed it behind my back. He stretched my body, my butt resting at the edge of the couch and my calves and feet bracing me on the floor. Ryan hovered over me, pulling my shirt over my head and removing my bra as his lips moved down my neck to my breasts. He didn't leave one inch unkissed. Once he reached my hips, he unbuttoned my jeans and slid them off while caressing my legs with his lips as he went down. Ryan traveled back up my legs to remove my thank-God-I-chose-Victoria-Secret-tonight panties, but this time his mouth stayed in place while his hands removed the garment.

I gripped the edge of the couch until my mind blanked, intense arousal and pleasure all at once. Just when I thought I would lose it, he stopped and stood. I opened my eyes, silently pleading for him to continue.

Ryan's eyes traveled from my eyes to the rest of my body and back up again. "Haleigh, you are beautiful." Any other naked moment in my life, I was self-conscious, even if no one was around to see my body. Rarely was I more focused on the person in front of me than my insecurities. But with Ryan, I *wanted* him to see all of me. Nothing to fear, nothing to hide. Clothes were a hindrance from our bodies finally touching. His clothes needed to be off, too.

I leaned forward and pulled Ryan closer, his knees drumming the couch between my legs. I raised his shirt to kiss his stomach, pulling it as high as my arms would allow. He took the fabric out of my hands and finished tugging it over his head. I unbuttoned his jeans and slid them down over his hips, pulling his boxers with them. Just as I reached for him, prepared to take him into my mouth, he grabbed my waist and lifted me off the couch, turning, and bending to place me on the rug. Ryan stepped out of his jeans and joined me, our bodies finding their match in the other person's. *Finally. Finally. Finally.*

My heart thumped against his chest, his knocked against mine. My nipples rubbed against his bare skin. Our stomachs grazed. Our thighs intertwined. Our feet scraped against each other like it was the most sensual thing in the world. The nerves throughout our bodies were throbbing enough for the Richter scale to confuse it with an earthquake. His hands brushed through my hair and traveled down all over my body once again.

Ryan kissed me as his fingers entered me, and I arched in response, desiring his entirety. My chest was going to explode if it didn't happen soon. I grabbed for him and pulled him in. The surrounding air was suddenly hot, thick, and full of voltage. Thrusts and moans, a synchronized dance to the strongest beat.

We didn't last long.

Josh crossed my mind afterward. Not that I missed him, but I realized this was another step in moving on, moving past what we had. Josh was gone so there was no going back anyhow; but this was like buying a one-way ticket to a new life. It felt right. Ryan's warm breath on my body, his sweat sticking to me, my hair stuck to his stubble, my leg draped across his hips. This was the best kind of right I had experienced. Even if the timing was still slightly wrong.

It must have been on Ryan's mind too, because after our panting died down, he separated from me to fetch water. I etched the memory of him walking to the kitchen in my mind, noting every curve of his body, his naked butt, the division of his tan lines on his upper thighs, the muscles in his back and the way his arms flexed automatically when reaching into the refrigerator. I was, without a doubt, smitten.

Ryan handed me a bottle and then guzzled half of his. As he stood over me, thirstily drinking the water, I thought, *Damn, this is the most erotic thing I've ever seen.* Fulfilling a basic need became sexy and confirmed I was a goner; Ryan had forever changed me.

He sat down next to me, propped on his side as he traced his finger down my stomach and around my belly button. I could see his mind working to form the words he wanted to ask. Finally, he spoke, "How are you feeling?"

I wiped a droplet of water caught in his chin scruff with my thumb. "Euphorically in love with you."

Ryan grinned, prepped instead for a response that varied greatly from that one. He caught my hand in his, opened my palm and kissed circles in it. Goosebumps shot up my arm. Ryan's voice became a whisper as though the words were a danger to the perfection built around us, "I know it's not prime timing. I just—"

"Shh…" I put my finger to his lips. I didn't want to talk about it. We had already broken the ultimate rule, and I knew a tinge of guilt would be layered underneath the pleasure. I wasn't ready to let the moment pass. I covered his mouth with mine as I crawled on top of him, immediately feeling him harden under my body as he grabbed onto my hips. "Let's just be us. Freely. Again."

CHAPTER TWENTY-NINE
YEAR 1 - FALL

Tangled up on the couch naked together, Ryan pulled a plush cream blanket from the back to cover us for warmth. It was a position I had seen in romantic movies, yet never thought I'd be in so comfortably. Josh was always quick to get up and shower after sex; however, Ryan didn't want to let go of me.

Ryan's strong arms wrapped around my waist. I brushed his arm with my hand, his arm hairs moving while I circled the small moles lining his skin. We continued playing our new game of Truth. That's it. *Truth.* Sharing what we've wanted the other person to realize, but couldn't say, or actions we always wanted to take but were restrained from.

"Remember when you surprised us by showing up at the bar?"

"Was that after my trip to Nashville?"

I nodded, my forehead grazing his chin with the movement. "You looked good. I mean, like *really* good." It was five years ago, and even though I couldn't remember what I did last week, I could describe exactly what he wore that day. Ryan had a burgundy and tan plaid button-down shirt with a black puffer vest on and unshaven facial hair that made him look rugged, like he had returned from a fishing trip, not a work conference.

As more people filtered into the bar behind him, they pushed him into our barstools and his hand gripped the back of my chair for stability. I couldn't take my eyes off his hand barely touching my shoulder and wanted to tug on his vest to bring him even closer. If I hadn't already acknowledged I had fallen in love with Ryan, I would have realized it that night. "You don't want to know the outrageous number of times I've recalled that image of you."

"I still have that outfit in my closet if that's all it takes to get you going."

"You should be happy I don't have an anime fetish. Like begging you to dress up like Pokémon or something."

"No, just a woodsman fetish."

I laughed at how true that may be. I always thought Ryan was sexier than Josh because of his woodsier features compared to Josh's sportier look.

Closing my eyes, I scolded myself for comparing Ryan to Josh again. I needed to stop. What Ryan and I had was something on its own, but if I kept bringing Josh into it, it wouldn't hold strong alone. I wondered if Ryan had any mental comparisons of Lindsay and me. The thought was unnerving.

"My turn. You know that first day we met, and I told you that my 'guess what type of person' line for you was something about how you're the type of person that volunteers at the humane society?"

I smiled at the memory, enjoying what once was a shameful reminder of a lousy night was turning into something I wanted to reminisce. Now it was about Ryan and me meeting for the first time, not one of the worst fights I had with Josh. "I do. I thought it was sweet you had me pegged for that when it was true."

"Okay, well, truth: that was a cover-up. My first thought was something different."

"Oh, really?" I sat up so I could see his face better. "What was your first?"

"I bet you're the type of woman that every guy could fall in love with."

I shoved him tenderly. "This is called *Truth*. Not exaggeration."

Ryan pulled his body to a sitting position, keeping his legs stretched out on the couch. "It's true, Haleigh. You have a certain look when you walk into a room. I saw you from the moment you entered the bar that night. It's a very steady, confident expression. As a guy in the room, it's breathtaking. We all hope your eyes will land on us. Then when they do, your eyes are unwavering, as though you see something deeper than what's in front of you. Even when you're not smiling, your eyes constantly are. Like there's a sweet little joke between you and us, and we want to know what it is so we can see that look from you again and again."

To know Ryan viewed me like that floored me. I wouldn't have thought I could carry that sort of presence.

I leaned my forehead into his forearm. "I can't believe this is all real."

Ryan's fingers played with my hair. "It's always been real."

Kissing his cheek, I started to bury myself under the blanket with him again. A knock on the door interrupted it.

"Oh, shoot. It's Mrs. Murphy across the hall. She's a sweet lady but usually needs help to get items out of the taller cabinets. I told her never to hesitate to knock when she needs me, and she's converted me into her cabinet boy."

"Cabinet boy?"

He shrugged with a smirk, "You know, like a pool boy." Ryan stood to pull his pants and shirt on. I started to do the same before he stopped me. "No, you stay naked in this blanket. I won't be long."

"Won't she see me?" It was hard to stay hidden in such an open floor plan.

Ryan grinned. "It'll be good for her to know I'm taken. Break her heart now before she gets too attached."

I threw a pillow at him.

Ryan's smile disappeared the moment he opened the door. "Lindsay? What's wrong? Are the kids okay?"

"I knew it!" Lindsay screamed, shrill echoes enunciating her words as she charged into the apartment, her all-black athletic attire making her look more like a robber than a distraught almost-ex-wife.

"What the hell are you doing here?"

Her eyes were bloodshot and tears lurked over the edges as she paced across the floor, shooting daggers at me, seemingly searching for something to throw. "How long has this been going on? Weeks? Months? Years?"

I shut my eyes, wishing I had hidden in the bathroom, or at least put clothes on. Her arrival was the last thing we expected. As much as I didn't get along with Lindsay, I couldn't handle the pain emanating from her. Her long blonde hair was pulled into a tight bun, making her look so frail that a poke of a thumbtack could shatter her. I reached for my shirt and jeans, trying to wiggle into them as best as possible under the blankets.

"You didn't answer my question. What are you doing here? Where are the kids?" Ryan demanded again, closing the door behind her.

Lindsay threw her hands in the air. "Like you give a damn about our kids right now."

Her unnecessary accusation scorched Ryan's face. "Don't you ever—"

She cut Ryan off before he could finish. "They are at home—OUR home—with my mom. I thought it'd be a nice surprise if you joined us for pizza and a game tonight so we could be a family again. I sent you several texts on the way over here. I didn't realize you were busy screwing your dead brother's wife."

"Okay, that's crossing a line." I rose from the couch. I would not allow her to degrade me or Josh's death or Ryan or us in that way.

"I crossed a line? Seriously?" Lindsay shook her long, perfectly manicured finger at me. "You two are out here rolling around naked while your husband is dead, and he's still married."

Ryan took a few steps closer to us, ready to interfere if needed. "We are separated, Lindsay. You knew I was dating someone."

"But you didn't say you were dating *her*! I expected you two to hook-up because you've been playing fucking googly eyes for years. But seriously, you couldn't grow the balls to date someone outside of your damn family?"

"I don't see why it matters to you who it is." Ryan monitored his voice to not add fuel to the fire, but his control was wavering.

"Do our children know you're screwing their aunt? Maybe that's why I give a damn."

Ryan opened his mouth and then closed it again. His chest rose and fell quickly. "Listen, I'm sorry you had to find out this way. It's not ideal for any of us. We knew as part of the separation that we would date other people. Who that is should not be a factor of your anger right now. If you're hurt, that's fine, I get that. There's no need to attack Haleigh."

Lindsay tucked her stray hairs in her topknot, searching for the next path to take. Her pink lips pressed together in a thin line. For a moment, I thought she may actually settle down and talk to us instead of yelling and cursing. But then she turned to me with eyes filled with hatred.

"Just because your marriage tragically ended, doesn't mean you have to ruin mine. No wonder Josh was ashamed of you and was gone all the time. He couldn't stand to be around you!" Lindsay then put her shaking hands against Ryan's chest and shoved him. "And *you*. What an asshole. I will make sure everyone knows how fucking low you two are." She glared at both of us one more time before storming out of the loft.

The door slammed shut, and the silence that followed was frightening, yet strangely liberating. It was the first person outside of Ryan and me who knew we were together. Although it was the last person I preferred to know the truth, our world opened up a little more, even in the middle of a hurricane. Ryan stood silently with his hand over his chest where Lindsay pushed him, stunned that she became physical.

I pulled out my phone, anxious to play damage control, my mind wild with theories on what she may do next. "Your mom. You know she will tell your mom." I could imagine Hunter in the background, listening to every word, casting judgment, turning into a problem child after that, blaming everything on this one situation that flipped his family upside down even more. I could see the crestfallen face of my mother-in-law as she called me a traitor, a disgrace to her family. "I should call her first. Or we should go there and talk to your mom in person." I typed in her name, but before I could hit the call button, Ryan grabbed my hand.

Shaking his head, he calmly took the phone out of my hand and set it on the table. "Come here," he pulled me into him, wrapping his arms around my neck. Despite his demeanor, his breathing was more rapid than usual, and a coat of sweat dampened his skin.

After a few minutes of silence, he finally asked, "Are you ashamed?"

I pulled back from him, looking up into his eyes and at his creased forehead. Lindsay's words stung him more than he was letting on. "I feel like I *should* be. We both know you still being married isn't the way we should have done this. But..." I searched for words, a strong retort to the conflicting emotions screaming at me that infidelity is wrong. I finally settled on, "No, I'm not."

A small smile tugged at Ryan's lips, "Me neither. It's not what I had planned for us. But it's you, and it's me." He swept my hair off my shoulders and wrapped the strands around his fingers. "I don't know, Haleigh... I feel like the world already knows."

If we were portrayed in a movie, the scene would cut to a montage of every moment we shared throughout the years with Jimmy Eat World's "Your House" playing in the background, highlighting the looks we thought were just between us and the noticeable change in the air when we were in the same room together. It all ran through my head at a rapid speed, a brightening light of revelations.

Ryan watched me with a grin. "We've always made sense."

Being publicly humiliated was a surprisingly easy pill to swallow. A horse pill, but digestible nonetheless. For several days, our social media accounts exploded. Lindsay was relentless and held nothing back. Our dirty laundry hung in the town square for everyone to see. I hated her actions but didn't blame her for her feelings. Lindsay was heartbroken from being blindsided and had every right to be. She retaliated in the only way she knew how which was using her title as the queen of hashtags to bring in new audiences that commented hateful things—even though they didn't know the details or have any ties to our story whatsoever. Some people troll just to troll.

Although heat flushed my face and spotted my neck from the accusations and the reactions to the allegations, it didn't take long to simmer down. One glance at Ryan was all I needed to feel rooted, like the most robust redwood tree that survives the worst storms. The number of responses from close friends and family that resembled "we aren't surprised" confirmed Ryan's comforting statement even more: we've always made sense, and we weren't the only ones who realized it, regardless of the atypical way we came together.

I was most angry that Lindsay exposed it to the world before I could gather what I would finally say to Hunter and Hannah. At least I knew what I had with Ryan was real, and I was ready for them to know about it, despite the circumstances forcing me to do it on a deadline. Hunter was peculiarly excited because he loved Ryan. His first question was, "Does that mean we will see more of Uncle Ryan?" I winced at his title, but it was the truth of our situation brought to light. Do they stop calling him Uncle Ryan? Probably not. And maybe that's not such a bad thing. It was the least of our worries in learning how to navigate these new family dynamics.

Hannah had a harder time with it. The idea of Mommy and Uncle Ryan being together meant no room for Daddy who must not be coming back after all. Ryan explained that death can seem like a trip at her age. Something that makes you say goodbye to someone, but you expect to say hello once again. The thought of someone never coming back again can be unfathomable. I was grateful Ryan was a familiar face to her. I couldn't imagine introducing the kids to someone new in that way. At least not yet.

My parents were surprised. I could see in their eyes they thought it was a rebound situation for the both of us. They didn't know the details about Josh or how he had left our relationship long before he died. They thought it was too soon, that I should still be mourning. But when does it become okay to stop mourning? Ultimately, it wasn't about anyone else understanding anything more than the simple truth that Ry and I loved each other. They didn't have to know our love was planted long before anyone saw it bloom.

Wanda was stunned into silence. Her first assumption was that Mike's and Josh's deaths impacted us too much to make a fair call on our relationship status since we were all in a "dark place." Ryan had to explain the grief felt from losing them wasn't the reason we were coming together, and it also wouldn't be a deterrent. We didn't explain to her that this had been going on for years because we didn't want her to have shattered memories of times when the family was all together.

"The grieving period never truly ends, Mom. It doesn't mean you can't grieve and still find love. They can both exist without being reliant upon the other." Ryan admitted he thought Wanda was siding with Lindsay more during their divorce anyway, and I could see that. She was at the house more often to help with the kids, and it was only bound to increase their communication and bond. Lindsay and Wanda were similar. That couldn't offend me.

Jessi freaked out when she had to find out through Chris's

social media feed. I received a call after her shock settled in, but instead of her saying hello, I was met with complete silence.

"Did you call to yell at me? Or to not say anything at all? I'm not sure which one is worse." I waited, wondering when I should give up and hang up the phone.

"I'm trying to process my thoughts," Jessi's words finally came through the speaker.

I waited patiently by pacing the floor in my living room, throwing toys in bins and putting books back on the shelf. Her silence was the worst punishment of everything so far. I felt terrible for not sharing anything with her. Ryan and I had needed time alone in our private bubble, and I trusted she could understand that.

I heard her whispering in the background with Chris.

"Chris says 'hi' by the way," she muttered as though frustrated he made her say anything at all.

After a few more minutes passed, she finally said, "Okay, I'm happy for you. And Ryan." She yelled something at Chris in the background before returning to the phone and divulging, "Chris says he's excited about you two and called it on Kimber night." I could imagine her rolling her eyes without having to see it.

"But?" I added, knowing what was next.

"But, I'm bummed I didn't hear it from you first. You're one of my best friends, and I thought I'd be the first to know if there was even an inkling of a romance blooming."

"I know, I know. Trust me, this is not the way I would have wanted anyone to find out. It's not like Ryan and I had talked about it or contrived it before acting. It just kind of happened. Then Lindsay walked in and made the decision that the whole world should know before we could even determine what we wanted it to be." I strained while explaining it to Jessi, barely skimming the surface of the truth and guilt-stricken for not being more transparent.

I wondered when the right time would be to reveal to Jessi the full story of what happened with Josh, of everything I discovered, of how it's always been Ryan instead of Josh over the years. I had been so careful to protect Josh's image, and although it was crucial to do with his mom and our kids, I wasn't so sure that Jessi shouldn't know.

"I'm done pretending anything is other than what it is. I'd love to tell you everything. There's more to this, and I've been holding it in for too long. Can I see you sometime soon? Where are you guys at?"

"Waiting to board a plane at La Guardia. We will be home in a few hours."

"Want to come over for a wine night? I'd like to hear about your trip, and we can finally talk about everything."

"Yeah, that would be great. I also have news to share."

I smiled, imagining how big of a rock sat on Jessi's finger now. "Engaged?"

She grunted, "What kind of girl do you take me for?"

"A hopelessly romantic one that has found hope in an equally romantic man."

"Well, I did get pretty lucky here. But, nope. Chris is moving in!"

I knew then it would only be a short time before an engagement. Jessi said she wouldn't live with a guy if he weren't the real deal. Ryan mentioned Chris had asked where the best place to get customized jewelry would be. I could not be happier for them and was eager to watch Jessi, the most expressive person I knew, provide details of their trip while her face would tell me more than any of her words could.

Just when I didn't think Jessi and I could get any closer, we did. When she came over that night, every secret was brought to light. I watched her go on the same emotional rollercoaster I did when finding out about Josh's hidden life, except hers were happening rapidly in the short time it took to recount everything I discovered and the timeline of it all. She was mad that I held it in, instead of letting her share the burden and helping me through it like friends do. I couldn't disagree. I should have let her be there for me.

Everyone closest to me now knew everything they each should know. No secrets. No darkness. Everything was as peaceful as it could be.

Yet, that's when I began to feel uneasy.

I still wasn't living my dreams like I had set out to do once the initial pain of Josh's death subsided. I was falling back into old patterns.

Ryan and I spent a lot of time together, trying to squeeze in everything we had thought about saying or doing with each other from the past decade. He was unlike anyone I had been with before. It was all different. I felt giddy and excited to be in a relationship, precisely like everyone said it should be.

The timing had always been wrong between us, and I still wasn't sure it was the right time despite the most obvious barriers no longer present. I had a son and a daughter now. They were my number one priority. I needed to set a good example and wanted to show them what it meant to be the best version of myself.

I still rollerbladed and attended Martial Arts classes to stay focused on self-care. But it was time to find a job. Every time I sat down to evaluate my options, I'd get distracted by creating a new playlist or watching a movie and dubbing a new soundtrack. It was such a passion of mine, and I was good at it. I researched record labels in Chicago, wondering if there was something I could do, even if it meant us moving to a new part of the suburbs or the city itself.

I wanted to be more. My kids needed to see dreams could come true by hard work and overcoming obstacles. I hadn't done a great job of displaying that, but I was ready to redeem it.

And there was the problem. I couldn't let anything stand in my way.

I had to figure out if Ryan was doing just that.

Chapter Thirty
Year 2 – Winter

One year.

It was the official one-year anniversary of Josh's death, the day life changed unpredictably. Everything was divided into two time periods: before Josh died and after Josh died. I wondered when the time would come that I no longer separated life in that way.

This was brand new ground that even Ryan's psychology background couldn't instruct how to best navigate. We weren't sure if it was better or worse to spend the day with each other and ultimately decided to spend it apart. Ryan would be with his kids and Wanda. I would be with Hunter and Hannah.

The kids and I did what made the most sense and went to visit Josh's grave. Hunter's maturity had been incredible to witness, but the way he grew up so quickly in such a short time was alarming and dismaying. I hoped he could still be a kid and enjoy his childhood, but a part of it had been stripped away, forced to understand death in the middle of the most freeing parts of his life. When he walked to Josh's headstone and placed a hand on it, leaning slightly into it as though comforting an old friend, I gasped with tears. It was like watching a grown man, taking a silent moment to appreciate the life of a dear friend.

Hannah edged her way to the grave, clinging to a teddy bear. I wondered how much longer it would be harder on her before it became easier, if ever. I knew there'd be times she would long for her dad, like for daddy-daughter dances or her wedding day. I saw in her eyes as she looked at the snow-dusted dirt in front of Josh's grave that she realized, maybe for the first time, this was where his body resided, and it would never move again.

I held her because it was all I could do. Hunter spent a while talking to Josh. I let him for however long he needed, keeping Hannah warm and protected from the biting wind. I didn't know what I would say to Josh this time. So much had occurred since our last visit here as a family. I wasn't sure I wanted to talk. I didn't owe Josh an explanation or details. I would let Hunter take care of that.

Thankfully, Hunter didn't ask me if I was going to talk to Josh. Despite such a young age, he understood the confusion that had come to exist in the past year.

My mom called when we were back home and warming up by the fireplace with hot chocolate. I turned on a movie for the kids so I could talk to her.

"Do you need us to come visit? We couldn't agree if we should get in the car or not. We didn't know if Ryan was with you," her voice quieted when speaking his name.

"No, Ryan is with Wanda and his kids today. You and Dad are always welcome to come by. You know that."

Mom sighed loudly, clearly displaying her feelings without the need for words.

I refrained from rolling my eyes, aware there was more on her mind than she was letting on. "Mom, say it."

"I don't know, Haleigh. It's all... unexpected. It might be more evident today than any other day. It's not that I think you're moving on too fast. I'm glad you're dating. I knew you and Ryan had a strong friendship, but I thought you'd date someone who wasn't a near twin of your husband."

"Mom, in all the times you have been around Josh and Ryan, do you really consider them to be alike? They may have similar features, but their personalities are vastly different."

"Yeah, maybe..."

I stretched and rounded my shoulder blades to push out the tension. "Are you ever going to be accepting of Ryan?"

Mom's fingers drummed on a table, something she did when holding back her first thought to filter her words. "What are the kids supposed to call him?"

"Whatever they want. Uncle Ryan. Ryan. Whatever," I steadied my tone, understanding our uncommon decision naturally impacted our families. I vowed to be patient as they came to terms with the changes. "Listen, I know this is unusual. Ryan and I have always had an undeniable connection. For the first time since the day we met, we can explore that. Sure, there are a lot of heartbreaking details that brought us to where we are now, but all we can do is keep moving forward. We are doing just that. We make each other happy."

"Well, that's something. He's the first man you've defended. In all your years, I've never heard you mention someone makes you happy."

"I'm confident in what we have. I won't go out of my way to prove it. I know in due time, you'll see it, too."

"The next time you drop the kids off, Ryan should come in with you. I'll make dinner for everyone."

I smiled, appreciating her attempt at acceptance. "We can do that."

But as relieved as I was to hear her speak those words, I knew I couldn't let things get too comfortable and routine before I considered changing it all again.

Since the temperatures dipped to the single digits outside, we turned the whole day into a movie marathon. I loved cuddling with Hannah and Hunter as we dozed in and out of sleep on the giant fort bed we created from every blanket and pillow we could find. I wasn't sure if we'd ever leave that spot as long as we had food in the house.

My phone frequently buzzed, receiving texts from people saying they were thinking of the kids and me on this day. I appreciated their sentiments; relieved people didn't disregard the impact of Josh's death just because Ryan and I found a relationship together.

When an unknown number came through, I took the opportunity for a bathroom break and figured I'd answer it.

"Haleigh?" That voice. It had been so long.

"Yeah?" I didn't want to reveal that I knew who it was. An immediate abundance of emotions came out of the woodwork.

"Hey, it's Kristen."

"Hey." I evaluated the millions of thoughts zooming through my mind. *Was I still mad at her? Did I hold a grudge? Did I want to talk to her on the anniversary of Josh's death?*

"I don't even know where to start, so I'm going to start, and if you hang up on me or stop me or whatever you need to do, just do it. I have so much to get out." Kristen was talking so fast I struggled to process her words. "I hope we can pretend I did this a year ago. That maybe even I did it before a year ago. I mean, wow, I have the worst timing. I am always too late in saying the things I should tell you. I want to be better at that. I will get better at that. I miss our friendship very much. I miss you. When I heard about Josh's passing, I didn't know what to say or do.

"I'm so sorry. I wrote you multiple letters I never sent. Called to have flowers delivered just to cancel them. Called you and hung up multiple times before it could ring, hoping my number wouldn't show. I even learned how to do this phone trick that takes me straight into your voicemail, but even then, I didn't know what to say. I'm so sorry about everything that has happened to you. I'm so sorry about his death. I'm so sorry I wasn't there as a friend or do anything at all that a friend should have done. I have thought about you nonstop, and I'm only now reaching out." She sighed.

"You would think the idea of death would have made me stop having so many regrets about holding back the words that I should say. Clearly, it hasn't. I just want to know that you're okay. Even if you don't want to say anything else, please tell me if you and your kids are all okay." She was out of breath, and I felt more exhausted than I was before she sprang into her apology, or explanation, or both—or whatever she intended it to be.

I didn't know what to say, so I found the only point I knew how to launch from. "Are you still in San Francisco?"

Kristen exhaled, relieved I would converse with her. "I'm in Los Angeles now, actually. Met and married a movie director out of all things."

"I'm assuming it's a little bit warmer there than it is here." The weather was a safe fallback when I didn't know what else to say immediately, but wanted to say something.

"Sunny skies and sixty degrees. Not too bad for the beginning of January."

"We are avoiding the blizzard outside if it says anything about the contrast."

Kristen chuckled, and the sound of her laughter made me ache for the nights we combined forces to save the world, one stray animal at a time. "I saw people post pictures of the snow on Facebook. Of all my regrets, at least I can say I don't regret leaving the Midwest." She cleared her throat as though scared to reminisce on our time together to avoid bringing up old feelings. "Are you still volunteering with Pet Angels?"

"I am." I dove into details of the changes that occurred since she was last there, and she told me about all the volunteer work in California and how much it differed.

We talked for two hours straight. I told Kristen I forgave her and as time went on that I understood how we were both at fault for the way our friendship disintegrated. I also told her about the lady who pierced my nose and how much she reminded me of Kristen, making me miss her even years after she left. She cried at that, admitting she had yet to find a friend she could connect with like me.

Kristen had found her new home in Los Angeles, among similar artsy souls who had endless opportunities to live their passions through various outlets from the music to the film and art scenes. Her husband had directed several indie flicks I knew well and was currently working on his first major motion picture.

"Listen, Haleigh. I have, like, twenty CDs of yours with the 'supposed to be in this movie, but they failed' soundtracks. Todd wants you to interview for a music supervisor position by throwing together some tracks based on scenes. He likes that you have a music business degree, but says there's a lot more to learn yet and wants to know if you have the drive to go after it."

I was tossing snacks in a bowl for the kids when I stopped mid-motion, the bag dropping out of my hand. "What?"

"Before I even brought up what you once wanted to do, he's the one who said you'd make a good one after we listened to a few of your CDs. Next thing I know, we are talking about it like it could happen. I know you have a lot back there with the kids and everything that has transpired, but I wanted you to know there's an offer out here to try it, if you were interested."

Jessi once told me that the moment I open myself to the universe, it'll open itself right back. I never understood how she could fling herself into a new city with no ties and yet everything worked out perfectly. Jessi swears by that advice. I would have thought it was too late for me, over forty with two kids to provide for, but if I had learned anything in recent years, it was that life is too short.

"Okay," I said confidently.

"Okay? As in, you'll do it?" Kristen's shock was evident in the upward inflection of her voice.

"Well, I'm guessing he wants to meet with me first, right? I don't want to assume it's happening yet, but I'm willing to discuss it more."

"You don't need to run it past anyone first?" It sounded as though she slapped her forehead when those words came out. "I'm sorry, Haleigh. I didn't think that through."

"Well, I do kind of. My kids. I mean, if I do this, now would be the time before they are rooted deeper into the school system and forge stronger friendships. I also want to have an honest conversation with Josh's side of the family. I owe it to them if I whisk the kids away." Ryan's face. That's all I could see. Ryan's brown eyes as I tell him our relationship is ending before it even has a fair chance to start. After all these years of waiting for the moment that was finally ours, I could be walking away. "Is there any chance to work remotely?"

"I asked that right away but he said no. He said there are way too many people eager to get their foot in the door, so why ruin the team dynamic by hiring someone who can't get their ass in the room? That is almost a direct quote."

"That's a bummer for me, but I get it. I don't want to lose out the opportunity and I haven't had any breakthroughs like this here."

Kristen squealed, "Eek! I'm excited you're open to this! I was so scared to call you. Shoot me over some dates you can fly out here, and we'll get it arranged on our side. You can stay with us, too, if you want. I'd love to have you."

"Yeah, that'd be great. As long as it's not too weird to stay with the man who might hire me. It would be great to see you."

"I'll kick him out if it is. We'll have a girls' night."

I laughed, loving that Kristen hadn't lost her tenacity. "I'll be in touch soon, okay?'

"Okay!"

"And Kristen? Job opportunity aside, I'm really glad you called."

I could hear the smile stretch across her face. "Me, too."

———

After many nights of debate, I decided to keep the interview a private matter. Even from Ryan. After everything we went through, I swore I wouldn't hold secrets from anyone, but this one felt too fragile. I told everyone I was going out to visit Kristen and get away for a few days. I didn't offer the details. I couldn't let anyone cloud my judgment on what this opportunity could mean. I had to keep an open mind. If I thought it was right, I'd have the conversations necessary to move forward. If it wasn't the right step, then at least I could decide with a clear conscience and no one's influence.

The warm weather was the first persuasive element I encountered. As soon as I stepped out of the airport with Kristen, I declared, "Oh my gosh, this is exactly what my pasty skin needs right now." The rays of the sun beating down on someone who had been clothed in thick sweaters and socks for months now (thanks to the Midwest winters) made me want to shed my clothes and walk around naked to soak it all in.

Kristen provided a tour of the city. I had thought Los Angeles would be congested and loud, but after living near Chicago, it exceeded my expectations. The views from the beach to the mountains and everywhere in between were incredible. I could smell the ocean from just about anywhere we stood. At least in the places she took me.

"I don't work right now, only volunteer. I can watch the kids while you're doing what you need to get started. Todd mentioned some classes may need to be taken, too. The kids can come with me to the shelter. It will be good for everyone. And good practice for me if we decide to have kids someday." We were already making plans about what life would be like if I moved out here. It didn't feel strange either.

"The wife of one of Todd's best friends is an excellent realtor.

She's coming over tomorrow night for dinner so you can meet her. You give her a list of what you need in a home, and she'll have options for you by the time you're ready. I can also go through any potential houses if you're not out here and give you the rundown or video chat the tours."

We ordered coffee before going back to Kristen's house. I paid for hers, recognizing I may be extremely dependent on her soon and wanted to start paying her back in any way I could. "I can't believe you're going so far out of your way for me."

Kristen squeezed my hand. "I'm not exaggerating when I say I've never found another friend like you. The possibility of you out here is a dream. It would make life complete." She sheepishly took a drink of her coffee. "No pressure, though, of course."

Todd was exactly the type of guy I'd picture as an indie movie director, and I instantly loved him and his relationship with Kristen. I couldn't help but have a flash of Josh when I watched them holding hands together, finding it strange that Kristen could have been interested in Josh. It was also many years ago, and as I've discovered, it can take time to come into your own and find a genuine love deserving of who you are.

After a tour around the movie set of Todd's current project, meeting with his team, and putting together tracks of a soundtrack with clips he showed me, I could tell he was pleased. "You do know there's a lot of negotiating and it's all very fast-paced, right? You will have to learn from people who excel before diving in, so the period before you're solo could be a while yet, depending on how quickly you pick it up and the connections you make."

I nodded. "Honestly, I'm more driven now than I would have been directly out of college. I have two little ones to take care of. I will work hard, shadow, study, and take all the additional courses I need. Whatever it takes. You get me started, and I'll run with it."

"Well, Kristen says you two are a lot alike, and if so, then I can only assume it'll be a short period before you're competing with the pros. Let's give it a run. When do you think you can get back out here? We have tight deadlines approaching."

———

Once I returned to Schaumburg, my first order of business was to have a sit down with Hannah and Hunter. I pulled out a map on my phone to show the distance between where we were in Illinois and where we would live in California. I also needed them to comprehend that we would be very far from our family and Josh's gravesite.

"We can come back to visit, though, right?"

I didn't know how much I would be working until I proved myself, so I didn't want to make promises I couldn't keep. I also didn't know how comfortable I'd be sending the kids on a flight by themselves until they were older. "We will try to come back as much as possible. I'm sure Grandma and Grandpa and Nana will all come out to visit."

"And Uncle Ryan?" My stomach dropped with Hunter's mention of him. Ryan would be my next conversation, then my parents after that, and Wanda last. If anyone could change my mind, it would be Ryan.

"Uncle Ryan will stay here with Brinley, Grace, and Adam. We will be sure to FaceTime them a lot, though. We can still talk to everyone even if we can't be around them."

"Will we make new friends?" Hannah's first concern as she was already proving to be a social butterfly.

"Of course, honey. We will get you involved in school and gymnastics there. You will make more friends in no time."

"What about the camping trip with Uncle Ryan?" It pained me that Hunter's primary questions involved Ryan. His attachment had expanded tenfold with the reveal of our relationship.

"We will make sure you come back for them. I promise you that one." I knew Ryan would be flexible in working around our schedule to ensure the boys could continue the tradition. I loved that Hunter already found it to be important and hated to take him away from the only other father-figure in his life. For a moment, I wavered before reminding myself there were single mothers worldwide who survived just fine without a fatherly role in their children's lives.

After several more questions, studying pictures of Los Angeles on the computer, opening the links for houses that the realtor already gathered, the kids' excitement flourished. "Wow," they said over and over again, especially when looking at the beaches. I knew it would be a hard transition no matter what, but we would find our fit, eventually. We proved we could bounce back from significant life changes and be as strong as ever. We were a family, and that would never change no matter where we were.

———

The knot in my stomach grew bigger until it felt like it would rip through my skin, which was about the same time Ryan lightly knocked on the door after the kids were in bed. He hugged and kissed me as though I was leaving, and not just returning from my trip. Maybe deep down he already knew the truth.

"I missed you," he breathed in my ear.

All I could do was kiss him back because I didn't want him to see the uncertainty on my face. Not yet.

We sat down on the couch over a bottle of wine as he asked questions about my trip. It was strenuous talking about it while ignoring the weighty truth cutting off my air supply.

Ryan pulled my hand onto his leg and played with my fingers. We were comfortable with each other and fit together so well. *Am I sure I want to ruin this? Do I want to walk away from a love I didn't believe existed until I found it?*

I squeezed my eyes shut tightly and forced the words out before I could take them back. "The trip was more than a visit. Todd is giving me a shot at being a music supervisor for his current film project and future works that his director friends have scheduled. He had me interview for it.”

Ryan's eyes studied mine while piecing together my rushed sentences. “As in, the job you went to school for and thought you'd be brave enough to take on someday?”

I smiled at how well he listened, quoting of my life stories verbatim. “Yeah.”

“And you'd move to Los Angeles, I assume?”

My smile disappeared. “Yeah. I asked if they would consider me working remote but it was a hard no.”

“Wow, Haleigh. Wow. I mean, that's incredible! I am proud of you for taking the risk. Hunter and Hannah are okay with it?”

I nodded, swallowing deeply.

“That's great. They'll adjust quickly. Especially Hannah. She'll be running for mayor of Los Angeles by next year.”

Studying the light in his eyes, his fingers gripping mine, his mouth as it held a smile, I waited for him to say more. But nothing came. I hastily stood from the couch, glared at him one more time, then marched into the kitchen for a glass of ice water.

Ryan joined me with wide eyes. “Are you *mad* at me?”

I didn't know how to explain what I was feeling. He was being supportive of me. It's precisely what I had hoped for in the scenarios I envisioned for how he'd react. But now that he was saying the right words, I was livid.

“I wish you wouldn't do that.”

“Do what?”

“Be so selfless! It makes this harder.”

Ryan was quiet for a moment. “I don't think it's fair to you if I immediately launch into all the reasons why you should stay instead of chasing your dreams.”

“Is that how you really feel?”

Ryan wordlessly traced the designs in the granite countertop.

I held my hands to my face, covered my mouth, and groaned. “Josh would have been pissed and told me I couldn't go.” As soon as the words slipped, I felt terrible. There was no reason Josh should have come to mind as though I insanely preferred his jealous reactions over Ryan's steady, altruistic ones.

Walking to Ryan, I reached for his wrist. "That was uncalled for, and I'm sorry. Adrenaline has been building in me all day, preparing me for the knock-down, drag-out fights birthed from these situations. You being so calm is not what I'm... used to encountering."

"I understand," he said softly.

Of course he does. Because he always does. "Do you ever compare me to Lindsay?"

Ryan squinted his eyes while anticipating my end goal of the question. "There's really no comparison."

"I mean, do you think about how what I do or what we are or whatever it may be with us differs from how it was with Lindsay?"

"Oh," Ryan took a moment to think about it before responding, "Sure. It's only natural. I was married to her for sixteen years. I would think you are regularly doing the same with Josh and me."

Maybe he's not as fazed by it as I am. "Doesn't that bother you?"

"I guess if I stopped to think about it, then a little. Only because he's my brother."

I pinched the bridge of my nose to fight the oncoming headache blaring a warning like a freight train. "Yeah."

Ryan grabbed my hands. "Nothing about us is typical, remember? You said that yourself."

"I don't want to be comparing you, though, Ryan. Not as frequently as I do. I've done that the entire time I've known both of you. I've always had thoughts about what you do that Josh doesn't do, and how you make me feel that he never did. It's not healthy to do, and I don't know how to break the cycle. It just makes it harder when you guys look so much alike."

Ryan spoke warily, "I can't exactly change my looks, Haleigh. Or my bloodline."

"I know. And that's not what I mean. You're perfect to me, and your bloodline and looks all contribute."

"Is this part of the reason for moving away?"

Rubbing my forehead, I considered if it was. "It's not contributing to the reasons, but it may be an added long-term benefit. Maybe I need more time to give us all we deserve. I don't want our relationship to feel dependent on Josh as the cohesion between us, or for it to fall into the same patterns we've been stuck in for years."

"What are you getting at?"

I reminded myself to breathe, forcing out the rehearsed lines about setting the best example for my kids, "I need to be more than a widow."

"You are. You're a mother among other things. The *best* mom."

"I love being a mom. I still need to become more of *me*, though. I was thinking about this part of my journey long before Kristen called. I didn't expect such an incredible opportunity to fall into my lap. But Jessi says—"

"The universe will open up to you when you open up to it." *Why did he have to continue to show his perfection?* He listened to every damn word I say.

Ryan leaned against the counter and looked out the window, avoiding eye contact with me. "I'm thrilled you get this chance to do what you've always wanted to do. You deserve it, and you should without a doubt take it. It's the right move for you."

I appreciated his support, but I also wished he'd fight for me.

Then he turned his piteous eyes to me, and my knees weakened at the sight. "Now that I've expressed what you should do, can we play Truth? When I look back on this moment, I want to be confident I said everything I could have said."

I was drained—exhausted with the decision, with the feelings, with the life I once knew and what remained. I was too tired to pull my eyes away, despite knowing they revealed the love I had for him, which could only make it more devastating. "Okay."

"Remember that no matter what I say, you need to go to Los Angeles and pursue that dream, okay?"

I nodded, biting my tongue because I knew this would hurt the most.

"I love you, Haleigh." Ryan ran his hand through his hair and down the back of his neck. "Am I supposed to wait for you?"

I responded with the first words to come to my mouth without pausing to doubt them, "I know that's not realistic. Not with kids in our lives. I don't know if this will be a temporary or permanent move. All I know is that I need to find my place, wherever that is, and it starts with finally becoming the person I've always known was inside."

"If you stay there, do you expect me to move out there, too?"

I sucked in my breath. I had been up all night talking to myself in the mirror in preparation for today. I needed to be ready so I didn't break, so I didn't do something in the heat of the moment that could remove the assurance I was making the right decision. I worried my voice sounded as robotic as I felt. "No. It's not possible as long as Lindsay is here, and I know that. The kids need to have both of you around." Also, there would be no way Lindsay would let him have any custody rights if he chased me across the country. She was bitterly ruthless. "Which is why you shouldn't wait for me. We just need to keep living our lives. Without each other." I grimaced at those words, sobs clenching my stomach, threatening to upheave every ounce of my being. *What was I doing? Why would I throw this away?*

"I can't just be cut off from you," his voice was barely audible. And this was the problem, we were still family regardless, part of the chaos that had everything entangled.

I nodded knowingly. "We'll make sure the kids still video chat. We may try to fly back a few times a year to see everyone, too." I knew the moment the words hit my ears how foolish that would be. I needed an extended break from Ryan. Standing directly across from him, I only had the strength to walk away once.

"I don't want you to leave." He finally murmured the words

that shattered me, the only ones that could be enough to break me, "Please. Stay. With me."

"Ryan," I fixed my gaze to be as unwavering as I could will it to be. Thoroughly gutted, I was no longer a person, only a shell of what once remained, an avatar. *Be strong, Haleigh, be strong.* "I have to go. I have to do this for the kids and me. I am moving to California."

CHAPTER THIRTY-ONE
YEAR 10 - SUMMER

Venice Beach was beautiful. Every morning, the kids and I went for a walk while our toes sank in the sand, and the sun broke through the horizon, magically transforming the water into shimmering crystals, singing of hope for a new day.

Our newly adopted golden retriever, Lapsie, joined us. Hunter found her while helping Kristen at the local humane society. It was instant love. Her chestnut brown eyes were so similar to Ryan's that sometimes I'd pretend he was there with us, too. Lapsie was an answered prayer as she helped the kids adjust to our new environment. They loved playing with her and showing her off. Their laughter with the dog bounced off the walls of our new house, which helped me ignore the initial doubt of my decision.

Learning the business of combining visual arts with music was tough at first. I hadn't worked for almost a decade, so that alone was a hard adjustment to make. Suddenly having to stick to the timelines and deadlines set by someone else was even harder. It was also a brand new world, culture, and lingo that I had to find my way in. I had to develop a stronger backbone as I learned how to say no, fight through negotiations and ending up with a deal that pleased all sides. There were many nights I cried to Kristen and on the phone with Jessi about my doubt that I was cut out for this intensity.

"Give it one year of hard work before you make a decision," was the consensus.

It was right at the year mark when I found my pace. Although my move to LA was too late to score the music supervisor position in Todd's big picture film, I attained the rights for all my chosen tracks to appear in his latest indie flick. The first time watching a screening was mind-blowing. The movie was about a broken relationship, a love rediscovered, and one lost yet again. I could relate. The songs I chose for the scenes made the actors' emotion and screenwriting even more powerful. While sitting in that small theatre, I stifled sobs.

That movie kick-started my portfolio and brought several other projects my way. My confidence was building, and when Hunter invited me to speak in his classroom for Career Day, I was the proudest I could be because he was proud of me, too.

We only made it back to the Chicago area twice in the first year after we moved to Los Angeles. Time quickly passed while we adjusted to new schedules and new lives. We were hesitant to leave Lapsie behind, which was another excuse not to go. Hunter took one more trip than Hannah and me so he could go on the camping trip with Ryan and Adam. He was only nine years old, so thankfully Kristen offered to fly back to see family and took him with her.

The most challenging visit was when Jessi married Chris in her Door County hometown. I was part of the wedding party, and so was Ryan. They had six attendants on both sides, three flower girls, and two ring-bearers, so it was easy to keep people between us and avoid close proximity.

Every time my eyes landed on Ryan, he was already looking at me, the magnetic pull between us so powerful that I had to fall to the ground to keep from being swept into his arms. I wanted to run to the one thing that would make the near-perfect life I was building absolutely perfect: Ryan. But I still had to work on me.

The family ties surrounding our relationship made it the most drawn-out and painful breakup that could exist. We couldn't avoid each other even if we wanted to, so we had to internalize the hurt. Hunter, Hannah, and I would FaceTime regularly with all of our family members, Ryan and his kids included. Ryan and I would sit back and let the kids talk to each other, limiting our interaction.

We only provided brief updates on topics the kids didn't cover, and that was it. After the first few conversations, I cried myself to sleep. Then over time, it turned into the norm. I didn't want details of his life, anyway. I couldn't handle the thought of him dating other women, although I hoped he was. I wasn't sure if my heart would mend, but I remained confident that Los Angeles was where the kids and I needed to be.

After a few years in LA, I had gone on several dates. I didn't make it past three dates with anyone though. I couldn't find the excitement that only Ryan had sparked in me. I also discovered I had trust issues that stemmed from my relationship with Josh that I had yet to heal or truly forgive. Those never appeared with Ryan because I trusted him with everything I had. Maybe it was another reason I needed to be out here, to close the wounds created by Josh that I didn't even know still festered. At least I could be grateful for kids who didn't mind only having their mom, and for a job I was in love with and getting better at each year.

Kristen was my lifesaver time and again. It helped that Todd was busy with his films because she had the availability and desire to throw herself into my life like a personal assistant. She took the kids everywhere, filled in when I couldn't, and helped me stay on track with their projects and activities that packed a schedule so tightly that it barely allowed time to eat or pee. In the beginning, I wondered if Kristen wasn't doing it to redeem the regret she harbored from previous years. But over time, I realized she was genuinely happy to help, and the ability to put her motherly instincts to good work was an added bonus. Once she got pregnant with their first child, I knew my extra help would end soon.

Hunter was a sophomore in high school, and Hannah was preparing for junior high by then. They were both mostly self-sufficient, which made the ability to work full-time easier. Work was in a rare lull since I was in between projects all of a sudden. Slowing down made the homesickness kick in. Eight years of being in Los Angeles, and I finally missed Chicago.

"I'm going back for a month."

Kristen awkwardly leaned backward to get comfortable on a lawn chair and struggled to do so. I reached for a throw pillow and tucked it behind her back. "Thanks," she gratefully sighed. "Ahh, that's the stuff."

She was gorgeous at seven months pregnant, all belly on her tiny frame, and ready for the baby to arrive. She had grown out her sun-kissed hair, blonde strands weaving with her natural brunette locks. Kristen stopped streaking it with rainbow colors, which was strange at first, but now it was obvious that the color served only as a distraction from her sharp features and striking face. People would stop and stare at her, debating if she was a model or actress. What I loved the most about her is that she didn't notice the impact she had on others.

"A full month? Do you think you can handle that?"

"I really miss it these days. Is that strange?"

Kristen waved to the ocean view from her extended patio. "Yes."

"It'll be good for me. Being back at my parents' house for a while, letting the kids run around freely in the country, seeing friends, all of that."

She smacked loudly on a pregnancy pop. Kristen had thirty-two straight weeks of nausea. "And seeing Ryan?"

Even after all this time, his name gave me goosebumps. "I'm sure we will at some point. The kids will want to see Adam, Grace, and Brinley. I want to see them. They're still my nieces and nephew, and it's been too long."

"Hmm," she studied me carefully. "Do you think you'll come back?"

I laughed, pushing away the morsel of regret with Ryan's name on it that still nagged deep inside. "It's a little too hard to pack up now. I'm committed to being here, at least until Hunter and Hannah graduate. I can't imagine having them start over again. They found their tribe." I was so thankful for their big circle of friends, all ones I approved of and even loved their parents. We were fortunate to fall into a school district full of LA transplants, all of us able to bond on that fact alone.

"Good, because I'm already counting on Hannah being a babysitter if this kid ever decides to enter the world." Kristen gently rubbed her belly and whispered, "But keep baking for a little longer, sweetheart."

"Well, Hannah owes you about eight years of free work with all the help you gave her mom."

Kristen slid her arm around my waist. "It was good for both of us. Trust me, you helped me as much as I helped you."

I sat down next to her and put my hand on top of her bump, imagining what the baby would be like as Kristen's protruding bellybutton rose and fell with her breath. One thing was for sure, it would be ridiculously loved. Kristen and Todd would be amazing parents.

The image of their perfect little family of three made me long for a time when I thought Hannah and Hunter would have two parents in the house. Life had not turned out anywhere near how I once expected.

Kristen noticed the twinge of grief. "Just don't be afraid to follow your heart, okay? I think sometimes you doubt it. Just because it steered you wrong in the past, doesn't mean it will continue to. You've made nothing but solid decisions for the past few years. Look at how much you've been rewarded because of that. You need to trust yourself a little more now."

I leaned my head into hers while gently tapping a song to the baby with my fingertips. "Yeah, I'll work on that."

———

Lapsie was entrusted into the care of Kristen while we were gone. Hunter and Hannah wrote her step-by-step instructions like leaving a child in a new babysitter's care. It was precious. Although they cried when leaving Lapsie and made Kristen promise we would FaceTime daily, they were excited to be back in the Chicago area for a longer period to spend time with their cousins and grandparents. Uncle Ryan, too.

I made Kristen promise not to have her baby until we returned. She made me promise once again that I would listen to my heart, which only inspired us to belt out Roxette as the kids plugged their ears in the backseat of her car. We said goodbye, entered LAX, and prepared for our flight to Chicago.

Hunter and Hannah were already texting their cousins, making plans for the beginning of summer vacation. From what I could gather, Adam, Grace, and Brinley would stay with Ryan for most of the time we were back. Lindsay married a businessman she met at her gym named Robert in a surprising move only five months after finalizing her divorce with Ryan. I found out about it two months after we moved to LA and was sick to my stomach that she did all she could to ruin Ryan and me and break us down in every verbal way possible, just to marry a different man mere months later. No one saw it coming. Lindsay and Robert regularly left for weeks or months at a time for his business trips. Ryan never seemed to mind since it meant not having to share the kids for those periods. He was an incredible dad.

Right before I switched my phone to airplane mode for take-off, I received a text from Ryan that asked,

> Would you be okay if the kids came to stay with me for a few days? It would give you some free time, too, and I really don't mind having them all. The house is stocked.

> Sure.

That was all I could text before the flight attendant commanded I turn on airplane mode or shut off my phone.

Once we landed, the first thing I did was turn on my phone with high hopes to see a response from Ryan. I spent the entire flight in anticipation, despising the eagerness he still aroused in me, yet unable to stop it. Nothing came through except a text from my mom letting me know they'd pick us up by baggage claim.

We took a few days to settle in at my parents' house, enjoying home-cooked meals made by someone else for once. The kids were at a better age to enjoy the outdoor toys around my parents' land, like the ATVs and fishing poles. "Lapsie would love this place," was said often as they dominated the eight acres, a luxury we didn't have in Los Angeles.

When it became clear I wasn't instigating it. Hunter and Hannah arranged a visit to Ryan's house on their own. I finally gave in and texted Ryan to confirm it,

Do you mind if the kids stay this weekend?

Sure.

His simple response stung. I let the kids work out the details on their own. In a day's time, I dropped them off at Ryan's new house in Lake Zurich, which was conveniently only fifteen minutes from my parents.

We stood at the door giving all the kids hugs. After they ran off to play, Ryan stuck his hands in his pockets, and my arms crossed, squashing invitations between us for physical contact. Eight years since our heartbreaking end, and tension still emitted from us like smoke signals.

"Your house is beautiful," I commented truthfully. It was quite a change from the loft, but presented a more mature version of Ryan with the rustic atmosphere framed by clusters of trees and a gorgeous wraparound porch I envied.

"Thanks," he said politely. Those brown eyes told me everything I needed to know. Ryan was dating someone; I could sense it. I knew him so well it hurt.

When it was obvious the conversation hit a wall, I told him I'd pick the kids up Sunday night. Ryan said "okay" and closed the door behind him, not looking back at me like he used to always do.

I drove straight to Jessi's house. She had been texting nonstop, and although I was excited to spend time with her, I was acclimating to how different everything felt. I was homesick for a place that was no longer the same as it was eight years ago. It was easy to overlook the changes when returning for quick trips, but being here for an extended period made it palpable.

Chris and Jessi rented a beautiful Victorian-style house on one of the oldest blocks of Schaumburg. The entire street boasted gorgeous older homes that had been renovated multiple times. Although I was surprised they moved out of the city, it fit their personalities perfectly. It was always Jessi's favorite street to drive down when she would come visit me.

Five years into marriage and they were more in love than ever. I admired the way Chris and Jessi spoke to and cared for each other as they traveled around the house doing everyday things. "You are happy." Three words with little impact but easily summarized Jessi's life.

Jessi beamed her million-dollar smile as she confirmed, "I am. I really am."

"And you're still feeling good about the no-children decision?"

Only last year they agreed to be a childless family. They deliberated for several years before finally giving way to a vasectomy for Chris. "I am. We love traveling too much. We felt more pressure from our families than any other motive. That's not a reason to have kids."

"I'm proud of you guys. That's a hard decision to make."

"But it feels right, you know? Everything with Chris has felt right from the beginning." She reached over to touch his hand as he rejoined us at the table with fresh coffee.

After I filled them in on life on the West Coast, I could no longer avoid another topic on my mind. "So, Ryan's new girlfriend…"

"I thought we weren't going to say anything!" Chris cried out.

Jessi's eyes widened. "That wasn't me. How did you find out?"

"I could see it in Ryan's eyes when I dropped off the kids. As much as I don't want to know, I also sort of want to know. But," I massaged the back of my neck while trying to separate the questions in my head from the pain scorching my heart. "Is he happy?"

Chris scooted back from the table and escaped to the kitchen, presuming it was his cue to leave even though he was Ryan's best friend and knew the most. Jessi filled in for him, "He's happy enough. We've hung out a few times. She's nice. A teacher at his school—"

I put up my hand up to cut her off. "Okay, that's about all I can handle."

"Do you regret leaving him?" Jessi cut right to the point as usual.

I knew the answer without having to think about it since it was a question I frequently asked myself in the middle of the sleepless nights when dreaming of Ryan's face was my only solace. "I wish I didn't have to leave him, but I don't regret our move. It's exactly what we needed. It's what I needed. We are happy with our lives out there. I like knowing I'm providing for our family with a job I love and was meant to do."

"But it'd be even better if you could have all of that and Ryan too."

I closed my eyes, wishing away the sorrow that wanted to come forth. "Of course. But you can't have it all, right?"

"Maybe," was Jessi's soft reply before Chris poked his head back in the room, asking if we wanted to go out for dinner.

I spent the rest of the night with them, crashing in their guest bedroom at the end, grateful to be surrounded by so much love. I ignored the nagging deep inside that told me I could have had that, too, if only I didn't move away.

———

The next morning, I woke early to seize alone time and walk while the sun was rising. Eventually, I ended up on the street of our old house to see what it looked like now.

In eight years, even a house can age regardless of the care. The two-story brick colonial looked so foreign, with bikes I didn't recognize leaning against the metal bars of the porch stairs, a car in the driveway that belonged to no one I knew, and curtains hanging in the windows that would not have been my first choice for decor. It was bizarre that I lived here for as long as I did, now feeling like a previous life. This house held many memories, tears, laughs, dreams, heartbreaks, and secrets. Hopefully, it had a second chance for a happier life. I was walking proof of how vital those second chances were.

My next stop was a place I purposely avoided during our return trips, outside of letting the kids run to see it while I stayed by the car. Josh's gravesite.

I leaned next to his headstone and put my hands on the cold rock, just like Hunter does when he comes to speak to Josh. "Beloved Father to Hunter and Hannah" was etched on it in harsh gray letters with his name, birthdate, and date of passing. I wondered how many people questioned why it said nothing about being a beloved husband, or if they overlooked that minor detail. When I chose the headstone, I didn't even know about Josh's affair, but our relationship had been broken for so long that I couldn't find it within myself to add it, partially fearful of eventual regret. However, after I discovered the truth, I was grateful for my reluctance.

I sank down on my knees, reached for the two beer bottles in my bag, and cracked them open. Putting one on top of his grave, I put the other straight to my lips.

"It's been a while, old friend." The leaves of the tree above me rustled as though responding to my greeting. I prepared myself for ten years' worth of conclusions that I needed to share with him. I pictured Josh's smile—his rare, genuine smile. The freedom in his soul when we went away to Jamaica together. It's how I imagined him wherever he was now. Unfiltered, unrestrained, happy.

"There's so much I wish I could do over with you. I wish we could have been best friends who made a pact to get together with the sole purpose of producing two beautiful kids. Then we could have co-parented like rock stars for the rest of our lives, with none of the complications that came from being married. Maybe Corinne and I would have been friends, too. Maybe she would have convinced you that Hunter should get a dog. Which we now have by the way, and we love her.

"Sometimes I still feel angry at how things played out. It's not entirely directed at you, though. We both made mistakes. You just went rogue and really went for your own happiness before I could. But how can I fault you for that? If we were friends, I would have told you to chase your happiness. To not give up. To go after that beautiful blonde that makes you be the best version of yourself. Even if she wasn't me."

I paused to sip my beer. Subconsciously tugging at the grass under my legs, I continued, "I found your letter written to me. You were right. I fell in love with Ryan. Maybe you knew before I did. I'm sorry for how that made you feel. It wasn't fair to you. I never meant to make you feel lesser because you weren't. You were very important to me and to the kids. We needed you. Ryan also loves you. If he had known how you felt all these years, if we all had known how you felt, maybe things could have been different.

"I can't help but wonder what life would be like if the two of you weren't in the car that day. What if you survived and came to me to confess? Sure, it would have been hard for a while. But would we have come out of it better? Would everyone be happier if only we had done things differently?

"I wish we made smarter decisions. I'm not sure if it would change anything. Everyone has an expiration date, right? But I like to think maybe we would have the power to. If only we kept fewer secrets. If only we were honest with each other. Endings don't have to hurt so much. We didn't have to hurt as much as we did.

"Anyway, the kids are incredible. We made some awesome human beings. You'd be proud of them. I hope that wherever you are, you're still holding Corinne's hand. Love like that is what this life is all about. I'm glad you found it."

Clinking my beer with the one on his grave, I leaned my head against his headstone, feeling lighter as true forgiveness washed away all my bitterness, regret, anger, and hurt. Forgiveness for Josh. Forgiveness for me. As I watched the squirrels play in the distance, I could feel Josh's presence more than I ever did when he was alive.

Chapter Thirty-Two
Year 10 - Summer

By the final week of our extended visit, I was emotionally exhausted. The trip had been more therapeutic than I expected.

Mom and I prepared to cook a huge four-course meal for all the kids as our final send-off. We drove to the grocery store to buy the needed ingredients a day in advance so we could wake up the next morning and start the marathon cooking. She hounded me with questions about my new career, finally understanding the reasons I left and pursued my dreams. Since the beginning of my trip, we had been more honest with each other. Our respect for each other grew, a natural development as we entered maturing stages in the life cycle between parent and child.

"I wish I had said something back in the day to make you believe in yourself more."

I shook my head. "There's no need for you to think that way. If I had moved to LA right after college, I wouldn't have been in that terrible accounting position and would never have met Josh. Then Hunter and Hannah wouldn't be here today. Everything happens for a reason."

Mom patted my leg. "You seem at peace."

"I am for the most part. It's comforting knowing that a scary decision at the time can lead to an incredible life."

"Hmph," she grunted. "I can understand that."

I looked at her questioningly. "You do?"

"Staying with your dad for all these years. The most frightening decision of my life for a long period. But some amazing things have come out of it as a result, including you, these grandkids, and finding myself among the hardships."

"Mom, can I ask why? Why did you stick with Dad when it got as bad as it did? I mean, I'm glad you did. *Now.* Now that I see how he's changed. But I have terrible memories of Dad when I was younger. I hated that you didn't fight back. That you weren't..." I swallowed before admitting the frank word, "...stronger."

"Oh, I wish that wasn't the case, honey. He tried as hard as he could to be a good dad and husband. He didn't have the best example set for him in the rough household he grew up in. Sometimes we don't always see the effort people put in because they do it in a different way than we expect them to. He and I spoke different languages for many years. Eventually, we learned how to translate. And now, we speak the same one."

I rubbed my forehead as the despairing parallels between their relationship and mine with Josh became clear. The memory of Josh dropping off the soundtrack he created after one of our biggest fights while dating stuck out the most. He tried to speak my love language. Maybe we never gave it the necessary time for us to sync up. If he hadn't died, if we stuck it through and worked past his affair, would we have eventually been like my mom and dad? Would we be looking like teenagers in love instead of at each other's throats? My stomach turned at the thought of how real that could have been, and how the outcome would have been different, namely with Hunter and Hannah growing up with their dad in their daily lives. But Los Angeles wouldn't have happened, and the growth that had evolved in the kids and me from that decision was immeasurable. Life has a way of presenting alternative paths, and I trusted I was on the right one.

"I spent many years searching for someone who wasn't like

Dad, only to marry someone who was exactly like Dad. It's almost like I continued to drift toward men that would make me feel insecure because that's all I knew."

"Oh honey, those cycles happen, unfortunately. It's the same reason your dad reacted the way he did for so many years. He knows only what he does, it's ingrained, even when you swear you won't treat someone else like that. You can only hope you do a little better than what you experienced, and eventually, the cycle will break."

My mom's insight amazed me, and it was something I never gave her credit for before, which made me laugh knowing that someday, Hannah may have the same thought.

"How are you getting on without Ryan?"

Surprised by her reference to him, I shifted in my seat. "Mom, it's been eight years."

"But he's still very present in your life."

"Okay, well, that's a different story. I thought we were talking about happy decisions."

Mom repeated her approval of my move to the west coast by saying, "You needed to leave to find the rest." I was relieved to know she didn't harbor a grudge since I took her only grandchildren thousands of miles away.

"You're exactly right. I had to put the kids and me first. Los Angeles has been incredible for us. I can't regret that."

"Don't you think you may eventually find someone like him?"

"I will try to explain this the best way I can." I bit my lip, confident there was no one like Ryan, and terrified to admit it out loud. "I once felt like a floating mess, just barely surviving day-by-day. But when I was around Ryan, he held me stable with one hand, rescuing me without knowing it. He reads me, he immediately reacts to what I need to help balance me, he's my steadiness." Leaves of swaying trees whipped by as we neared the grocery store. I admired their dependency on the wind, unable to go anywhere unless blown, unable to steer their path, but fully trusting the source that carries them. "Everything I have and everything I have yet to hold... my past, present, future... every single detail, every truth, every possession, every thought, every feeling... I would put them all in Ryan's hands with complete trust. With him, I don't worry, I'm not scared."

"You found your person," she paraphrased.

The unforeseen, modern-day summary from my mom was one I couldn't deny. "I did. The timing has never been right though."

"Sweetie, sometimes in life, we get a little misguided. It's as though you and Ryan have been drifting toward each other, but all these distractions arose, and you took them as signs of something else, rather than what they should have been. Life isn't over for you two yet. There's always a chance you may find each other again."

"Maybe..."

"Your mom can be wise sometimes." She grinned as she turned off the ignition. "Have a little hope. You never know. There may still be a day I can say 'I told you so.'"

———

The kids planned one last cousin sleepover, so Ryan dropped off my nieces and nephew so they could stay at my parents' house and enjoy the countryside with Hannah and Hunter.

My mom wiped her hands on a dishrag as she kissed the cheeks of Grace, Adam, and Brinley. "Ryan, you should come in and eat dinner with us."

"No, I—" Ryan frantically looked at me as he scoured his mind for an excuse.

I sent telepathic waves to my mom to tell her to stop. "Maybe he has other plans, *Mom*," I emphasized, hoping she'd get the point.

She purposely ignored me and steered Ryan into the house without another word.

Ryan worked with my dad to get two more tables set up to allow space for all the extra bodies. I set the tables while my mom put the finishing touches on the meal. As we sat down to eat, I soaked up every minute with Ryan's kids, listening to their voices and stories, knowing that the next time I see them, there'd be a very distinct line between leaving childhood and entering adulthood. The speed of passing time was best reflected in the faces of our growing children.

Once dinner was over, the kids ran upstairs to the attic to search for treasures concealed among random boxes that had been stored for years. Mom hid various trinkets and a few dollar bills to make it more exciting for the older ones. Ryan helped with dishes while my dad asked if I could step outside with him.

"I don't really care to smoke one," I told him, tilting my head to the cigar.

"Just follow me," he gruffly demanded as he stepped out on the porch.

Dad lit his cigar as we watched the fireflies drift across the yard. "Listen, sweetheart. Last night, your mom told me the things you shared with her. I want to set the record straight on some of it."

He coughed to clear his throat. "I know I wasn't always there for you, and when I was, I was harsh. But it wasn't meant to bring you down. I wanted you to do better than me. You were meant for more than what your mom and I have done." He kicked at the dirt on the porch with his boot. "You're our only child. I didn't know what I was doing. Still don't. I had a lot of growing up to do. I know I didn't do it right. I have regrets. But it's why I love watching you with those kids of yours. You're doing it right. The way we should have. I'm proud of who you are."

It was the only time in my entire life I had received a straight compliment from my dad. Tears welled in my eyes and a lump rose in my throat.

"Don't go getting all sappy, you know I don't handle that well." Dad cleared his throat again. "Ryan is a good one. He fits well. He's a better man than I am. It's something to think about." With that, he stubbed out his cigar, blew on it, and put it back in his shirt pocket. His words and his skill in avoiding burning a hole in his shirt equally astonished me.

Before Dad could walk back into the house, I grabbed his hand. He stiffened, and didn't turn his head to look at me as though he sensed what was coming. "Hey, Dad? I forgive you for leaving us. I forgive you for all the things you did that you didn't know how to do better. I forgive you because I know you're no longer that person and you would do it all differently if you could."

I could hear him swallow deeply three times. Still without looking at me, he said, "Thanks, honey." And then he disappeared inside.

Processing the most words Dad had spoken in one singular moment, I continued watching the blackness of the night. When the door clanged behind me, my body froze in place. I could sense him before he spoke.

"I'm heading back, but wanted to say goodbye before I left." Ryan's voice was gentle as though speaking too loudly may cause a window to shatter, or my heart.

I bit the inside of my cheek, refraining from saying anything I may regret later, but hated filtering my words to someone I once poured everything out to. "I'm glad you're happy, Ryan." And I meant it. There wasn't any bitterness in my words.

"And you? Are you happy?"

"As happy as I can be with everything I have in my life out there." That was truthful. I was happy there. When I was here, my heart ached the most, the emptiness of Ryan no longer in my life the way I wished he was, the desperation to feel the love we once had that was so special. We only tasted it for such a short period, but I was beginning to fear I would spend a lifetime searching, only to never find it again.

After a moment filled with the distinctive serenity of the countryside, Ryan reached over and grabbed my hand, gently squeezing it inside his. I looked down at our joined hands and back up at his sparkling brown eyes as a tear slid down the bridge of his nose. I focused on the lines in the side of his eyes as he squinted through a benign smile. The lines were deeper in recent years as he forced himself to stay positive, to be the rock for me, his mom, his kids, my kids, and everyone when we all needed it the most. Ryan was the strongest and most selfless person I knew. He deserved his shot at love, too. Just like I wasn't able to give it to Josh, I was unable to give it to Ryan, despite yearning to be the person who could.

Ryan leaned in, his lips softly brushing my cheek, lingering. When he pulled back, his chestnut irises were dilated with the unsaid words. He slowly descended from the back porch. I thought about running after him, but what good would that do? We were thousands of miles apart. He was dating someone else. Time had shifted. We weren't the same as we were eight years ago.

———

On our last day in Lake Barrington, Ryan arrived early in the morning to pick up Adam, Grace, and Brinley from their sleepover. He was taking them straight to Wanda's house since he was flying out for a three-day work conference.

While the kids loaded into the car, he rolled down the window and said, "Listen, I'll be back this way in about an hour. Can I drive you to the airport? My flight out is a few hours after yours. I really don't mind going early. It'll save you all a taxi ride."

Before I could object, Hunter called out, "Yeah! That's perfect, thanks!" He saw a documentary on TV once about the dirtiness of cabs when examined by a blacklight and had since avoided using them at all cost.

"Sure," I accepted his offer with my lips pressed together. Mom and Dad planned to take us, but I didn't correct him. The trip to the airport combined with our dinner last night would be the most time I had spent with Ryan in years. I was grateful for Hunter and Hannah's presence to keep me grounded.

By the time Ryan returned, we had exchanged our hard good-byes with my parents. The month-long visit deepened our attachments and repaired any underlying misunderstandings and brokenness that had existed for years. My relationship with my dad was especially sturdier, an unexpected perk that made me even more grateful for our return trip to Illinois.

The drive to the airport was the worst. I couldn't stop staring at the center console. Ryan's elbow rested on it as always. A long time ago, mine would lean against his, our elbows grazing each other's skin because we couldn't stop touching. I wanted to put it there so badly, to feel the heat of him, to make it all *good* again, but I recognized the little self-control I had. At least Hunter and Hannah in the backseat were great distractions as they talked Ryan's ear off about all the upcoming events they had planned once we returned to the coast.

Standing in the security line with Ryan, Hunter, and Hannah, I daydreamed we were all going on a trip together. Everything felt as natural as it always had. As the minutes ticked by, the touches between Ryan and I increased in frequency. It was difficult not to be physical with someone I was naturally and profoundly connected with. Ryan touched my elbow, then my lower back as my touches went from his shoulder to his bicep. Insignificant to anyone watching us, but potent.

"I'll see you in a few months, right?" Ryan exchanged a complex fist bump with Hunter, created years ago on one of their camping trips.

"Can't wait," Hunter added before giving Ryan a quick, manly hug with thick pats on their backs. I couldn't get over how he would soon be driving. I only hoped Ryan was conducting meaningful guy talks during the camping trips, preparing Hunter and Adam for what was to come that only a man's perspective could give.

Ryan bent down to Hannah, kissed her cheek, and said, "You

will change lives with that smile of yours, do you know that? Don't hold back from showing the world who you are." She gave him a hug and called out, "I'll miss you, Uncle Ryan!" I thought my heart may stop beating right then.

I expected Ryan to simply wave goodbye before leaving, but he stood by my side as I waited for our boarding group to be called. We were the last group, and I purposely stalled in line to marinate in Ryan's presence, unsure if I'd get the chance again if he and this new girlfriend became serious.

"Haleigh," he exhaled. Our eyes dissected each other's, begging for insight into what was going on in the other's mind. "I'm glad you visited for this long. It was nice to see more of you." He was being formal, but I noticed his words broke at the end of each syllable.

I smiled knowingly. "Don't. Let's not do this anymore, okay? We've always been real. Let's keep it that way. Please. No more fakeness."

"I've missed you," Ryan came right out and said it.

"I've missed you, too, Ry. A lot. I don't know everything that's happening in your life, but I wish I did. After all this time, you would think it'd be easier to figure out how to balance our past with our present. But it's not."

"I know. Seems like no matter what we say or do, someone could end up hurt."

I scoffed at how true that was. Him, me, our kids, our parents, his new girlfriend, Lindsay, Josh; so much was continually riding on the line with us. We were always at risk of hurting someone else.

"If someone ends up hurt no matter what, when do we decide it's not worth us hurting anymore?"

Ryan thought carefully before responding, "When do the kids graduate?"

"Hannah has seven more years."

"Brinley only has six."

I grinned as hope tickled the depths of my stomach. "I hear Los Angeles is a little warmer than the Midwest."

He feigned surprise. "Oh yeah? Maybe I should take a sabbatical after Brinley graduates and seek sunshine before the empty nester's syndrome kicks in."

Before I could reply, the ticket attendant interrupted, "Ma'am, we're about done boarding with only three seats left. Are you all four on this flight?"

Ryan held up his ticket. "I'm on a different one."

"Whew," she commented in her southern drawl. "I was afraid we overbooked. Alright, well you three with tickets for this flight need to get on now before it takes off without you."

Hunter and Hannah scanned their tickets and waved to Ryan once more before disappearing through the tunnel.

I gazed at Ryan with his soulful brown eyes, his hand gripping his ticket so hard that it was wrinkling, his teeth biting his lower lip, and his heart, though unseen, beating in perfect synchronization with my own. I didn't stop loving him and never would. Despite our chosen paths keeping us physically apart, we remained together, an invisible string connecting us mentally, emotionally, and spiritually. An eternal connection like that couldn't be broken.

I loved pursuing my dreams and would never regret moving to do it. If I had stayed with Ryan through the distance, I would have left LA that first year when the transition to a new state and new career was difficult. I wouldn't have given it the time needed to turn LA into the best decision I could make for myself and my kids.

But men like Ryan were rare.

Stepping back so I could find the power to walk away, Ryan softly repeated the words he once admitted was his initial thought the first day he met me, "I bet you're the type of woman that every guy falls in love with."

My heart stopped and with every ounce of strength that

remained, I willed my hand with the ticket to lift so the attendant waiting for me could scan it. I could stay. I didn't have to leave.

But Los Angeles was where we needed to be. We built a life there. A happy one. I had to trust what I knew to be true.

Before I walked under the threshold of the gate, I darted back to hug Ryan and whispered in his ear, "I bet you're the type of man a woman never stops waiting for."

The ticket attendant loudly cleared her throat, hinting at the urgency for departure, so I forced myself to let go of him and pull back.

Ryan was mine.

I knew it the day I first met him.

And I will always be his.

Ryan's eyes shined, tears mixed with relief. He knew it wasn't the end.

I'll be with you again, Ryan Claystone, I affirmed silently, grinning as I walked backward.

"I'm not going to say goodbye," he called out, that perfect smile appearing again. "I told you I'll never break a promise to you."

I gave him one last look meant only for him and mouthed, "Good."

Maybe all those romantic movies Jessi made me watch were onto something after all. Some people are truly meant to be.

Epilogue
(Written by Hannah Claystone)

I knew that day would change everything for me.

The day Uncle Ryan stepped through the door and kissed Mom like that was the breath he needed to live another second.

The way she gazed at him afterward, stunned, lost in their embrace, gently stroking his stubble with the tip of her thumb.

Both seemed to forget that twenty-two eighteen-year-old girls and a cluster of Hunter's friends surrounded them, standing still, looking at me for guidance to applaud or launch after this man who captured Mom.

None of them had met Uncle Ryan. In fact, none of them knew that we had been waiting for this day, every step in the house, every ring of the doorbell, every knock on the door, were spent waiting for this exact moment. Mom never said it. But we knew. Because we wanted it, too. The underlying beat of her heart for fifteen years was waiting on him, for their timing to align.

For years, I had secretly invited Uncle Ryan to every party and event we had. He would kindly decline and send me a gift in the mail. Every time I went back to Illinois to visit, he'd apologize for not coming. I told him I understood. I didn't really, but I wanted him to always feel welcomed. To feel free to change his mind at any point and come chase after Mom like I knew he wanted to.

I was used to his response by now. Somewhere in the past few years, I stopped hoping as much. I was focused on applying to colleges and the next stage of life.

So I didn't expect him on *this* birthday. I opened the door and tears immediately sprang to my eyes. I stepped back to let him see who he really came for. My mom. My gorgeous, strong, patient mom who risked her heart so we could have this life that we love in Los Angeles. She gave up Uncle Ryan for us and her dreams. I shouldn't say that she gave him up. She knew they'd be together again. I could see it in her eyes after the dates of every man she had met since. No one would have her heart like Uncle Ryan would.

There he was. Finally. In our foyer, holding a bottle of wine and a small package that I knew was a book for her. Just like their very first date, as Mom told us. His hand was trembling as he reached for her, and the energy between them was electrifying. Everyone in that room could feel it.

That was the day that changed life as I knew it.

It was the day I turned to Joe and whispered, "I think we're done now," ending our three-year relationship.

The day I pulled my acceptance from Stanford University.

The day I booked a one-way ticket to Nashville.

Seven years ago, I met a boy at music camp who changed me. I've never stopped thinking about him. I ignored his old-fashioned letters he sent for fifteen months in a row, yet cried when he stopped writing.

All I knew about love is that the truest of loves ended like a bad curse. That's all I had seen with my mom, and I didn't want any part of it.

But my heart breathed hope again when I saw Uncle Ryan and my mom finally together.

They made me believe in fairytales.

Now, I'm going to chase mine.

Acknowledgments

The storyline in this book wouldn't exist if it wasn't for Jimmy Eat World's Bleed American album. One of my top favorite albums for the past two decades, I listened to it hundreds (maybe thousands) of times while outlining and writing this story. Every single important scene was inspired by a song on that one precious album, hence the references to "A Praise Chorus" and "Your House"—among others I didn't name. If you love this book, please go listen to the album and imagine this entire story unfolding— the perfect soundtrack pairing.

As always, I would never write if it wasn't for the support of my family first and foremost. My mom has been my biggest cheerleader since I wrote my first story at eight years old. She has read every version of everything I've written a million times each, criticizing when needed and praising when equally needed. She pushed me when I was ready to let my dream slide, and I can't thank her enough.

To the rest of my family, I'm grateful for your love, support, and belief in me. Every day, I strive to make you proud.

Thank you to Allison, Kellee, and Erin for helping me edit and make this book the best it can be.

And to everyone reading the story I want to tell you: THANK YOU for choosing this book. I will forever be grateful for you, and I hope you enjoy the rest of the Second Chance Spark series!

ABOUT THE AUTHOR

Lauren Eckhardt is an award-winning and best-selling author, ghostwriter, and book coach and the CEO of Burning Soul Press. She has has a particular love of writing stories centered around second chances in life and the self-strengthening journeys of the characters through them. She's also the mama to two little guys who are her why that drives her every day to create a better world through the stories that inspire and empower others, while bringing light to those who need it the most. Lauren lives in Nashville, TN surrounded by many, many books.

Be sure to check out the other Second Chance Spark series, all standalone books that bridge characters throughout.

www.LaurenEckhardtWrites.com

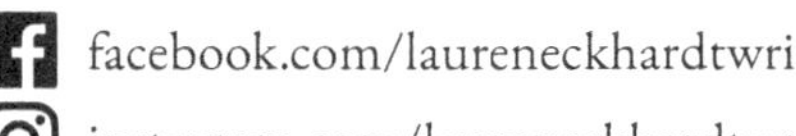

facebook.com/laureneckhardtwrites

instagram.com/laureneckhardtwrites

Also by Lauren Eckhardt

The Second Chance Spark Series
Women's Fiction

The Remedy Files
Young Adult Dystopian

Other Books

www.ingramcontent.com/pod-product-compliance
Lightning Source LLC
Chambersburg PA
CBHW050753190726
48285CB00005B/1643